"Keep it casual but m
Against the wall."

Arlo caught on quick. He turned his head slightly, his lips brushing the edge of her brow. "What am I looking at?"

Kerrigan fought the instant awareness of him, the subtle tick of his breath against her skin shooting sparks.

"I'm getting really bad vibes off the dude, over near the entrance. About six-three with the leather vest, arms crossed."

He held his part, playing her doting date, but she sensed the tension in him and the shift of his attention across the room.

"I can't get a solid look at this angle."

Scenarios flashed through her mind, one rapid frame after another, even as one kept flickering as the right choice. "Remember that compliment you gave me earlier? About how good I am at staying calm?"

"Yeah."

"Stay calm, Arlo. And try to keep up."

Without giving him another opportunity to respond, she wrapped her arms around his shoulders, shifting them just enough so he had a view across the room.

Then she pulled down his head, their lips a fraction of a breath apart, and took.

Dear Reader,

Welcome back to the 86th precinct in Brooklyn and the second book in my **New York Harbor Patrol** series. I'm having so much fun with these books, imagining all that lies beneath the waters surrounding the city I love and call home.

In this book we meet Detective Arlo Prescott, a hotshot at the 86th and one of the precinct's brightest talents. He's coming off a big case and is pulled into an investigation when Officer Kerrigan Doyle finds bodies in a shipwreck.

Kerrigan has recently joined the police diving team that works out of the 86th. She transferred in from Queens and loves the people she's working with. She's especially intrigued by the case and wants answers.

Arlo and Kerrigan are paired up to uncover the mystery of the bodies on the boat, and his seniority and experience do much to help season her youth and ambition. But along the way, they're fighting a building attraction for one another as well as the growing danger around them.

Because a threat *is* growing. And the person behind it is power hungry and very, very determined to run the city's drug trade at all costs.

I hope you enjoy this new book in the series about those who make their living protecting the waters in and around New York City. Their courage and drive to defend the home they love run as deep as the waters that surround it.

Best,

Addison Fox

PERIL IN THE SHALLOWS

***

Addison Fox

HARLEQUIN

ROMANTIC
SUSPENSE

HARLEQUIN®
ROMANTIC SUSPENSE™

Recycling programs
for this product may
not exist in your area.

ISBN-13: 978-1-335-59396-2

Peril in the Shallows

Copyright © 2024 by Frances Karkosak

For questions and comments about the quality of this book, please contact us at CustomerService@Harlequin.com.

Harlequin Enterprises ULC
22 Adelaide St. West, 41st Floor
Toronto, Ontario M5H 4E3, Canada
www.Harlequin.com

Printed in U.S.A.

Addison Fox is a lifelong romance reader, addicted to happily-ever-afters. After discovering she found as much joy writing about romance as she did reading it, she's never looked back. Addison lives in New York with an apartment full of books, a laptop that's rarely out of sight and a wily beagle who keeps her running. You can find her at her home on the web at addisonfox.com or on Facebook (Facebook.com/addisonfoxauthor) and Twitter (@addisonfox).

Books by Addison Fox

Harlequin Romantic Suspense

New York Harbor Patrol

Danger in the Depths
Peril in the Shallows

The Coltons of New York

Under Colton's Watch

Midnight Pass, Texas

The Cowboy's Deadly Mission
Special Ops Cowboy
Under the Rancher's Protection
Undercover K-9 Cowboy
Her Texas Lawman

The Coltons of Colorado

Undercover Colton

Visit the Author Profile page at Harlequin.com.

For my new editor, Emma. I know this is the start of a beautiful partnership.

Chapter 1

Kerrigan Doyle loved the water. To this day, her mother still told the story of Kerrigan's first trip to Coney Island and her squeals of delight as her father dipped her toes, over and over, into the lapping waves of the Atlantic one late-August afternoon.

It had been a solid quarter century since that first dip, but she'd never lost her soul-deep, unceasing desire for her first love.

Too bad she hadn't figured out a way to find any other loves, Kerrigan thought, before chastising herself for the mawkishness.

It wasn't like she'd put that much time into the dating scene. A fact that her best friend, Laverne, had berated her for this past summer.

"Get out and live a little," her friend had told her. "You spend all day with those hot divers, Kerr. Can't you spend a few evenings with one, too?"

While Laverne only had her best interests at heart, her friend's work at one of the large accounting firms in Manhattan insulated her from some of the more challenging aspects of the modern dating scene. Laverne was a working city girl, out most nights of the week with an ever-rotating crew of fellow twentysomethings who all had a steady paycheck, a love of martinis and an expectation of "work hard, play hard" as the foundation of their lives.

For all her progressive thoughts and go-get-'em excitement for her friend, Kerrigan was well aware she couldn't enjoy the same lifestyle. She believed it was essential to maintain a reputation as a damn good cop instead of as a man-hunting twentysomething.

She'd seen it happen before. It might not be fair, but the woman ended up on the short end of the stick when things went sideways.

And while she hadn't been one of New York's finest all that long, she'd seen enough crash-and-burn relationships to recognize that was a potential minefield she wasn't interested in navigating.

Chicken.

That inward voice whispered the word, even if it wasn't the most apt moniker for herself. She'd completed the police training course *and* the diving course for the special division of the NYPD with flying colors. And she'd had the best times for a female recruit in department history. *And* in the nearly two years since she'd joined the special arm of the NYPD that specialized in underwater work, she'd built a rock-solid reputation for herself.

One that had paid professional dividends, such as the dive she was part of today.

The waters around New York City held their own challenges, as the hard-flowing currents and the confluence of freshwater and saltwater ensured her dives were always interesting. That she was considered one of the experts who not only knew how to navigate those waters, but also work within them, was a source of deep pride.

Her work challenged her and constantly kept her on her toes. It might be all-consuming but working under the water required her full focus. She'd explained this to Laverne repeatedly, to little effect.

Shaking off her rambling thoughts, she keyed into the quieting chatter as their lead detective, Wyatt Trumball, stood on the deck of the small boat. They were currently bobbing in the water between Governors Island and the solemn face of the Statue of Liberty, rising up in all her green splendor from the grounds of Liberty Island. Ellis Island was a bit farther in the distance and Kerrigan felt a small shot of gratitude for her intrepid ancestors, who'd been processed through that small spit of land after arriving from Ireland more than a century and a half before.

Driving, cold rain beat down on the exterior of the boat and Kerrigan sunk a bit deeper into her sweatshirt. October in New York was a tough month—the weather could be damn near perfect, or it could be a dire example of all Mother Nature could toss, including hurricanes.

They'd been close to the latter all week, as the residual effects of a storm that had hit farther south had made a total mess of the entire coastal region. She could already imagine the conditions for the day's dives.

Wyatt was clearly aware of the dangers as he began their briefing.

"A suspected drug boat went down here around four a.m. Our good friends in the Coast Guard gave solid chase, but ultimately lost them to a couple of hard waves the perpetrators didn't know how to navigate."

"Coast Guard didn't try to engage?" Gavin Hayes asked, concern on his face.

"They did and called for NYPD backup. But the overnight storm and the tail end of the hurricane that hit Florida three days ago didn't do anyone any favors."

She heard the grumbles and even a bold curse that their water-based comrades could have done more when Wyatt held up a hand. "The fact the drug runners set the boat on fire to avoid detection sealed the decision to call off the op. Especially once it sunk and the Coast Guard already had the coordinates of its location in hand. They've also kept a team in place all night, despite this lovely weather we're having, so let's cut them some slack." Wyatt's grin was more grim than humorous.

The grumbles quieted, and Kerrigan didn't miss the downward cast of a few gazes as Wyatt finished up.

"When it became clear there weren't survivors, the focus shifted to our work today. We're on recovery duty."

More muttered curses went up around her and Kerrigan already knew why. Recovery was a nasty business under the best of circumstances, but a deliberately torched boat left a serious mess behind. In addition to mutilated bodies, the accelerants used needed to be handled with extra care and caution.

She let out a small sigh of her own as she imagined her descent into the water and the approach to the boat.

She braced for what they'd likely find. Already brackish water would be thick with the accelerant and the evidence was likely in multiple pieces, or heavily decomposing from the fire and then time in the water.

And the bodies…

It was part of the job, and she would willingly complete it, but dragging the dead off the floor of the ocean never made for an enjoyable aspect of her work.

But it *was* the job. Along with evidence recovery, bomb checks, standard patrol and any number of routine duties that were required when living in a city surrounded by water.

Wyatt continued his briefing. "You're going out in pairs, four to a Zodiac boat. The goal here is to get in and get out as safely and as quickly as we can. The harbor's a bitch today and she's not looking too happy to give up her secrets. Soon as we get the bodies and a recovery area set up around the boat, we're pulling out."

"You don't want us to secure evidence?" Gavin asked.

"If it's in easy reach and you can safely secure proof, you're cleared to do so, but the entire boat's coming into impound and will be scoured top to bottom once retrieved."

Kerrigan considered the orders before returning her attention to the full briefing on her tablet. Wyatt was thorough, as always, but there were some additional details on expected dive conditions, the specs and size of the boat, theories on who was navigating the cache of drugs through the waters and the ultimate destination of said drugs.

Endless, Kerrigan thought. The battle against the criminals who sought to ply their trade in New York never stopped. Or even slowed, really. There was an element of hopelessness to it, and she worked hard not to let it creep in too often. But something about the deeply gloomy day and the useless loss of life dragged at her.

It was an invisible weight they all bore and most days she handled it just fine.

So why was today any different?

Shaking it off, she scanned the high points of the briefing once more, pictured the area she'd go out on the Zodiac boat and how she and her dive partner— it looked like she was working with Jayden Houston today—would split up the search-and-rescue.

And then it was time to go.

"We're partners today, Kerr."

She smiled at Jayden, his dark brown eyes crinkling at the corners in return. "We are, on an absolutely glorious day for a dive."

"Come on now, you mean you don't love diving in dark soup with a side of rip current?"

"We're living the dream, Officer Houston."

Jayden slung an arm around her neck as they walked onto the soaked deck of the police boat, the light rain that had accompanied them from their headquarters at the 86th Precinct now coming down in torrents. "That we are, Officer Doyle. A fact I tell my husband, who is currently ensconced in his very comfortable and, might I add, warm office uptown. And I still wouldn't have it any other way."

She patted a hand on his impressive chest before slipping from beneath Jayden's arm and crossing to her equipment. She efficiently loaded it all into the waiting Zodiac boat, mimicking the work of her fellow officers as they all got ready to face the mission. And as she nestled her gear into the inflatable that would lead them to the dive site, she had to admit Jayden had a point. With a smile she couldn't hold back, Kerrigan stared through the rain that poured in near sheets over New York Harbor, the city skyline barely visible in the distance.

She really was living the dream.

An absolute nightmare stared back at her from the harbor floor. She and Jayden were the second team down, following Wyatt and Gavin by about four minutes. The detective had radioed up the condition of the boat and the suspected location of the bodies, so Kerrigan and Jayden had made that quadrant their focus.

Only to find a tangle of nets, discarded boxes and a clear effort to ruin the crime scene before the boat had inevitably gone down.

They limited voice communication whenever possible because of their breathing apparatuses, but Kerrigan didn't miss Jayden's sharp intake of breath. "This is bad."

"Nightmare."

Their words were garbled but she'd done this work long enough—and had more than enough contextual clues—to understand and be understood.

And this was monumentally bad.

The realization that the boat was going down in the storm had obviously driven the drug runners in their last moments. A significant portion of the boat had been doused with fuel, then set on fire. The water was thick with gas, and she could catch light whiffs of it, even with her breathing apparatus.

With steady, deliberate movements, she swam closer to the boat. The always restless water was churning even more than usual with the continued aftereffects of the hurricane. The harbor was never particularly clear, but the agitated waters ensured her headlamp barely made a dent in the dense, murky depths.

Jayden voiced his location and what was in his view, and she responded with what she could see. Although they weren't more than ten feet apart, the most she could make out of her partner in that short expanse was an outline of his body in his thick diving suit.

All the more reason to find what they'd come for and get out.

Wyatt had warned them the dive would be difficult. The continued agitation of the water, pressing on her body as she fought to keep her position, and the general condition of the torched boat only added to the overall challenge of making the recovery.

"Got something, Kerr." A hard curse followed, very unlike her normally jovial dive partner.

Kerrigan voiced a quick reply and worked her way through the thick muck toward Jayden.

Only to come face-to-face with two charred bodies, lashed haphazardly to the still-intact railing of the boat.

Detective Arlo Prescott watched the sheets of water run off the edge of the police boat and burrowed more deeply into his NYPD-issued jacket. The weather had been a mess the past three days, with puddles the size of small lakes springing up at every intersection in Brooklyn. He'd done his level best to keep his head buried in work, but he had to go home sometime, and the late October nor'easter had given the city a solid dousing.

The only plus side, he mused as they drew alongside a couple of Zodiac boats, stopping to allow their occupants onto the larger NYPD vessel, was the decided lack of street crime, since the lingering storm had driven most people inside.

Unless the bastards were dumb enough to try a water escape. Arlo sighed to himself as he saw his closest friend in the NYPD, Wyatt Trumball, climb out of the Zodiac and into the police boat.

Which, based on today's outing, those idiots most certainly had. Proof once again that crime happened on the water just as it did on the streets.

"You look like a drowned rat, Trumball." Arlo offered the man a hand, pulling him into a close, one-armed hug. "A freezing-cold drowned rat."

"You should see the other guy." Wyatt stepped back, his gaze already scanning the rest of his crew disembarking from the now-tethered Zodiacs. "Or guys, I should say."

There was a second police boat in the water, dispatched to manage the evidence recovery of the drug runners' fishing vessel. And then there were the smaller speedboats that would keep lookie-loos out of the surrounding water as they dealt with the bodies.

Arlo had already been warned these bodies were more gruesome than the Halloween decorations beginning to line the houses in his Red Hook neighborhood.

It never failed to amaze him that even in the worst weather conditions nature could throw at them, there'd still be some dumb jerk who wanted to watch the show. The grislier, the better.

"Hell of a way to go," Arlo said as he considered his friend.

The past few months had been a challenge for Wyatt. A series of safes strapped to bodies he and his dive partners had recovered from the waters had ultimately led to an even bigger mystery. One that had blown the 86th wide open, shaking the precinct to its core.

As Wyatt's investigation had progressed, it had become clear the bodies and the safes were a diversion for the cops, one meant to keep eyes focused on the water and off the drug smuggling running through Sunset Bay. The plan was also designed to shake faith and trust, when it had been revealed the masterminds had a long-standing vendetta against the retired chief of detectives, Anderson McCoy.

A vendetta that had started nearly thirty years ago with McCoy's willingness to look the other way so his own son could avoid prosecution.

They were all dealing with it, Arlo admitted, in what had come to be known as the Nightwatch case. Working through that betrayal was something they were all struggling with, but no one more than Wyatt. He'd not only found the bodies that kicked off the case, but he'd also fallen in love with Anderson's granddaughter, Marlowe, in the midst of the explosive revelations.

Proof, Arlo thought as he watched his friend help the rest of the dive team onto the boat, that responsibility might carry weight, but love did, too.

It was a stark reminder of why he avoided it himself. Love might work for some, but he wasn't interested in the responsibility. His job and his commitment to the city of New York were the only unassailable commitments he wanted in his life. He'd learned the lesson young that people might be loyal to their job or their ideals or their friends, but not necessarily to their family.

Not one single bit, he thought as a ready reel of images flipped through his mind on a loop. Family was easy to walk away from.

Too easy.

Because when something was taken for granted, it was always easy to walk away.

The last diver came up from the Zodiac boat and Arlo mentally counted off how many individuals had been needed for this mission before he stopped, every last thought fleeing his head. A tall, statuesque, neoprene-clad form hovered at the entrance to the boat, long dark hair spilling out of a swim cap. The goddess/diver pulled off the cap, crushing it in one hand. Long, slender fingers ran through her crown of hair in a one-handed shove out of her face, and what was left behind were high cheekbones, lush lips and dark brown eyes that were nearly black in the overcast mist on the boat deck.

Damn, but she had a heartbreaker of a face.

Heartbreaker everything, he amended.

He'd never considered dive suits particularly attractive, especially the ones the NYPD used for their missions. Thick, and designed to withstand both the cold and the often disgusting and unhealthy mess beneath the local waters, the woman wore it well.

Better than well, Arlo thought.

She wore it like a second skin and he felt his breath catch as she started to strip out of it.

"Yo, Prescott!"

Wyatt's bellow had him shifting his stare and Arlo caught the woman's gaze, then he quickly ducked his head. As attractive as she was, he'd be damned if he wanted to stand there like he was ogling her.

But, wow, she was a knockout.

A fascinating one, if the dark look that came into her eyes at his perusal was any indication.

Arlo gave Wyatt his full attention, tamping down the rush of interest at the goddess on deck. The team had wired in the news they'd recovered bodies, so he'd already braced for what was coming off the floor of the harbor. But even the advance warning couldn't quite prepare him for what they'd discovered, now laid out on tarps beside the entrance to the boathouse.

No time like the present, Arlo mused as he dropped into a crouch to assess what the dive team had pulled up. The effects of the saltwater and the active marine life near the wreck had already done even more damage than the deliberately set fire, but he could make out the solid strength of the bodies. There was a visible neck tattoo on one that the medical examiner's office would capture and document, as well as the basic quality of clothing and shoes.

These guys had been prepared for the trip into the water, as their feet were clad in waterproof boots. Both men also wore thick, wind-breaking jackets that would have kept them relatively dry as they went about their work on the boat.

The stench of gasoline filled the air, rising off the bodies along with the distinct scent of death. But it was the quiet voice behind him that had Arlo looking up, right into those fathomless brown eyes.

"If you turn the bodies over, Detective, you'll see the cause of death."

Arlo was a cop who favored humor to manage the job, and he couldn't quite hold back the sarcasm. "Drowning, wasn't it?"

"I'd say the bullets to the back of the head were far quicker."

Chapter 2

Since joining the academy and making the commitment to police work, Kerrigan had spent a lot of time managing her personal judgments as well as her assumptions that she knew why or how people got mixed up in crime.

Part necessity and part personal attitude, she'd joined the NYPD to make a difference. She wanted to believe in the good in people, despite the continued evidence to the contrary.

And she'd come to accept that for those who made bad choices, there was a system in place so they could atone for those decisions and—hopefully—make a better life in the future.

Naive? Maybe, she often admitted to herself. But it was a belief she *needed* to do the job and do it well.

Yet none of it could prepare her for days like this one.

Whatever these two men had involved themselves

in, their choices were inexorably tied to the brutal, terrible acts human beings could perpetrate on each other.

"Bullets?" the new arrival asked. "You recover any casings under the water?"

"No, but I saw the condition of the bodies as my partner and I removed them from where they were tied to the boat railing. Both men were tied up with haphazard knots obviously done in a hurry."

"Would you help me? I want to see those wounds."

Kerrigan realized her mistake as she crouched down beside Detective Arlo Prescott.

She knew who he was, of course. Most everyone in the 86th knew of the hotshot detective who'd developed a reputation as one of the NYPD's best detectives. He also did a considerable amount of work with the harbor team, so it was inevitable she'd come into contact with him from time to time. Up to now, though, she'd only seen him from a distance.

Although she'd helped out on dives throughout the city since joining the team, her home base had been her precinct in Queens. She'd only become a full-time member of the harbor team out of Sunset Bay, Brooklyn, about six weeks before.

Which meant she'd better get her heart out of her throat and get used to seeing the very able-bodied, dark blond, blue-eyed detective.

Not that his eye color mattered one whit to her.

Even when the full heat of those baby blues had been focused on her, snapping her to attention as she'd stripped off her dive suit.

It was something she did several times a day, but never before had the action seemed fraught with meaning, or the remotest trace of sexiness. Yet, somehow, getting caught up in one look from Arlo Prescott meant that routine had become so much more.

Since Laverne's voice and her friend's steady admonishments "to find herself a hot cop and enjoy herself" had grown a bit too loud in her head, Kerrigan kept her attention focused on the grisly forms in front of her.

They were in a covered area of the boat, designed for privacy in handling recovery work, but the thick rain outside the space had left the deck wet and slick. The atmosphere was cold enough to have them both breathing out puffs of air as they spoke.

"Help me roll him to his side."

Arlo did as requested, the waterlogged body even heavier than the two-hundred-pound-plus frame would suggest.

And just as she'd promised, the work of a single bullet was evident at the lower base of the skull.

"Damn." Arlo let out a low whistle. "No honor among thieves."

"Apparently not." Her voice was dry, a side effect of her breathing apparatus and the stress of the dive. She resolutely would *not* believe any hints of breathiness could be attributed to the sexy man currently holding a dead body with her and giving off glorious heat where his body crouched close to hers. "Other guy's the same. I think he was the second shot because his bullet wound isn't quite as clean."

Arlo laid the body back, wiping his hands on his slacks as he turned to her, still in his crouch. "What's that?"

Once again, that attention was laser-focused on her,

but this time she didn't see any traces of interest. Instead, all she saw was cop.

And that, she knew what to do with.

Pointing toward the other guy, she expanded on the theory she'd puzzled through as she and Jayden had worked to free the bodies and bring them up to the surface.

"The second one." She pointed to the other man, who was still lying face up, untouched. "If you look at his wound, it's low on the back of the head, too, but it's clear he moved in some way. The shot isn't nearly as clean or even. I'd guess he figured out what happened to his buddy and braced to fight."

"With a third crew member. One who left no traces in the boat."

And there it was. That nagging, mental toothache that suggested the case had grown even more complex than they'd first thought.

"That's what I thought when we brought them up. There had to be a third person."

"One you didn't find?"

"No," Kerrigan replied. "No trace of anyone else."

Arlo nodded, obviously working through the problem as he spoke. "These two might have doused the boat, but neither of them thought they wouldn't get out."

She exhaled hard, affirming Arlo's hypothesis. "It appears that way, and while I'll leave it to the medical examiners to make the final assessment, I'm sure they'll find traces of the accelerant on the victims' hands that suggest the same. These two were destroying evidence, but in full expectation they'd get off the boat."

"Looks like."

He pointed toward the other body. "Help me turn him. I'd like to take a look at that gunshot and then we turn them over to the ME to see if we get an agreement there, too."

Kerrigan moved with Arlo, resettling into a crouch beside the second body. This man was a bit smaller than the first in heft, but roughly the same height. And just as she'd assessed on the recovery, the bullet wound wasn't as clean—the shot had shifted at the base of the skull with the man's movement.

"Hell of a way to go." Arlo shook his head before gesturing to let the body back down. "And you've done a proper assessment, Officer…?"

He let the question hang there, obviously waiting for her name.

"Officer Doyle, Detective Prescott."

"You got a first name, Officer Doyle?"

It wasn't protocol, per se, to ask her first name, but she'd addressed him by his rank and he'd technically done the same.

"Kerrigan. Kerrigan Doyle."

He nodded and then surprised her when he reverted back to her rank. "This is good work, Officer Doyle. I'm more than happy to have you on this case if you want to see it through."

"I'd—" She broke off, the small bubble of happiness at having his professional attention popping at the remembrance of the way his gaze had settled on her when she'd stripped off her suit. "Thank you, sir. I'd appreciate the opportunity."

Something dimmed in his gaze, but it fell away after that quick flicker. And then he nodded, tilting his head toward Wyatt. "I'll clear it with Detective Trumball. This is very good work."

He got to his feet, stepping back as he spoke. And before she could say another word, he turned on his heel and left.

She wouldn't feel bad for that flash of frustration that he might have only asked her out of some misplaced sense of attraction, but she could honestly acknowledge that she was a bit disappointed as he walked away. She wanted to progress in the NYPD and working with a celebrated detective was one of the pathways to do that.

But what if he'd only asked for her help because he liked how she looked wet?

It was a harsh assessment—and possibly an unfair one—even as she still shivered from the memory of that intense stare. It hadn't been lascivious, but rather, she'd seen real, tangible interest in his eyes.

A two-second glance, Doyle? Get it together.

She'd have to, she realized as she stared down at the two vics. Because working with one of the lead detectives in the 86th would be a huge boon to her career.

Kerrigan consoled herself with that as she crouched down beside the bodies once more, her gaze roaming over the charred clothes and the premortem wounds. And as she pictured those gunshots—one clean, one not so much—she couldn't help but feel there was one more thing she was overlooking.

But what?

There was a third person on that boat, and that meant they had a lead. A lead she'd been given the opportunity to see clear through to its inevitable end.

It wasn't much, but it was something.

Something, Kerrigan knew, that she was determined to make into everything.

Arlo knocked on the door of the ME's office, a large box of doughnuts in hand. He knew the rules of order and waiting in line—and was well aware his harbor bodies weren't the only priority in the medical examiner's office—so he'd come bearing a gift.

He'd given the ME more than a day, after all.

Thirty-six hours, to be exact, to give proper time to examine the bodies and allow that team to do their essential work when the bodies still had fresh tales to tell.

He'd still brought breakfast.

For those who were smart and paid attention, a truism could be learned very early in a law-enforcement career: copious amounts of sugar could, and often did, work miracles in a cop shop.

A fact his new "partner" on the harbor case must have known, because Kerrigan Doyle was gesturing with a heavily glazed cruller toward their chief medical examiner, Lorelei Mayes, who at this very moment had a jelly bear claw in hand.

"Officer Doyle? Dr. Mayes?"

Both women glanced over at him, their irritation at being interrupted smoothing away as their gazes landed in unison on the box in his hands.

But it was Lorelei who smiled first, a gleam in her eyes.

"I see the bakeries in Brooklyn have been busy this morning."

Arlo shot her a wry grin. "Or as I prefer to say, great minds thinking alike."

He didn't miss the slightly guilty flush that added color to Kerrigan's cheeks, and he kept his smile in place even as a shot of annoyance skated over his skin.

She'd done nothing wrong, yet the sexual politics at the precinct likely made her feel as if she had. And he knew why. Some people—hell, more than some— would have been frustrated with Kerrigan's early arrival, effectively beating him to the punch with the doughnuts, but he was far more pragmatic than that.

Whatever got the job done.

And it was also one more notch in the column that the woman had a real future as a detective. A rank she could still make on the harbor team, just as Wyatt had. Career progression was readily available to all cops in the NYPD, but they made adjustments by pairing the experts in the harbor team with the "landlubber cops," as Wyatt had often called him.

The fact that Kerrigan Doyle had taken on the work with him for this case in addition to her dives was a sure sign she wanted that career. Her ideas and careful consideration of the victims pulled off the harbor floor were more indicators she was smart and focused. But that she'd arrived early this morning told him all he needed to know.

The woman was as bright as she was ambitious. But more than that, she was determined. He'd take a partner or a trainee any day of the week who showed that level of commitment to the work.

"Well, the bribery was unnecessary this morning, despite the sweet, delicious flakiness of this bear claw." Lorelei's gaze still twinkled with some amusement. "My team and I worked late to finish up your water rescue last night."

"Thank you."

Lorelei waved a hand. "It was our pleasure. The storm's been nasty, and this crime had an extra layer that bugged all of us."

"And we were waiting for you to discuss the specifics," Kerrigan quickly added. "I only just got here."

He didn't miss the quick answer or her eagerness for him to know she hadn't usurped the chain of command.

"As Dr. Mayes knows, I'm not particular on how the news gets shared. The more good minds working on this problem, the faster we catch our killer."

"I did finally figure out what was bugging me," Kerrigan said, seemingly more at ease with his acceptance. He was pleased to see that momentary concern over jumping rank had settled, and her natural eagerness was rising back to the surface.

"What's that?"

"The third person. They had to be quite a bit shorter than the two victims. The angle of the gunshots coming so low at the base of the skull."

Once more, she'd impressed the hell out of him. Her quick, thoughtful assessment on the boat and now this. She was observant, a necessity for police work. But she was tenacious, too.

Which shouldn't have been a surprise. It was a key trait of any good cop and Arlo had observed long ago that it was beyond essential for the men and women who worked the harbor. His own knowledge was limited more by what he knew of Wyatt's work than his own experience, but the harbor team was top-notch. They worked in unceasingly harsh conditions, in a city so large that crime in and around the water was a forgone conclusion.

Yes, the NYPD had made impressive strides over the last several decades to ensure New York was one of the safest large cities in the world, but it still held millions of people within its border. Not all of them were content to skip to work and turn in early for a good night's sleep.

An image of the dead drug smugglers rose in his mind, something that had happened regularly for the past thirty-six hours.

"That's good, Officer Doyle. It'll add to the profile of the killer and it's one more piece of the puzzle."

"I'd also agree with the officer's assessment," Lorelei added. "The angle of the gunshot is consistent with someone of lower stature. Especially since we found no gun residue on either victim, it wasn't a situation where one vic turned on the other, then was turned on by a third. Assessment indicates it was the same gun, same general angle."

"And what about Officer Doyle's other hypothesis?"

"Other?" Lorelei turned to look at Kerrigan. "We hadn't gotten that far."

Arlo nodded, encouraging Kerrigan to continue. "Please, Officer. Give Dr. Mayes your full assessment."

Kerrigan reached for a napkin, then set down her half-eaten cruller on top of it on one of Lorelei's pristine counters. She grabbed a second napkin and wiped her hands as she spoke, all purpose and efficiency.

"I believe the victim with the neck tattoo was shot second. His wound was consistent with the other one, but the hole is irregular, as if the victim became aware of the perpetrator and moved to fight him off."

Lorelei's attention never wavered as she moved toward a small laptop. She set down her own doughnut—

right on top of the surface—but did wipe her hands before tapping on the keys. After reviewing a few files, she stepped back.

"That's a strong deduction, Officer. I'd agree with that assessment as well. We'd noted the difference in wounds in the file but hadn't added that level of insight. It's a good one. And I'd say it means you're looking for one cold-blooded son of a bitch. Shots to the back of the head at point-blank range show determination and a certain sort of willingness to quickly end a life."

Arlo had already moved into the case with the same assumption—he'd even briefed his captain the day before with a similar description—but the affirmation still sent a shudder down his spine.

What were they dealing with?

He never assumed a criminal wasn't capable of humanity's worst sins, but that didn't mean there wasn't a hierarchy to what they dealt with. While there was considerable premeditation in the crimes he and his fellow officers worked, there were a lot of crimes of opportunity as well.

But this one?

This one had greed, avarice and a determined willingness to do evil at all costs.

Shaking off the second shudder, he gestured toward the files still up on the laptop screen. "You get an ID?"

"We got a hit on one of them. Jordan Bilks, age thirty-four," Lorelei recited, using the computer's track pad to scroll through the report. "Spent time upstate and got out on good behavior about fourteen months ago."

"I guess *good* was the operative word there." Arlo said. "Which one was he?"

"The first fired on, if we work under Officer Doyle's theory."

"For now, we do." Arlo didn't miss the slight creasing of Kerrigan's lips that she fought back into a straight line.

"We'll keep working on the second."

"Even with the neck tattoo, there's no hit in the database?" he asked.

"No, which was a surprise. I expected we'd get something off that tat," Lorelei said, working through a few more screens. "But nothing's popping on the ink."

One more mystery for them to puzzle through, Arlo acknowledged. While the bodies had decomposed considerably prior to coming to the surface, there was a harshness to both men that suggested career criminals to him. It was a snap judgment, but one he trusted all the same.

Yet, no hit on the second vic.

"You have a sense of age on the second one?"

"Estimates put him between thirty and thirty-two. His overall health and muscle tone are consistent with that age range, but he was a smoker and that had begun to take a toll. I'd put his initial tobacco use as early as eleven or twelve."

Lorelei never ceased to amaze him, the smallest details part of her evaluation and assessment.

"Looks like Officer Doyle and I have our work cut out for us."

"My team does, too." Lorelei turned her attention away from the computer and picked up her doughnut once more. "I want to run some of the details on their clothes and that tattoo has some specific markings to it.

The skull in the lower left corner of it has some meaning."

"Gang?" Kerrigan asked.

"Possibly, or some sort of badge of honor. I want to see if we can match any aspects of it to other known criminals."

"It's appreciated." Arlo tapped the lid on the box he'd brought in. "Please give the team my best and tell them to enjoy."

"Will do." Lorelei nodded.

Arlo glanced at Kerrigan once more. "Officer Doyle, let's go update the captain on what we've got."

"Of course."

She followed him quickly, waiting until they were nearly to the elevators before turning toward him. "I am sorry if it looks like I jumped the gun. I just wanted to see what they had."

He stopped short of the elevator bank, turning to face her and the anxious expression that put small crinkles around those dark eyes.

Pretty eyes, he realized as he stood there. It was an observation that shouldn't happen with a fellow cop he'd taken on to offer a bit of in-the-field training. But he couldn't deny the thought, either.

Vowing to think about it later, he keyed back into her underlying concern. "Are you under the impression I'm upset?"

"This is your case. And I'm thrilled to be a part of it."

"Officer Doyle. Part of police work is having the sheer tenacity to keep at something. I'd hardly discourage anyone from wanting to solve a crime as quickly as possible."

"No, I didn't mean you would. It's just that—" She broke off, letting out a small sigh. "I just know there's protocol and earned rank, and I don't want to give any impression that I don't appreciate your experience or your seniority."

"Tell you what." He hit the button for the elevator. "You focus on learning what you can and if I have a problem with anything I'll be sure to let you know."

"Oh. Okay."

"We're square." He gestured to the elevator door as it opened. "Now let's go talk to the captain."

Kerrigan wasn't a shy recluse, and she didn't back down from going after what she wanted. So what was it about Arlo Prescott that had her twisted up?

The late-afternoon recovery and the wait on the ME's office had kept their communication to nothing beyond email for the past thirty-six hours. It had been a buffer, she realized now, giving her some space to ratchet down that initial rush of heat when she noticed how attractive he was.

Moreover, she'd diligently avoided thinking of how he looked at all. She'd worked several dives the day before and had only checked her emails as time permitted between her duties. The opportunity to investigate the case wouldn't interfere with her work, which was something she'd assured Wyatt of when he'd let her know he'd approved the pairing with Arlo.

Everything was fine *and* she had the support of her boss to expand her skills.

So what was it with all these weird, mixed emotions?

Maybe because the man's damned attractive.

A thought that had slammed into her as he'd strolled into the ME's space with that box of doughnuts.

Especially since she'd immediately flashed back to the heat in his gaze when he'd watched her after she'd come out of the Zodiac boat.

She didn't need this. A crush on a coworker wasn't in her best interests. One on the superior who was offering her career growth only doubled down on the bad idea.

Which meant she had to bury it.

Crushes were nothing more than flights of fancy, anyway.

She'd nearly convinced herself of that fact when he followed her into the elevator, the doors closing them into the small space.

She wasn't a small woman—her tall frame usually put her at eye level with most men. But with Arlo, she had to look up slightly. She'd have to settle her arms on his shoulders if they kissed.

Not helpful, she mentally admonished herself. And since the bad-idea train was dangerously close to stopping, she searched for something innocuous to focus on. "You like the doughnuts at Sunset Bakery?"

"They're my favorite. Nobody makes a Boston cream like they do."

"I haven't been in Brooklyn very long but I'm partial to Cake Brothers."

He shook his head, a grave look covering his face. "The Rosetti boys have nowhere near the light touch Josie and Cora Callahan do."

"Come on, you heard Dr. Mayes. That was a delicious and flaky jelly bear claw."

He extended a hand as the elevator door opened,

keeping the conversation going as they walked to the captain's office. "You've got a lot to learn, Doyle."

"Duly noted, sir."

She heard the note of sass under her own words and was pleased and more than a little surprised when he turned back to her, a broad grin splitting his face.

"But I think you'll do."

Chapter 3

Arlo was still trying to figure out those peculiar moments discussing doughnuts in the elevator fifteen minutes later as he and Kerrigan brought Captain Dwayne Reed up to speed on the case. He hadn't found his footing yet with her, so the shots of wry humor underlined with just the right bit of cheeky wit felt like a start.

He was the elder statesman here and he'd taken her on for training. She'd earned it, but he was the lead, all the same.

Even so, the responsibility for her sat heavier than he'd anticipated.

Because she was a woman?

Or because, no matter how hard he wanted to push aside that fact or ignore it, he *was* aware of her. And, even more to the point, attracted to her.

Which had made jokes over doughnuts a strange yet comforting way past all of it.

He'd always been known for his sense of humor. It came easy and often, and he'd always believed that the ability to laugh was a necessity in life. Especially in a job where staring at murdered and burned bodies was all part of a day's work.

How refreshing—and unexpected—to find it in Kerrigan.

Like I have the corner on the market? he wondered to himself, even as he glanced at his trainee, standing straight and tall, respect for their captain stamped in every inch of her body.

It was novel, Arlo admitted to himself. And a reminder that while he respected his fellow female officers, he had never partnered with one. Where he'd exchanged jokes, often bordering on ribald, with his male colleagues, he would never dream of doing the same with a female officer. Yet, she had a solid streak of good humor all the same, one that didn't need the gross or the sexual to make her point.

Humor she had the maturity to keep in check. Here she was now, pivoting quickly to demonstrate proper deference to their captain, the job and all that lay before them in the case.

Captain Reed asked several questions and each time, Arlo had nodded his head, suggesting Kerrigan provide the response.

Dwayne focused on Kerrigan. "Your instincts are solid, Officer. And that was excellent work, evaluating the body before ascending to the surface. That couldn't have been easy."

"Thank you, Captain."

Dwayne smiled, the deep grooves around his dark brown eyes creasing. "I've told Trumball over and over

I don't know how he goes down in that water, day in and day out. But I can't deny the miracles you all work when you're down there."

"It's an honor, sir. I love my work."

Dwayne's eyebrows shot up. "And you still want to be partnered with this one?"

It was the first time Kerrigan gave Arlo more than glancing attention, her focus now fully on him as she responded to their captain. "I'm wholly committed to my work for the harbor team. But I'm also a cop and I'd like to continue the progression of that aspect of my career as well. Working with Detective Prescott is a huge benefit to learning that part of the job."

"So noted."

"Wyatt cleared it as well," Arlo added for no other reason than to assure Kerrigan. He well knew their captain missed nothing when it came to his team at the 86th.

"Trumball already let me know." And then without a pause, Dwayne was on to the next topic. "You have any sense yet what group this might be associated with?"

"No." Arlo shook his head. "I've run all the usual suspects and no one's popping as having a boat with those specs. Or the sheer stupidity to try manning it in waters churned up by an October hurricane."

Which, in and of itself, was strange. Boats cost money and effort and had pesky little things like serial numbers on them. Simply torching one—with cargo *and* men—meant there was someone operating in the harbor with a lot of cash to burn. Literally.

"Talk to Vice and see if anything's hit for them. Any new turf wars they're aware of or anything suspicious," Dwayne said.

"Of course. Initial efforts are already underway to run down the boat's owner. The team at Impound has instructions to send over any noticeable markings or serial numbers as soon as they find them."

Dwayne nodded but had already returned his attention to Kerrigan. "You've only been at the 86th for a few weeks. How are you finding it?"

"I'm very happy with the move. Detective Trumball leads a good team."

Which explained her earlier comment over doughnuts that she hadn't been in Brooklyn long, Arlo noted. *Interesting.*

Ambitious, hardworking cop.

Most people found comfort in their home precinct, yet she'd put in for a transfer. It wasn't completely out of the ordinary, but it was another notch in the ambition column. Especially if she felt she wasn't getting enough opportunities a few years into the job.

He vowed to ask her later before Dwayne's words registered. "Thank you for the dedication to seeing this through, Officer. Detective?" Dwayne's dark gaze was laser-focused on him. "I'd like a few more words, please."

"Of course."

Kerrigan stepped out and Dwayne waited a beat before speaking. "You think it's wise to bring in someone who is, essentially, a rookie?"

Arlo respected Dwayne in every way, aware their captain carried the burden of leadership in a way that only ever reflected positively on his team. He fought the hard fights and protected his people from the more political aspects of the work.

Which made his question something of a surprise.

There was no one at the 86th—and Arlo would even go so far as to say the entire NYPD—who wanted to see their team progress and succeed more than Dwayne.

"You have a problem with my partnering with Officer Doyle?"

"No problem. But she's new and all the evidence suggests some dark stuff is going on. Shot and burned bodies?" Dwayne's mouth firmed into a hard line. "That's personal and final."

"Especially to henchmen who were seemingly loyal."

"Exactly," Reed agreed. "To go out in a storm like that? The payoff might be good but there's an undertone of loyalty, too. And to be done like that? Cold-blooded shots to the back of the head, execution-style? This one doesn't sit well, Arlo."

It didn't sit well at all, especially with Dwayne's perceptive additions.

"All I'm asking is if you're sure you want to bring her into this. Her first big case."

Arlo considered the calm, collected woman who'd stood on the boat two days ago, helping him roll dead men in the rain. "She pulled up the bodies. Had the wherewithal to assess the gunshots and formulate theories, all while swimming in the morass of a storm and the leftover mess that was a doused and torched boat. She's earned it, sir."

"No doubt about that. But I want you to proceed carefully. Whatever we're dealing with, it's not going to be an easy case."

"No, it won't be."

"Officer Doyle's got incredible promise. I never want to see any of my brethren harmed in the line of duty. But the bright, eager ones? The ones with a future?"

"Yes?"

"I always worry it's that brightness that puts them at most risk."

The joke was nearly out of his mouth, a glib response that he was one of the brightest and he'd survived, when he caught Dwayne's serious gaze.

He *was* one of the brightest. And he'd proven himself to the 86th, over and over.

None of it could stop the nightmares that still came like clockwork over his first big case. He'd been bright and eager once, too.

And it had nearly killed him.

Kerrigan took the captain's dismissal in stride, but she couldn't deny the raging case of curiosity at whatever he and Arlo were talking about in his office.

The captain seemed pleased with her contributions but that didn't necessarily mean anything. The harbor team was small in size, and he might not want her stretching her time like this, no matter how complimentary he was with her work so far.

Which was just like her, she admonished herself, and forced calming thoughts through her mind.

Other people knew how to do their jobs, too. And no matter how determined she was to prove herself, the captain could talk to any member of his team however he wanted. The man's rank gave him that privilege, but so did reputation. If he hadn't wanted her working this one, she'd have heard about it by now, not a few days into the case.

Dwayne Reed held the responsibility of leadership comfortably on his shoulders and she'd do well to keep her eyes on her own paper and not worry about his.

Metaphorically.

A point that she'd do well to remember against her earlier flights of fancy, too. There was nothing to gain by looking at Arlo's deep blue eyes or slim waist or appealing height as he stood beside her in the elevator.

This was her shot and the reminder to keep her eyes on her own paper applied to attraction, too. Even more so than worrying about the captain.

The discussion with Reed filled her thoughts once more and gave her focus. Once Arlo came back, she'd offer to keep up the grunt work running down the boat's ownership and free him up for whatever else he needed to do.

She wasn't afraid of hard work. And while she had no expectation they'd find out the owner was one of the murdered men, they'd at least have a trail to follow.

Arlo left the office, closing the door behind him, and headed her way.

That lingering shot of awareness floated through her. *Damn it, how was the man's walk even sexy?* But with force of will, Kerrigan tamped it down and focused on the tasks that lay ahead.

"I hope you don't mind I waited. I can head down to the squad room and start on the boat research."

"Yeah, about that."

"You'd rather I did something else?"

"Actually, I was thinking your expertise on the water meant you had to have some familiarity with boats."

Once again, he'd caught her off guard. She hadn't come into this assignment thinking she'd be dismissed, but she also hadn't expected to be taken on as such a partner. Yet here they were, and Arlo seemed genuinely interested in tapping into her knowledge.

"Well, yeah. I mean, we train on all types of water-craft and I also grew up near the water. My dad has a boat. My uncles have boats." She smiled as she thought of her big family and weekends throughout the summers of her life spent on the water. "I have a pretty decent working knowledge."

"Know any boat sellers we can go talk to? I want to get a sense of how someone could essentially make a major asset with serial numbers, ownership and docu-mented provenance disappear out of any and all data-bases. Because I've been running that boat for a few days and nothing's coming up."

Her mind was already whirling with the possibili-ties, but there really was only one choice. "Let's go see Big Will at Brooklyn Yacht."

"*Big* Will?"

"Yep. Big Will Gentry. The man's six-nine and about three hundred and fifty pounds." At Arlo's widened gaze, she rushed on. "He's a gentle giant. He's owned the business for about forty years. His father owned it at least thirty more before him. Rumor has it his sons will be taking over but Will's not too excited to retire."

"Let's go."

The rain that had blanketed the city for a week like a thick, soupy mess had given way to a perfect fall day as they headed out of the precinct and toward Arlo's car.

"Did the rest of the meeting go okay with the cap-tain?"

At the sound of the locks unclicking, she pulled open the passenger-side door, cursing herself for div-ing straight in. His meeting with Captain Reed was none of her business.

And just because it happened after their debriefing didn't mean it had anything to do with her.

Arlo didn't respond right away, as he buckled in and then navigated out of the 86th's parking lot. It wasn't until he'd reached the entrance to the highway, heading onto the expressway, that he spoke. "The captain's good with you working this case, if that's what you're worried about."

"I'm not usually so—" She sighed, letting the words fade away.

She wasn't so what?

Wishy-washy?

Afraid of going after what she wanted?

Attracted to her coworkers? A small voice whispered that at the end.

"Not so what?" Arlo asked, his gaze, blessedly, on the late-morning traffic.

"I know my value and I know what I want, Detective. I'm a hard worker and I've wanted to be a cop since I was a kid. I'm just afraid it'll be taken away and that's on me to figure out how to navigate."

"Taken away how?"

"You've got a reputation for being the best. And I'm thrilled and terrified to be partnered with you. I want to do my best."

There.

It was out. All the way out. Or most of it, anyway. The failing-him part did terrify her.

And the rest?

Well, she'd manage the attraction. She had no choice.

It had been a long time since he'd trained someone so new, but Arlo still remembered his own feelings at

that stage of his life. The ones that had pushed him to
be the best and terrified him, both at the same time.

It wasn't a comfortable place to be. Arlo recalled the
push-pull of emotions vividly, but it was necessary to
progress in the job.

To keep moving forward.

Which was why he wasn't going to BS her or dismiss
her questions. "Captain Reed is good with you on this."

"Why do I sense a *but* in there?"

"Because he's worried about the really dark, violent
overtones of this case."

Dwayne's words had haunted him since he'd walked
out of the man's office. He hadn't quite gotten his equilibrium back yet.

*And to be done like that? Cold-blooded shots to the
back of the head, execution-style?*

Arlo had tried to shake it off, but even the bright,
sunny day couldn't chase away the darkness on this one.

"He doesn't think I can handle it?"

"Not at all. But it's his job to carry the burden of
leadership over his squad. And I can tell you straight,
he's worried."

Traffic was heavy, but moving, and Arlo risked a
quick glance over at her. Her mouth was set in a grim
line, the good-natured smiles of earlier vanished.

"I can understand that. The weight of responsibility
on him must be enormous."

He heard the hesitation beneath her words and opted
to keep quiet, giving her time to puzzle through the
details.

"I just have to ask if he'd be as worried if it were
Jayden on the team. Or any other male colleague, for
that matter."

"I get why you have to ask, but I've known Dwayne Reed a long time. He's fair and he plays it straight without consideration of gender. What I haven't seen much of in all that time is this level of concern over a case."

Or he hadn't, Arlo admitted to himself, if he didn't count the Damson job.

"Any murder would raise questions. What was on that boat?" Kerrigan let out a long, low sigh. "It's brutality on a whole different scale."

"Which is the cap's point."

In another ten minutes they'd cleared the traffic and were exiting for Sheepshead Bay. Kerrigan navigated him through the streets toward the water and in the distance he saw the sign for Brooklyn Yacht.

"This is a bit late to ask, but I'm assuming Big Will sells more than yachts."

"Most definitely. He's probably sold a quarter of all the pleasure boats in the area."

Arlo pulled into a spot in front of the entrance and glanced around as he got out of the car. He'd always been an observer, a skill that had set him up well as a cop, but he'd honed the practice over nearly fifteen years on the force.

Sunlight glinted off several boats visible in the docks behind the building. They shimmered in the distance, floating on the water.

"What did they do during the storms?" Arlo nodded his head toward the docks as Kerrigan met him around the back of the car.

"Same thing anyone else with a boat does. Tie down what they can and pray for the best."

"Sounds like a tough way to make a living."

"Big Will has a good business. He's got volume on

his side, which also helps. But the small mom-and-pops? It's definitely a challenge but they put up with it." Kerrigan grinned then, that smile lighting up her face before settling deep in her eyes. "People who love the water really love the water."

"A fact you, Trumball and the rest of you harbor nuts prove every single day."

The heavy moments in the car seemed to have faded as she tilted her head toward the building. "Come on. Let's go find Will."

Arlo followed her into the cavernous showroom and was amused to realize it had a similar look and feel as a car dealership. Which only reinforced that, regardless of a person's reason for buying a boat, it was still a vehicle that got you from point A to point B.

"Kerrigan!" The bellow emanated from the back of the showroom mere seconds before a large man who could be no one other than "Big Will" emerged from an office.

Arlo's first thought was that the man was aptly named. His second was the clear and obvious affection between Big Will and his newest partner.

After a quick round of introductions and a confirmation from Kerrigan that they were there on official police business, Will waved them both into his office and shut the door.

"That was some bad business that went down in the harbor." Will shook his head. "And your team found the bodies."

"We were assigned to the recovery, yes."

"You know about the downed boat, sir?" Arlo pressed. It wasn't a surprise, exactly, but it did mean news of the drug smugglers' demise had moved into the community quickly.

"Word travels." Will shrugged. "And a boat like that going down? There's interest."

"Will, if you know anything that can help us, we'd appreciate it." Kerrigan's respect for the man was obvious, but so was her tenacity to do the job right. "We'll do our best to keep your name out of it, but if you know something, we need to know."

The man was at least seventy and he'd clearly spent many of those years out on the water. Time, sun and water had weathered his face into craggy lines, but knowledge was a bright beacon in his blue eyes.

"I'll help however I can but let me guess. No serial numbers?"

Kerrigan remained silent, leaving a confirmation to Arlo. Even more impressive, she didn't turn toward him for verification. Instead, she was all cop, handling official business with her partner. It was a reminder of why she'd gotten this opportunity in the first place. And whether she stayed on the water or eventually moved inside the precinct, Arlo had no doubt the woman would make a damn fine detective.

She was cool where it mattered, and her instincts were rock-solid.

Taking advantage of the runway she'd already created, Arlo nodded his head. "No, sir. All provenance was removed. We have reason to believe that was handled by the current owner before going out on the water."

Will's inhale was sharp, his expression grim. "We don't keep track of everything we sell after it leaves here. I'd expect other sellers are the same, but the rumors in the business are strong. Word has it a drug-smuggling ring has been trying to get its hooks into the local trade. My sons and I have been careful. We do all the standard credit checks, but we've been keeping a close eye on new buyers."

"You think smugglers are working with boats from around here?"

Even as he asked the question, Arlo recognized the situation carried the potential for even bigger problems than they already faced.

A local smuggling ring?

He had no reason to doubt Will, but he was going to have a few words with his colleagues in Vice. How the hell was it possible an entirely new node on the drug trade was operating and no one had caught wind of it? All too often, it felt like they were just trying to keep up. But this? How could this level of crime go so completely unnoticed?

"No." Will shook his head. "The boats are likely coming up from farther south. Somewhere along the way they're going through the standard chop-shop process, retrofitting amped-up engine parts and erasing serial numbers and key markings."

Once again, the sheer ingenuity of criminals never failed to both impress and dismay. And proved, as always, there were people who *wanted* to live in the shadows.

"I really do appreciate your taking the time to talk to us."

"For you?" Will beamed at Kerrigan. "Anytime. And I will keep an eye out. I can promise you my sons will, too. There's too much crime in our city as it is. Polluting the water with this sort of bad goings-on?" Will let out a low whistle. "It's immoral."

"I wish there were more who felt just like you, sir."

Will took the acknowledgment in stride and promised to share anything else he might think of. With a quick light returning to his gaze, he offered to show Kerrigan a new addition to his fleet and Arlo waved them on.

Although he knew next to nothing about boats, Arlo took his time strolling around the showroom. Their proximity to lunchtime meant the place was pretty empty, but he saw a well-dressed woman on the far side of the room talking to an older couple.

Keeping his head down, he made a show of casually looking at a few of the speeders they had positioned around the large show floor. Beyond identifying the ship's wheel and the throttle, he had very little understanding of what he was looking at.

Which gave him that much more time to surveil the rest of the building.

Additional offices ran along the back wall, adjacent to Will's office. A small kitchen was visible in the back corner, and he saw someone puttering around at the sink, clearly occupied with their task.

Everything appeared in order. A prosperous business managing through a quiet part of their day.

He went back to perusing the boats, feigning interest as he waited for Kerrigan. Despite recognizing very little, he nearly missed the movement in the back of the showroom. Would have missed it, Arlo suddenly realized, if he'd stared any longer at the list of manufacturer upgrades posted on the side of the boat.

But whatever it was that grabbed his attention,

once caught, he listened to his instincts that something was off.

A younger man, not nearly as tall as Will but still a familial match, stepped out of the office beside his father's. He glanced at Will's open door, obviously hesitating, then ducked into the office on the other side.

Arlo didn't like jumping to conclusions, but he couldn't deny his interest when the man not only shut the office door behind him, but also snapped the floor-to-ceiling shades covering the office window closed.

A closed office meeting wasn't a crime.

Far from it.

But he'd already been curious when Big Will shared that he knew about the sunk boat and the bodies in the harbor *and* rumors of a new drug-smuggling ring.

Now his son was holding closed-door meetings the moment their father stepped out of sight.

With the other son Kerrigan mentioned?

Was it a coincidence?

Kerrigan's smile was bright as she walked back into the showroom from the dock area. She hadn't seen the man slip into that other office and he considered asking her about it.

"You ready to go?" she asked.

"Where's Will?"

"He got into a discussion with one of his mechanics. I let him know I could see myself out."

Arlo glanced once more at that closed office door and considered saying something right there, but then thought better of it.

He had no concerns about Kerrigan's honesty, but maybe it was time to do some digging on Big Will and his sons.

Not every hunch paid off.

But one that carried dark insinuations about her friends? Well, he'd handle that alone, come what may.

Arlo shook off the small stabs of guilt as he and Kerrigan walked out of the showroom.

His decision was made, and he'd do what he had to do.

Chapter 4

Kerrigan walked the perimeter of the boat debris spread out with numbered markers noting various pieces of evidence. She had several afternoon dives, but opted to start her day looking at what the salvage team had hauled up from the harbor floor.

She had her memories and what she'd observed on the dive, but it was time to look at the drug runners' boat in the light.

The evidence-management team worked around her, and she was careful to keep her distance to avoid any risk of contamination, but what they'd managed in only a few days was impressive. The sheer volume of items and boat debris laid out in a cavernous room of the evidence warehouse was stunning.

The port side of the hull was mostly intact, and it had been placed at the far end of the warehouse. She'd spoken briefly with an arson investigator brought in from the fire department who was consulting on the work as they'd walked it together. The woman's congenial approach and willingness to share what she knew had been a good start to the morning. It had given Kerrigan a few things to consider as she now navigated the pieces that had already been separated from the boat.

Namely, that the majority of the damage was isolated on the starboard side, along with the bodies. More to hide? Kerrigan wondered. Or had they just run out of time?

It was the starboard-side pieces where she was standing now.

Recovery photos had already been sent to her and Arlo, the first step by the evidence team before any aspect of the boat was touched or pulled apart. Although they would continue to photograph and record as the boat was reviewed and, in places, disassembled, those initial photos were the best record of what actually came off the harbor floor.

She'd studied them late into the night, now trying to associate the pieces before her with what she remembered in the images.

"It's a massive job."

The low voice over her shoulder was friendly, congenial even, so why did that husky timbre manage to send a wave of shivers low down on her spine?

Kerrigan whirled to face Arlo, determined to shrug off the ridiculous reaction. "Detective." She nodded. "Good morning."

"Good morning, Officer Doyle. Looks like we're both getting an early start."

"I spent a lot of time with the photos last night, trying to associate them with what I saw on the dive. But we were also so focused on the body recovery that I didn't get a good look at much."

"Recovery in the midst of a hurricane's lingering effects, I'll add."

She didn't miss the clear note of approval in his gaze, and she found herself looking a few beats too long in those dark blue eyes before coming back to her senses.

"It's not the easiest to see in the depths of New York's waterways on a good day, so that's a fair point."

Even now, she could conjure the feel in her mind of being down in the dark on that dive. The water had been flowing hard, pushing on her and Jayden as they did the work. Every dive required her full focus, but that was one of the ones where she'd truly earned her keep.

"What do you see now as you look at this?" Arlo asked. She had to admit just how excited she was to share her theories.

And if it led to more of that approval she saw in his eyes...

"The deliberate setting of the fire obviously impacted the whole boat, but there's more significant damage on the starboard side." Kerrigan gestured to the pieces of the boat railing, where even now she could remember the way the bodies had been lashed to it. "Jayden and I had to remove the bodies from that railing."

"That's where they were tied down?" Arlo kept his fair distance, just as she had, but he did move to examine where the evidence team had laid out the boat railing.

"Yes." She pulled the image from the dive fully to her mind. "More than six hours under the water had already done a lot of damage but their hands were bound to the railings, and both were sort of slumped over it."

"That takes some work on the part of the killer. Especially if the gunshots had already taken care of them."

Kerrigan weighed that remark. "You're right. That's a lot of unnecessary work. Why go to the trouble to lash them to the railings?"

"One more question we have to figure out."

They moved in and around the debris but Kerrigan kept coming back to the railing, Arlo's observations racing through her mind. Why did the killer attach the bodies? It wasn't like a man was a threat with a bullet in his head?

Theater?

"Arlo." He glanced up from where he was standing among various pieces of decking and walked over. "Come look at this."

Although she knew the starboard side had sustained more damage, upon closer review it looked like the boat had burned in layers.

"Look at this here." She pointed toward a large piece of decking. "See that arc of charred wood? It looks like the flames followed the pour of the fuel as the deck was doused."

"It makes sense. The boat went down pretty quickly so while the fire would consume if given the time, the rain, as well as the harbor water, likely put it out."

"But then look here." She gestured toward a piece of decking that was still attached to the base of a seating banquette. "This looks like fuel was poured straight on it. Like it had a wider mouth from the fuel container."

She was already glancing toward the entrance, ready to flag down the fire commissioner, when Arlo spoke.

"Seems like a funny coincidence. Two bodies and more fuel."

"It's possible it's just because this was the last area where the victims were. Like maybe they had emptied the last of their fuel?"

"But you don't buy it?" he asked, his voice neutral as he pressed her to work it through.

"It just seems as if it could be more deliberate. Like the area was doused with more fuel."

"The ME didn't note any additional fuel on the clothing. I think we'd have seen more burn damage on the vics if that had been the case."

Kerrigan considered his statement. "Maybe just more fuel on the ground, beneath them. This had to have happened fast, and methodical behavior starts to go out the window."

"I suppose it does."

"I'm going to go get the arson investigator. I'd like her take on this."

"Calhoun. She's good. I spoke with her on my way in." He moved into a crouch beside the piece of decking. "Let's see what she says."

He got back to his feet. "And then let's go get some breakfast. Despite the grisly subject, I'd like to talk this one through."

She could hardly deny the suggestion when her stomach chose that moment to let out a large growl. Arlo hadn't missed it, either, his wry grin at the ready. "I guess you agree?"

"Sure. I could definitely go for some breakfast."

It was only as she headed off to the other side of the warehouse that Kerrigan recognized the challenge now before her.

Having breakfast with her partner wasn't a crime. Nor should it be a problem. She and Jayden had eaten any number of meals together, just as she had with the rest of the harbor crew.

But this was different, Kerrigan knew.

Whether she wanted it to be or not.

Because no matter how she wanted to slice it, dice it or try to wish it away, she didn't get a funny little flutter low in the belly when she thought about sitting opposite her other male colleagues sharing a meal.

Arlo had learned his first week on the job that coffee was damn near sacred to a cop. Drinking coffee and eating doughnuts might be an age-old police cliché, but it was for a reason.

He'd played a game with himself from that first week, often trying to guess how a fellow officer might fix their cup.

Coffee regular? It was a New York standard for a reason, with milk and two sugars dropped neatly into a steaming mug of joe.

Just black? Some of his best friends consumed it that way, including his first chief of detectives, who'd drunk roughly a gallon a day.

And then there were the rare few, heaven forbid, who drank decaf. An awful waste, in his opinion, in any possible combination.

But Kerrigan?

The heavy cream, dumped in until the coffee resembled the color of oatmeal, along with four sugar packets, was a surprise.

"What?" She glanced up as she finished off the last swirl of her mug with a spoon. Sunlight filtered in behind her, haloing the crown of her head, and he was just fanciful enough to admit he was a bit dazzled.

Which was why his tone likely came out a bit drier than he intended. "How can you possibly drink that?"

She glanced down at her mug. "My coffee?"

"More like sugar and cream with a splash of coffee. Is it even hot?"

"First you pick on my doughnut choices and now you piss and moan about my coffee?"

"Consider it more a surprising observation."

"Over my coffee?" Her dark eyes sparkled but he could also see the genuine curiosity there.

"I guess I took you for a black coffee type?"

"Oh?"

"You divers are tough. Seems you'd take your coffee the same way."

"Obviously not."

She looked about to say something, then seemed to think better of it, so Arlo pressed the point.

"What is it?"

She hesitated by taking another sip of her coffee before sharing her thoughts. "The harbor team seems to have a special reputation."

"A well-deserved one, I'd say."

"But it's like we're held separate somehow. The words are always complimentary, but we're still seen as something other from the department. I noticed it with the captain earlier. And, truth be told, it comes up often."

"What you do is special."

"Sure, I get it. But it's also cop work in a city surrounded by water. Somebody's got to do it."

"But not many people do. Diving work is special under any circumstances. But in the waters around

New York? Which, and I realize we're about to eat, and you live it on the daily, but they're horrifically nasty. Wyatt's told more than a few stories."

She sniffed, her affront at an assessment held by oh, basically *everyone*, oddly sweet. "They're not as bad as they used to be."

"That's like saying toxic waste only has a half-life of a century."

"Well, it's not the Caribbean, but what is?"

"Not much." Arlo settled his scarred menu in the small wire holder against the window.

Why was he pushing this?

He'd spent the better part of the past day feeling ill at ease for his decision to run Big Will and his family. It had seemed like the right decision inside the showroom, but once he'd begun running queries and checking files in the database, it didn't feel quite so cut-and-dried.

Kerrigan was his partner on this.

Yet he'd kept her out of a line he was tugging because of what? Concern her feelings could get hurt?

Or, worse, that she couldn't handle it?

He wasn't one to run from his mistakes and he nearly said something right there, anxious to clear the air, but he didn't want to lose the momentum of their conversation.

Nor did he want that lone choice—made in the moment—to negatively color an opportunity to help her get past whatever it was that was gnawing at her.

So he'd save it for another time.

"My point's still valid. The job's impressive, just like the cops who choose to do it, day in and day out."

"But it's the job. It doesn't deserve special attention. Or not to the degree everyone seems to put on it."

Arlo did understand the special attention. While it was an ego boost, it could be a bit much at times. He'd been fortunate to have a strong run of closed cases, and while he more than appreciated the attention for it, closing cases was his job.

Police diving was hers.

And too much attention could mess with your head if you let it.

Which made her overall reticence interesting. Because the anxiety he kept sensing in her didn't seem at all tied to cocky behavior or an overabundance of attitude. Instead, there was an obvious processing on her part as she tried to find her place in the department.

"It's important to you, isn't it? To know where you fit."

The sparkle vanished from her gaze, even as she held her voice steady. "Isn't that important to everyone?"

"Yes, but I can see you working through it. It's okay, to be part of the team and still have a specialized role. You can have both. Be both."

"I'm not trying to sound ungrateful."

There it was again. That subtle insinuation that having an opinion or ambition or thoughts about what she was doing was somehow ill-advised.

Which meant he had to tread carefully.

Someone had made her feel that way.

She had far too much competence and inner drive for it to have simply surfaced without provocation.

"You don't sound ungrateful. You sound like you're trying to figure it out."

Although she was toying with the handle on her

coffee mug, she kept her attention focused on him. Direct. Solid. A willingness to stick to it, even if it was difficult.

"Not everybody thinks a woman belongs on the force. That goes double for specialized services."

"Has someone said anything to you? You have problems with other officers?"

"I know how to take care of myself. But it doesn't mean there isn't pressure. It also doesn't mean there aren't men concerned about going down on a dive with a female partner. Or other cops, male or female, worried about going out on an op with a female partner. It's real, Arlo."

"You were trained, same as me. Same as the other divers. What does the rest matter?"

She shrugged at that, but he saw the slightest smile return to her gaze. "You're a detective. A damn smart one best as I can tell. Don't suddenly develop a case of ignorance as if you think it doesn't happen."

"Doesn't mean it's right."

His comment hung there as their waitress brought over their breakfast orders. His stack of pancakes along with eggs and bacon and an omelet and wheat toast for her.

She prepared to dig into her breakfast when he pressed the point again.

"I meant that. You belong on the team."

She took another sip of her coffee, obviously marshaling her thoughts. "I'm not trying to dismiss your question, or dance around it. I suppose I am a bit tetchy about my role. I'm here because I want to learn. I want harbor, yes, but I want more. I want the detective's badge."

"Why's that? The tetchy part, not the badge."

"I joined the NYPD to make a difference. I have a love of the water, so Harbor Patrol was a natural choice, but I'm a cop to the core. I love this city and I want to see it shine."

"Then why worry what others think?" When she looked about to argue, he held up a hand. "Hear me out."

She nodded but didn't say anything.

"You work hard. You do the job. Expertly, I'll add. No one who partners with you can argue you don't pull your own weight, especially when I saw you drag a body out of the harbor and then saw you use your mind to work through the puzzle of that same body's gunshot wounds.

"Lean into that. Lean hard, because from where I'm sitting, you're doing the job and then some."

"Thank you."

"You're welcome." He nodded, aware he'd veered dangerously close to elder-statesman, speech-giving territory. "Now let me eat my lumberjack breakfast in peace."

"You got it."

Arlo's words were still occupying Kerrigan's thoughts that afternoon as she and Gavin prepared to descend into the spiky waters of the Harlem River around the Macombs Dam Bridge.

"Some moron tosses a gun over the bridge and we have to go hunt for it." Gavin was one of her sunnier colleagues, so the fact he was complaining was out of the ordinary.

"It's the job, Gav."

"I know." He shook his head as he did a final check

of the gauges on his oxygen tank. "I know it is. But life would be a hell of a lot better if people'd quit shooting one another."

"I won't argue with you there."

"Fifteen." Gavin sighed. "It's the young ones that get me. Fifteen damn years old and he gets in a fight after the Yankees game. He's too young to just be a moron. He's a kid."

Only the child who tossed a gun used to kill another wasn't a kid anymore, Kerrigan thought as she did the final check of her own equipment. And wasn't that nearly as sad as the loss of life the fifteen-year-old's gun had inflicted? Two lives ruined, with one simply left to exist above ground.

She shook off the dark thoughts—there'd be time for them later—and focused on the dive. The water ran a bit easier here than farther south, but it was still a tough dive. All the waters around New York were, Kerrigan thought as she dropped her mask over her face and fitted in her breather. With no more preparation left, she sunk into the water, reorienting herself to the immediate shifts in sound and physical weight.

They had a limited field for the search. The likelihood the gun was within a ten-yard radius around the perimeter of the bridge was in their favor. Witnesses hadn't been plentiful and the kid who did the shooting still hadn't talked, but video from the bridge's shelter house had indicated the gun fell straight down versus being tossed.

Gavin took the north side of the bridge and she'd taken the south. She used her thickly gloved hands to sift the silt at the bottom of the river, working in slow, progressive movements. Visibility was limited,

as usual, but the sun was bright and filtered in a bit
from above. She settled into a rhythm, communicating with a quick confirmation of "negative" to Gavin
every ten feet or so. Other than his *negatives* in return,
the work was quiet.

Steady.

Which gave her far too much time to think about
breakfast with Arlo.

*Lean hard, because from where I'm sitting, you're
doing the job and then some.*

She *was* leaning hard, damn it.

So why was she so far in her head?

She was devoted to her job and she'd willingly taken
on the additional work with Arlo. She had confidence
in herself—she wouldn't do the job if she didn't—so
why was she second-guessing herself over everything?

Those last few months in Queens had been bad but
she'd survived. The Internal Affairs investigation had
been unfortunate but necessary, and she'd simply done
her job.

But it had left scars.

And despite getting the rep as the team snitch, she
was the one who'd been left feeling betrayed.

None of it had anything to do with her work now.

Hell, it hadn't had anything to do with her work
then, either. She'd just been made to feel as if it did.

With that fire lit in her belly, she focused on the task
at hand and off the voices that kept racing through her
mind. Arlo was perceptive and he'd hadn't taken long
to notice her concerns and that lingering sense of in-
justice she hadn't fully shaken.

Which meant it was time to shake it.

High time, she thought.

This wasn't her precinct in Queens any longer. She'd only been here a matter of weeks and she'd already had more opportunity to progress than the entire two years before. She might not have liked the reason she chose to leave, but she was damn glad she had.

Silt filtered through her left hand as her right hit something.

Immediately keying back in, she recognized the distinct shape and, as she picked it up, weight of a gun.

Gavin's "negative" filtered in through her comm unit and she replied a garbled "I've got it" around her breathing apparatus.

A "great job" filtered through her comm unit from Jake Sewell, the officer manning the Zodiac, and Kerrigan began her ascent. Sunlight greeted her as she broke the surface, even as she felt the cold swirling in the air.

Fall was definitely here, the weather taking a real turn after the rain the week prior. Before even getting out of the water, she dropped the gun into an evidence bag Jake already had out. Once she'd ensured the transfer, she climbed into the Zodiac and got to work stripping out of her gear. Traffic rumbled above them over the bridge, those passengers unaware of anything that had transpired in that very spot the night before.

It was a strange counterpoint to her memories of her time in Queens, yet oddly comforting.

The information she'd given to Internal Affairs was confidential. Her new colleagues had no reason to know what had happened. They had no reason to judge her. Just like the passengers up above on the bridge, they were oblivious, too.

She'd be sure to keep it that way.

"Kerr." Gavin caught her attention as Jake navigated

them toward the waiting NYPD boat about a quarter mile downriver. "Great work."

"Thanks."

"Come out with us tonight once shift's over. We're all heading to that new bar in Sunset Bay."

"Bulldog's?"

"That's the one."

She'd avoided any fraternizing up to now beyond a couple of beers at a retirement party last month, but she recognized the offer for what it was.

Camaraderie.

Partnership.

And a big step in the right direction to firmly put the past behind her.

Chapter 5

Arlo pulled up in front of Wyatt's house in Park Slope and his friend walked out with his new love as Arlo came to a stop. Although he'd seen Wyatt briefly in their chief-of-detectives weekly meeting, they hadn't spoken much since the harbor recovery on the boat.

He'd known Marlowe was coming out for the evening and while he was looking forward to seeing her, he'd already considered how much he was willing to discuss the case. Since she was the granddaughter of a cop and now the girlfriend of one, she understood the requirements of the job. The fact she was a civilian who did a lot of work for the NYPD as a locksmith added more weight.

And still, he struggled with how much to say to someone outside the department.

Like you've got the time to quibble, Prescott. Or a hell of a lot to say.

He was stuck. Or *they* were stuck, he corrected himself, since Kerrigan was certainly a part of this.

Despite digging, questioning and making calls up and down the eastern seaboard to every boat expert he could find, he had nothing. Kerrigan had been pulling her weight as well, reviewing a number of case files from the past decade that had any resemblance to their current situation, no matter how tenuous.

It was tedious work, yet she'd done it willingly, balancing it with her dive work and writing some of the most thorough reports he'd ever read.

And still, they had nothing.

Their lack of leads was an increasing frustration, one that had begun to eat at him. Even the quiet digging he'd done into Big Will's business had proved fruitless. Not finding the man engaged in criminal behavior was a positive outcome, even if it meant Arlo was also now trying to figure out how to discuss that one with his new partner.

His decision to run the boat salesman had seemed rather straightforward in the moment. Now it felt like he'd held out on Kerrigan, and he didn't like the way it had settled low in his gut. It didn't help that he still had to write up his report on his findings, so the clock was ticking to handle this one.

Not the best headspace to have on a free Friday evening.

Wyatt pulled open the door, gesturing Marlowe to take the front seat, but she pressed back. "You sit with Arlo. I'm sure the two of you have a lot to discuss."

Wyatt looked about to argue when Arlo heard the lightest whisper of Marlowe's voice float in the open car window. "Take the time to talk to him."

They settled into their seats and Arlo navigated through the neighborhood toward the main thoroughfare between Park Slope and Sunset Bay. As miles went, it was just over two to the bar, but with Friday-night traffic, they practically crawled, light after light.

"Brooklyn sure looks different from when I was a kid." Arlo loved the renaissance the borough had enjoyed over the past decade—it was now an epicenter of young professionals, trendy hot spots and activity.

He might love it, but navigating it was an entirely different matter.

"It's amazing, isn't it?" Marlowe added. "I grew up here and there are days I wonder when I got so *un*cool."

"You'll always be the coolest to me." Wyatt shot her a grin over his shoulder, to where she was sitting in the back, behind Arlo's seat.

"You sweet talker." Marlowe blew him a kiss.

"You're both googly-eyed," Arlo said, but he couldn't deny how good it was to see his friend happy.

"And you're both cops," Marlowe added. "Talk shop while I check a few emails."

"How's the case going?" Wyatt asked.

Whatever reticence Arlo had evaporated, as Marlowe's understanding went a long way toward settling him. He did need the thoughts of a fellow cop and Wyatt was one of the best. Plus, their friendship gave them a sort of short-handed communication style and Arlo unloaded.

"No leads. No provenance on the boat. No chatter, at all, despite having two drug runners torched in the middle of a freaking storm." Arlo shook his head. "Nothing about it makes sense. People talk, Wyatt. And no one's saying a word about this one."

"Somebody should have blabbed by now," Wyatt agreed. "Or at least gossiped in a way that indicated someone knows something."

"And yet there's nothing." Arlo fought a sigh as he turned onto Fourth Avenue.

"How's Kerrigan working out?"

It was nearly out of his mouth, that decision he'd made on Big Will's business, when Arlo pulled it back. He'd dug that hole and he'd dig himself out of it. Especially because sharing that small detail would likely put Wyatt's antennae up.

"She's fantastic. Eager and smart and she's got a good eye."

"She does. I've kept a watch since she came into the team a few years ago. She's smart and incredibly prepared and has been a huge asset to the harbor team. I'm glad we've got her at the 86th."

Wyatt inadvertently gave him the entry he needed, and Arlo took his shot. "I read her file. She's quickly making a name for herself. Her assessment of the bodies, especially the ballistics, was smart."

"I believe it."

"Why'd she transfer in?"

For the first time, Arlo saw his friend clam up and Arlo knew he'd hit on something.

"Had a bit of trouble at her old precinct. She handled it and that's about all I know." Wyatt only paused a beat, then added, "You said you read her file."

"Broad personnel overview. Her experience and her résumé's about all. Key cases she's worked."

"That's too bad, Arlo," Marlowe said from the back seat as Arlo saw the sign for the bar come into view on the next block.

"What's too bad, sweetie?" Wyatt asked, turning to face the back seat.

An unmistakable note of humor laced Marlowe's words. "Looks like Arlo's going to have to pump his new partner if he wants to know her backstory."

Kerrigan took a sip of her beer and considered her surroundings. While she'd hardly call Bulldog's a cop bar, there were a heck of a lot of off-duty cops from the 86th there tonight.

It made sense, she admitted to herself. Bulldog's was a new hot spot and it was a Friday night. For all their pride in being an elite group of people who had their own watering holes and eateries, she'd yet to find a single cop who didn't enjoy a fun night out.

Sunset Bay's newest bar definitely qualified. Especially after word had spread that a group was heading out this evening to check it out.

"Fancy seeing you out tonight." Jayden sidled up to her, his smile broad as he extended his longneck in a gesture of cheers against her glass of chardonnay.

"Right back at you. I thought you and hubs had date night tonight."

Jayden frowned, even as it didn't fully reach his eyes. "He had a client come into town who decided they wanted to enjoy a Friday night in New York and he's on deck to help entertain. We moved date night to tomorrow."

"That stinks."

"Since it's a client Darius brought in *and* that win was responsible for his rather lovely holiday bonus, I'm hardly in a position to complain."

"And I bet you upgraded your reservations to an even swankier place for tomorrow night, too."

"You know me so well." Jayden's grin went positively Cheshire. "Speaking of knowing, how's working with Detective Prescott?"

"It's good. The case is an endless series of dead ends, but the work's good and challenging. I'm learning a lot."

"Hmm." Jayden took another sip, his warm brown eyes anything but innocent as he looked over his beer.

"What's that supposed to mean?"

"Nothing at all except the man's attractive and re-portedly single. As are you."

"Jayden!" Kerrigan fought the rush of heat that flushed her face and worried that her voice had gone a bit too loud.

As in get-the-neighborhood-dogs-barking loud.

"You know that doesn't matter," she said in a qui-eter voice.

Her friend shrugged, even as all traces of teasing dried up. "It does matter, even when we don't want it to. But why does it have you so bothered?"

"I'm not bothered. I'm trying to do my job and make a name for myself. Not a reputation."

"Your rep and good standing is unassailable. You have to know that."

While she appreciated his support and suspected Jayden knew more about her Internal Affairs dealings at her old precinct than he let on, she couldn't see her way to his optimism. "It can all go away with one bad deci-sion. I'm not interested in making one with my boss."

"Partner and elder statesman, maybe, but not boss. There's not even a whiff of boss in there and you know it."

Perhaps it was because of his support of her and

their strong friendship that Kerrigan was a bit surprised Jayden continued to press the point.

"He's my new partner, nothing more."

"Well then, let's put that to the test."

Jayden's knowing grin was back as his gaze settled somewhere over her shoulder. She turned to see what he was looking at, only to find Arlo already weaving his way through the bar toward them. Wyatt and the woman Kerrigan knew to be his girlfriend, Marlowe McCoy, followed close behind.

Kerrigan wanted to curse Jayden for his perceptiveness, but even she couldn't quite deny the pure shot of heat that lasered through her as she took in that tall form, blondish-brown hair and firm jaw.

What struck her even more than how he looked was the way his eyes roved around the bar, assessing as he moved.

He was all cop and she found something about all that protective focus deeply compelling.

About as compelling as Jayden's words, which hadn't stopped rattling around in her mind.

There's not even a whiff of boss in there and you know it.

She did know it and it didn't help.

Arlo reached them first, his smile broad. "Kerrigan. Jayden."

She'd begun to get a sense of him over the past week and while the smile was genuine, there was a distinct sense of tension hovering beneath the surface. She didn't get the feeling it was because of her and Jayden, but she sensed it all the same.

"Arlo." She nodded before turning her focus to Wyatt and Marlowe. She'd met Marlowe shortly after the Nightwatch case closed and the woman had lived up to her reputation. She had a cool look about her, the sleek blond hair and slim figure accentuated by the habitual black she wore. Her kick-ass job of safecracker added to her intriguing persona. If asked directly, Marlowe would have introduced herself as a lock-and-vault technician, but safecracker was way cooler.

Not to mention, a description that fit.

What also fit were Marlowe and Wyatt, Kerrigan thought. They were a matched pair and as someone who'd known Wyatt since joining the harbor team, she'd never seen him happier.

"This place is hopping," Wyatt said after he and Marlowe had both leaned in for a quick hello kiss. "They've gotten a reputation as Sunset Bay's hottest nightclub in a very short time, and I can see why."

"It took us ten minutes just to wait for the valet," Arlo added.

That lingering sense that something was bothering Arlo continued to nag at her, but he kept his conversation as light as his tone and she finally resolved to ask him about it at work. It was Friday and if he was working through something, she couldn't expect him to spill it during an evening out.

"Why don't we go get some drinks at the bar?" Wyatt deliberately glanced at her and Jayden's drinks. "We'll get refills for you both. You want to stick with what you've got or change it up?"

After confirming the same drinks would be fine, Jayden followed Wyatt and Arlo to the bar and Kerrigan was left alone with Marlowe.

"It's good to see you again." Marlowe started in immediately, her warm words at odds with the cool look.

"Wyatt's been singing your praises. I know you all had a tough dive with that horrific storm."

"It had its moments."

"Burned boats and people?" Marlowe shook her head. "It's moments like that when I admit to myself that my life is boring and I'm okay with that."

"It's a tough way to die."

"Which means it was a tough way to live." The other woman appeared to hesitate for a moment before she pasted on a wry smile. "Don't mind me. I'm still working through the reality of losing a loved one to bad choices."

Although it was the Nightwatch case that had brought Marlowe and Wyatt together, the case had also led to her father's murder while in prison upstate.

She might not have anticipated being the person Marlowe would share such personal information with, yet she also understood the impulse.

In a lot of ways, Kerrigan and the rest of Wyatt's team were a safe space. All of them were aware of the case and its outcomes. There wasn't any need for explaining or providing backstory, since the cops at the 86th already knew all the details.

Marlowe had been open with her. Kind, too. And Kerrigan was determined to give the same in return.

She put a hand on Marlowe's arm, hoping the compassion she felt for the woman's situation—and the resulting heat on her grandfather's decisions to hide his son's sins—was clear. "It takes time. Grief doesn't just evaporate."

"Wyatt keeps telling me that. He's always saying it comes in waves." Marlowe let out a small laugh as she brushed the tips of her fingers beneath her eyes to wipe away a few stray tears. "And that's not diver-speak."

"He's right. And while it's not intentional diver-speak, it is pretty accurate. Some things just have to be felt. And they don't come on a set timetable or, sadly, often with any warning."

"I know you're right. You're both right." She took a deep breath, straightening her spine. "Which is why I'm going to enjoy my evening out and not be a wet blanket."

"You're not being—"

Marlowe stopped her with a raised hand. "Yeah, I am. But that's okay since I'm hoping to play on your sympathies and ask how things are going with Arlo."

"Arlo?"

"He's impressed with your work. You can consider that the highest compliment."

"I take it that way. His reputation as one of the department's best detectives is why I feel so lucky to be working with him."

For someone who'd been so forthcoming up to now, it was interesting to see how Marlowe quieted, obviously weighing her words. The timing coincided with a shift in the energy in the room as a song ended, and her words came in louder as she spoke.

"He's definitely good at the job. And I know you all are. It's an aspect of being a cop that's sort of embedded in what makes you who you are. But there's a lot of weight on him. On Wyatt, too. I saw it after Nightwatch. And I guess what I'm saying is that no matter how dedicated or driven, you're human, too."

While it was an incredibly astute observation, Kerrigan wasn't quite sure what to say in response. They *all* were focused on the job. And if she was honest with herself, she liked it that way.

She wanted to go under the water with others who were as committed as she was. Same went for going out with a partner or facing down a possible perp.

If you weren't fully, wholly committed to it, how did you ever get up the courage to go through the door? To make the dive? To do the work that carried inevitable risk?

But the job carried weight. A heavy one, that had to be figured out along with the rest of their lives.

"It is the job, Marlowe. It carries weight because we are talking life and death on both sides. As well as that in-between limbo where we're chasing people who are lucky to be alive, but they're ruining the life they have."

"Doesn't it get tiring?"

"Some days."

"And others?"

"It's the others I live for. Those are the ones when I know exactly why I was called to this job. Yes, it carries weight, but it's a privilege, too."

"I told you she was great."

Arlo's voice filtered in behind her, loud enough to make it through the pulsing, throbbing background of the club, but still low enough that it sent a few shivers skittering down her spine.

When had they come back with the drinks?

And how much had he heard?

Since he'd obviously heard some of what she'd said, Kerrigan opted to hit it head-on as she set her empty wineglass on their small, high-top table and took the fresh glass Arlo extended. "Don't mind me. I'm just waxing poetic on police work."

"Wax away," Arlo said, and for the first time since he'd arrived, she saw an easing in him. In the set of his shoulders and the small light that now danced in the deep blue depths of his eyes. "It's what makes you a good cop."

Kerrigan reached for her glass of wine and took a sip. It was already more than she'd planned, promising herself on the way over she'd only have one drink.

But, damn it, she didn't want to leave.

Didn't want to walk away from that appreciation in his gaze or his support of her chosen profession.

His support of her.

"Kerrigan was just telling me about how she gets through the hard days," Marlowe added, leaning into Wyatt before looking up into his eyes. "Seems like devotion to the job runs rampant in this crew."

"You know going in that it's not easy work." Wyatt wrapped his free arm around Marlowe's shoulders. "But it's meaningful work. In the end, I've come to realize that's all that matters."

Wyatt's words lingered in his mind as Arlo took a pull on his beer. It wasn't easy work. They all knew that going in and even as far back as the academy, when everyone was shiny and eager, their instructors made sure everyone understood what they were signing up for.

Yet he'd still made the choice.

So had Wyatt and every other cop on the force.

And so had Kerrigan.

He'd been caught off guard to see her already inside Bulldog's and the walk to the bar had given him a few moments to settle himself. To cover up the instant hit of attraction he'd felt at seeing her long dark hair waving around her face before falling like a dream down her back.

Why was it easier to see her as a partner when they were on the job? Now all that professional distance had seemingly vanished.

He'd had female partners before. Not many, especially since he'd worked with his first partner, John, for more than six years of his career. But he had worked with women and none of them had gotten under his skin. They'd been valued colleagues, nothing more.

And now he had someone under him, training with him, and he was having a hard time keeping any sense of distance.

Was it that first moment, when their eyes had met across the boat?

Before he knew who she was or recognized her profound desire for the work?

Because no matter how he sliced it, he kept coming back to that single instant in his mind. That moment of sharp awareness that went soul-deep.

Since he was at risk of looking like he'd zoned out of the conversation, Arlo lifted his beer toward their small circle. "To doing the hard and the meaningful work."

"Hear! Hear!"

The light clinking of drinks echoed up from their group and in short order several more cops joined their circle, the conversation turning more casual with the excitement and enjoyment of a night off.

The new additions were welcome, shifting his focus off Kerrigan and onto various friends and acquaintances.

"You must be riding high after taking down that big drug ring." David Remus, a fellow detective at a nearby precinct in Brooklyn Heights, was quick with the compliment as he moved in next to Arlo and Wyatt. "That was a big catch, Prescott, and outstanding work."

"It felt good to get that much product off the streets."

"Heard you got a lot of the low-level dealers out of circulation, too."

"We did."

"That must feel pretty great, too."

It did, and Arlo wouldn't say otherwise, but for all the hype and excitement others had about the big bust, he still felt oddly ambivalent about it.

Yes, they'd removed a lot of product. Thousands of kilos of heroin and cocaine as well as a sizable bust of fentanyl off the streets meant huge benefits for the community. And those lower-level dealers often led to bigger busts when they turned on higher-ups.

But beyond removing the product, not much else had transpired in the past two months. The lower levels had been strangely reticent to squeal for a deal.

"Admittedly, I'd have liked a better hit rate on the upper echelon. The worker bees are satisfying, of course."

"But they're not the real prize," Remus affirmed before taking a sip of his drink.

"You've still got the year's big bust," Arlo said, curious if David had felt that same lingering sense of dissatisfaction. "How'd it feel after?"

"It felt pretty good. But we also got lucky and took down one of the big dogs."

"That's right," Wyatt said, his eyes lighting up. "You got the Papa."

David's takedown had included the head of a drug cartel nicknamed "Papa" by both his rank and file, and the media. He'd been a seriously big fish and Wyatt's quick thinking added another piece to the puzzle. The same one that had eluded him and Kerrigan for more than a week.

Because getting the Papa had been a big deal. But with such a powerful leader off the market, the drug corridor was open to new players.

Was that what he was dealing with? People who'd switched loyalties and were still trying to figure out where they fit into their new organization?

It was a new line to tug and he was suddenly anxious to discuss it with Kerrigan.

"Arlo, do you have a quick minute?"

He turned to find her standing there and the moment was strangely sweet, almost as if he'd conjured her up.

"Sure."

"I won't be long but let me get you a refill on that beer while we're at it."

He didn't doubt the generosity, but it was curious that Kerrigan obviously wanted to pull him out of the conversational circle. He followed her in the direction of the bar. It was only after he was in line that she leaned in, her voice urgent.

"I'm sorry to seem like I was eavesdropping, but I was standing right behind him, and I keyed into David's comments. His takedown last year? What if it's tied to our boat? And maybe to your bust a few months ago, too?"

Since it played so closely to his own thoughts, he ran her quickly through his theory as they waited their turn at the bar.

"It makes a lot of sense, Arlo. Not one single lower-level drone has turned on the higher-ups from your bust. That has to mean something."

"It's definitely an angle."

"What if it *is* the angle?"

"How so?"

"The two dead guys on our boat. They were awfully loyal to end up done that way and no one's talked for over a week? It goes back to the lack of chatter. Just like none of your lower-level guys turned witness after that last bust."

It made sense. Hell, it made a lot of sense, Arlo admitted. "We need to find a leak."

"There's a new leader in town and whoever they are, they've got everyone running scared."

Chapter 6

Kerrigan felt the adrenaline spike in her system as clearly as she felt the thumping bass emanating from the DJ's booth. She and Arlo finally had a lead to chase.

Even if it had come at the expense of a personal evening out.

They'd opted to abandon the wait at the bar and head back to the precinct, both anxious to review his last case and bump it up against the boat murders. Wyatt and Marlowe had been quick to wave them on, confirming they'd take a ride service back home later.

And here they were, Kerrigan inwardly sighed, an hour later and still looking for any semblance of a clue, a lead or even a criminal with a suspicious hangnail.

They had nothing.

"There has to be something there," Kerrigan said, shocked at the level of disappointment that coursed in her veins. "There's no way there's not a link. Even if it's something small, or a midlevel dealer jumping to a new organization."

"Whoever's replaced the Papa, they've buried their tracks well. You and I've been running that boat down all week."

"And we don't have a damn thing to show for it." She fought the curse that tinged the tip of her tongue and kept on with her depressing list of proof. "The boat. The dead victims. And maybe worst of all, the complete inability to follow where the product is moving."

She would own the fact that it had been a busy week, and a long one, but there had been a real shot of hope as they talked it over waiting in line for their turn at the bar.

And now for there to be nothing?

She might not have the level of experience Arlo did, but she was a trained cop. There was no way they were circling around the same thoughts and coming up this empty.

"Hey there." His eyes were a dark, fathomless blue as he stared at her across his desk. "We'll find something."

"We should *have* something. Anything. This is just maddening."

"Maybe the fact we're here on a Friday night, giving up a free evening, is influencing our attitudes."

"Bulldog's really was something." Kerrigan thought about the bar they'd left, one more example of how Sunset Bay had been changing. Now there were young people thronging to businesses and restaurants and snatching up every available apartment a matter of hours after it went on the market.

As she thought about the crowd of people six deep at the bar, filling every interior table and spilling out to the heated decks at the back that overlooked the water, Kerrigan recalled something else she had seen in the files.

"Wasn't there a bar at the center of your last takedown?"

"Yeah, McNulty's."

"That's only two blocks from Bulldog's, right?"

"It is." Arlo's gaze had sharpened. "You think there's something there?"

"I realize downtown continues to expand and grow and hot spots are a part of that, but nightclubs and bars? They're places that deal in cash. They all become real easy places to clean money."

Arlo shot her a smile. "You sure you haven't been working Vice?"

"Nothing beyond my academy training and a deep devotion to police procedurals in book or TV form."

Arlo placed a hand over his heart. "Which means you no doubt see me as your grizzled partner, while you're the young ingenue determined to solve the case."

She couldn't help laughing at that, especially because it was a definite trope in the detective shows she loved so much.

"I wouldn't quite say *grizzled*."

Once again, that dark gaze captured her, drawing her in, as he asked, "What would you call me?"

"Why don't we go with *seasoned* and leave it at that?"

"I guess I can live with that."

Their locked eyes added too much weight to the air between them. Kerrigan glanced down at the notes she'd scribbled on a notepad as they'd reviewed his prior case.

"It's still early." She tapped the notepad. "Why don't we pop over to McNulty's? See how they're handling taking second place to Sunset Bay's newest hot spot."

"You think something's there?"

"Yes. No." She shrugged, not quite sure why she was suddenly curious about the other bar.

Or why it suddenly felt so important to *move*.

To push back against the desire that gripped her when she looked at him for too long.

"I'm not sure, but something seems…unfinished about your last case."

"I won't argue with you there."

"You want to go check it out?"

He was already standing before she had the words out. "Let's go."

Arlo drove back in the direction they had come from earlier, the traffic just as busy as the start of the evening. He was still processing his thoughts on those quiet moments with Kerrigan in his office, but even he couldn't deny there had been a few moments that were…fraught.

If it was simply a matter of his own awareness, he'd feel better. Or so he consoled himself.

But there was something in the deep brown of her stare that made him think he wasn't alone in how he felt.

And *that* was another matter entirely.

He was training her. He'd taken on the professional responsibility for her growth. To turn it around or, worse, come off like he was taking advantage of the situation and hit on her?

Technically, it wasn't against the rules for them to date. He wasn't her boss and they'd done nothing inappropriate.

And yet, he couldn't quite get a handle on how he'd gotten himself into this situation.

Or maybe a better question, why he couldn't separate this swirling attraction for her from the work?

"This traffic is something else. I know it's Friday night, but we've barely inched these last few blocks."

It was just the inane sort of small talk he needed, and Arlo grabbed at it like a lifeline.

"I know they say the city never sleeps, but I still remember the day Brooklyn had a little bit of lazy in her."

Kerrigan's laugh was quick. "Not anymore. This is now a young professional's paradise. 'Work hard, play hard' seems to be everyone's motto."

"That it is."

"Does it bother you?"

He came to a stop at a red light and used the physical pause as a chance to turn and look at her. "Bother me how?"

"Progress is great, but it does come with change. And not all change is welcome."

Did she speak from experience?

He nearly pressed her on it right then and there, but held back, somehow recognizing he'd have better luck letting their conversation play out instead of immediately seeking answers.

"I'd say it's more good than bad and it is fun to be a part of. If my grandparents could see Brooklyn now…" He let the thought hang there, even as he imagined his sweet grandmother who used to hang wash out the back of her side of a double house in Red Hook.

"Have they passed away?"

"Sadly, yes. Both my grandfathers when I was young, one of my grandmothers when I was in high school and then my last remaining grandmother a couple years ago."

"I'm sorry to hear that. I know it's the natural order, but I also know I'll be devastated when I lose mine."

"You have all of your grandparents?"

"I do. My mom's parents are out in Suffolk County on Long Island and my dad's parents retired to Florida."

It was interesting, he realized, but this was the first somewhat personal conversation they'd really had. They had talked quite a bit about her diving, which obviously veered into the personal, but nothing that spoke of family.

"Are you close with them?"

Kerrigan let out a wry chuckle at his question. "Are we close? Let's just say we're the Sunday-dinner, family-text-string, all-the-way-up-in-each-other's-business sort of close."

"That's nice."

"Most of the time. But sort of like change, it's not always welcome."

"By you?"

She hesitated briefly and even though he wasn't looking at her, since the light had turned green, he sensed she would have preferred to pull back the observation.

"By outsiders. People see my commitment to my family and either don't understand it or get disillusioned about it really quickly."

"Others? Boyfriend others?"

"Just…others. People outside of that close-knit family structure."

He turned onto the block to McNulty's and realized once again that he had an opportunity to keep pressing or let the conversation ride and see what she shared.

Or, more to the point, what she was comfortable sharing.

"What about you? Is your family local? Do you have brothers and sisters?"

He fought the punch of disappointment that her willingness to share details about herself had wisped away like smoke, even as he understood self-preservation as much as the next person.

"Two brothers. Two half brothers. My father and stepmom live in Virginia and my mother is divorced and living her best life, as I understand it, in Sedona."

"Do your brothers live around here?"

"My half brothers still live with my dad. My older brother is in Boston and my younger brother followed him a few years ago. Said there wasn't anything left in New York for him."

"You're here."

"I guess I am."

As answers went, it was as vague as her earlier comment about "others" and Arlo realized he wasn't interested in sharing any more.

Funny how much more interesting it was to ask the questions than to be on the receiving end.

"We're here." Arlo effectively put an end to their conversation as he scanned the crowd milling around on the street and in front of the bar as they waited for the valet. "They're not pulling a crowd the size of Bulldog's, but it's not empty, either."

"This bar was central to your takedown, yet they're open and still doing a steady business." Her attention was focused through her window as she shared her observations. "A competitor might have dealt them a financial blow, but being at the center of a bust didn't?"

"The bar owner wasn't involved. In fact, he was shocked by what was running out his back alley."

"And you bought that?"

It had been a long time since he would have called himself offended but the sensation was strong before he caught her eye.

She side-eyed him back, her expression more than a little satisfied. "That one was too easy." And then her grin turned into a saucy laugh as she turned her full attention toward him and off the scene outside the car. "I'm messing with you, Arlo. I read the files and I know you did thorough work. The bar owner was clean and you more than proved that."

The arrival of the valet prevented him from saying anything else and he judged the interruption to be a good thing as they both climbed out of the car.

He'd observed several times now Kerrigan's uncanny ability to focus on the work and still maintain a broader awareness of the moment. She could be as serious as needed or equally as light-hearted.

She had proven herself unique and unexpected from the start and clearly Kerrigan-on-a-Friday-night was another level of fascinating.

And you like it, Prescott. A whole damn lot.

The truth was, he did like it. He'd more than enjoyed his hard-won reputation at the 86th, but over the past few years, as his case record had grown bigger and gotten better, people had begun treating him with kid gloves. What had felt good at first had begun to feel forced, like he was somehow unattached from the team.

Elevated in a way that felt separate instead of honored.

Which could easily be a big layer of self-delusion, but he'd felt it all the same.

Kerrigan's subtle poking and seeming willingness to tease him and keep him on his toes was…

Well, hell, it was welcome.

"For the record, we did run the bar owner," he began once he was out of earshot of the valet.

Kerrigan had gotten out of her side of the car as he'd handed off his keys and was now walking beside him toward the entrance to McNulty's.

"Extensively. I read the case file."

Arlo nodded at that as they closed the last few yards to the bar's entrance. "He was just a local guy who made good. Got sick of his big-city job and opened a bar that catered to the after-work crowd."

He'd thought it curious at the time and had pressed the owner angle repeatedly in his investigation of the leadership of the gang. Yet, no matter how he looked at it, the guy was clean.

It had been Captain Reed who'd finally suggested Arlo ease off.

Sometimes people are exactly who they show you they are, Arlo. I know the job works hard to beat that out of us, but don't let the work take that away from you.

Sort of like Kerrigan?

Because up to now she'd shown herself to be rather straightforward. Even those few insecurities she'd carried at first had been real and shared outright instead of hidden away.

While cops were driven and called to the profession, he had worked with those who'd let a natural and normal amount of fear override their common sense. It wasn't incurable behavior, but it did bear attention.

And addressing it head-on was one more feather in the captain's hat that Arlo had always admired.

Dwayne trusted his team, but he also made sure they were armed with the proper tools. Both the physical pieces they carried as well as the often more important tools. Their minds and their ability to think through a problem.

"You do that well."

"I do what well?" Kerrigan looked up after edging around a couple obviously into each other and oblivious to the crowd navigating around them on the sidewalk.

"Your balance. The good-natured teasing with the need to be serious. Your quick assessments and your ability to remain level-headed. It's a skill that often takes time to develop, yet you seem to innately manage through each situation."

"Thank you." Kerrigan's expression had gone slightly hazy, those always expressive eyes clouding a bit. "Really. Thank you. Any compliment from you is welcome but that's an incredibly nice thing to say."

"I mean it. I suspect a lot of it's your natural intuition, but I have to imagine your dive training also serves you well. You have to stay calm and in control at all times, yet you have to move fast and make decisions quickly."

"Well. Yeah. I guess I do."

He could see the flustered satisfaction in her face as pink heightened her cheeks. It made him glad he'd said something even as he couldn't deny it was also fun to stymie her as the tiniest bit of payback for her teasing in the car.

"It's a trait I see in Wyatt as well. That ability to stay

calm, even when things are going to bits around you, is an incredible skill. Lean into that."

"I'll do that."

He nodded as he pulled the bar door open for her. "Good."

Dyson Gentry avoided glancing over at his brother, Decker, even as fingernails of ice scraped up and down his back. He'd known this was a bad idea from the start.

Damn it, he'd *known* it.

But he'd gone ahead with it all, anyway.

The family business was a good one, but it never changed. Hell, they already sold a ton of boats every year. There was nowhere else to go. No new revenue streams to make them feel like they were moving forward. And no amount of pleading with his old man had convinced Big Will Gentry to expand the business beyond their very large dock in Brooklyn.

Only Dyson's dreams were bigger than that.

But it was Decker who had the ambition and the balls and just enough frustration with their father's unwillingness to expand to put it all into motion.

Now that they were sitting here, beneath that unrelenting stare, he had to admit his brother had been the one to take the initiative and he'd been grateful for it at the time.

Only now…

Now the partnership that had seemed so promising was balancing on the thinnest of wires.

"Can you please explain to me how the police have managed to identify your business establishment as the purchase location of my boat?"

Dead eyes.

It was all Dyson could think as he stared across that desk. He wasn't sure he'd noticed it before, yet as he looked now it was all he could see.

Flat, dead and as cold as the Atlantic in February.

"The cops have no idea your boat came through us. They had a casual conversation with my father and asked a few basic questions about boats. There wasn't any hint they thought of us as the supplier at all—"

"We weren't made," Decker added, cutting Dyson off. "Our father doesn't know about our side work. Because of it he came off like the always congenial, good guy he is."

Dyson's shred of hope that his brother had finessed things fled on swift wings, even as those icy fingers skimmed his back once more.

Was that really Decker's voice?

They weren't twins but close enough in age that most people figured them for it. He'd always believed he knew his brother, but ever since going in on this deal he'd had those strange moments of awareness when he realized his brother had thoughts he didn't share.

Even more, he had *knowledge* of things he didn't share.

It had been a bit awe-inspiring at first, but Dyson had quickly come to the conclusion that there was an edgy layer there in Decker he wasn't comfortable with.

Nor did he fully recognize his sibling because of it.

We weren't made.

Who said things like that? Thought like that? Or, maybe more troubling, when had his brother begun to talk like that?

"There were cops inside your establishment asking about my boat. I don't care if your father's the damn mayor, you promised me anonymity. Not one single thread, invisible or otherwise, tying me to Brooklyn Yacht."

Decker leaned forward and there was just enough menace in the physical position that the two goons who'd stood sentinel, flanking the wall, moved forward. "You're not tied to anything."

"See that it stays that way."

Dyson took a moment to glance at Decker, not entirely sure if they'd been dismissed or if they needed to stay put.

He didn't need to wait long for the answer.

"Now. There is one final matter I'd like to clear up."

"And what would that be?" Decker asked, even as he shot Dyson a sharp glance to hold his tongue.

Although his own curiosity was running high, Dyson couldn't deny that once again he questioned how much he really knew about his brother.

It had increasingly nagged at him since they'd gone in on this deal, working with a chop shop down in Maryland that specialized in this sort of boat work. They'd supplied the pieces and the parts, and Decker's contact had put it all together.

Rather easily, Dyson thought.

And more proof that the man sitting next to him had become someone else. Someone he'd never even known existed.

How had he missed this side of his own brother?

"You will replace my boat."

"We procured it. You destroyed it. Find someone else." For the first time, Dyson heard the quiver of concern beneath his brother's attempt at a casual response.

Those dead eyes remained unwavering, seeming to both take them in and stare them down all at once.

"No, I really don't think so. You're in this now and you're going to see my boat is replaced. I will, of course, pay for your services. But I want it in New York by next Friday."

"That's impossible!" The words were out of his mouth before Dyson could stop them and in his outburst he realized his mistake.

A mistake that had opened a door he'd never have thought existed when he started down this path.

"Nothing's impossible, Mr. Gentry. Not with the right motivation."

Although a strong streak of self-preservation welled up inside, he still pressed on. There was no damn way they could get an unregistered, hot boat up here in a week. "As my brother said. We helped you. We secured the merchandise you needed. It's not our fault you torched it to get out of a tough situation."

"Funny, but I see it different. You told me that boat could handle the waves."

"You took her out in a hurricane," Dyson pointed out.

"Hardly. We took her out in a storm I was assured she could handle. She didn't, so now you'll work to secure me a replacement."

"It can't be done that fast." Dyson shook his head. "We need a month, minimum."

The lightest sigh drifted across the desk. In it, he should have recognized the absolute lack of sympathy or understanding.

It was only when that small utterance was followed

by the scariest of truths that Dyson recognized they had made yet another misstep.

"Big Will's been talking to all and sundry about the cruise he and your mother are taking for their anniversary. I find it a bit silly, actually. A boat seller taking a vacation on a boat but—" shoulders lifted in a delicate shrug "—to each his own. They leave in two weeks, I believe?"

The cold ice that had merely skated down his back up to now wrapped a tight, unyielding fist around his spine. "He's not in this."

"But his sons are. It would be such a shame for their parents to meet a dreadful end as they headed out on the start of a loving adventure."

For the first time, Decker moved, his hand covering over Dyson's forearm.

"You'll have the boat by next Friday."

"An eminently reasonable response."

With the flick of a hand, Dyson knew they'd been dismissed. He stood, surprised to find his knees were wobbly.

One of the goons standing guard duty against the wall gestured them to exit the office and follow him down the hall. Dyson did, his brother's footfalls solid and heavy behind him as they exited the same way they entered, through a door into an alley behind the bar.

It was only as the door slammed behind them that Decker let out a hard breath.

Dyson turned to his brother. "What the hell are we doing?"

"We made a deal. We're now seeing it through."

"Threats against Mom and Dad? And where the hell are we going to get an unregistered boat in a week?"

"I got us into this mess and I'll handle it. I knew what I was getting us into."

"What do you mean 'you knew?'"

He still had enough sense to keep his voice low, but Dyson wasn't willing to let Decker off so easily. His brother might have been the brains behind what they were doing, but he'd questioned the job and the partnership.

"I knew going in that we'd have to see this through."

"See what through?" Dyson asked.

"The deal we made with a stone-cold bitch."

"Nice place." Kerrigan let her gaze roam casually around the bar as she took the glass of wine Arlo extended her way and tried to infuse a happy-go-lucky vibe into her demeanor.

"Upscale. Trendy. Nice thick wood bar, well-polished brass and welcoming barstools." Arlo took a sip of his beer, his own gaze returning to her from where it had settled over each item on his list. "It's solid."

"Is it what you remembered?"

"They've cleared out some of the tables to make way for another pool table in the back but otherwise it's the same."

"We keep staring like we are and the whole bar's going to make us as cops."

"Cops get nights off, too."

"You don't want to stay further under the radar?"

"At this point, if there is something suspicious going on I'd like to draw out an attack. It's been damn near a week and nothing's turning up. Maybe it's time some of the low-level rank and file know we're looking."

Kerrigan knew it bothered him—that distinct lack

of chatter about the boat and the dead dealers—and she suddenly had a sense of what he was after.

"Are we putting ourselves out here as bait, Arlo?"

"Bait's too subtle. I want the whole damn neighborhood to know the cops are out looking for the perp who did that boat. Someone needs to trip up and if we can force them to fall sooner, I'm all for it."

They hadn't come in here with a well-baked plan, more a hunch that they wanted to take a look at the same place the last drug bust went down and see what they could find. But his reasoning made a certain sort of sense.

Whether there was anything to see at McNulty's wasn't really the point.

What was the point was the idea that the cops were out in full force, turning over stones and hunting for answers. The more people who lurked in the shadows recognized that, the bigger the chance someone would get scared and start talking.

She saw a small standing table open on the far side of the room and gestured him toward it. They'd have a good view, yet still be able to keep their backs to the exposed brick wall that made up the eastern end of the building.

They settled their drinks on the table and Kerrigan was surprised to look down at her watch and see it was still just shy of ten o'clock. They'd covered a lot of ground and still had most of the evening ahead of them. Which somehow shot Jayden's earlier wisdom right back to the forefront of her thoughts.

Partner and elder statesman, maybe, but not boss. There's not even a whiff of boss in there and you know it.

There wasn't a boss relationship here and she'd do well to remember that. Both for the romantic aspects Jayden was overtly pressing for as well as how the two of them managed the case. She was his partner on this and her thoughts and ideas were welcome.

Necessary, even, to a successful outcome.

She could appreciate his tutelage and his willingness to guide her, but ultimately solving this case was about the two of them working it together. What she hadn't banked on was the level of personal involvement that would permeate that partnership.

A fact that seemed even sharper with Arlo's own admission on the drive.

My older brother is in Boston and my younger brother followed him a few years ago. Said there wasn't anything left in New York for him.

You're here.

I guess I am.

It sounded lonely.

He sounded lonely.

As someone who was so close to their family, she recognized she had a bit of a biased view on how much families could support and stand behind each other. Especially when life reinforced the point over and over that many weren't nearly as fortunate.

But she hadn't expected Arlo was living that reality.

Was it his reputation? Or his obvious ease and ability to build relationships, which she'd seen clearly with Wyatt and even with Captain Reed?

Either way, it was unexpected and—

Her train of thought skittered away as Kerrigan keyed in on the sensation of being watched. It was a subtle wisp of awareness that shifted rapidly, as her gaze met a dark one on the opposite side of the room.

Was he security? Another bar patron?

Whatever it was, she felt the threat as clearly as she knew her own name. Determined to remain casual, she leaned into Arlo, her lips brushing the edge of his ear before she caught herself and pulled back slightly.

"Keep it casual but my eight o'clock. Against the wall."

He caught on quick, his voice low as he turned his head slightly, his lips brushing the edge of her brow. "What am I looking at?"

She fought the instant awareness of him, the subtle tick of his breath against her skin shooting sparks.

Damn it, Doyle. You've got a bigger problem at the moment than your partner's sexy lips grazing your skin.

"I'm getting really bad vibes off the dude, over near the entrance. About six-three with the leather vest, arms crossed."

He held his part, playing her doting date, but she sensed the tension in him and the shift of his attention across the room.

"I can't get a solid look at this angle."

Scenarios flashed through her mind, one rapid frame after another, even as one kept flickering as the right choice.

"Remember that compliment you gave me earlier? About how good I am at staying calm?"

"Yeah."

"Stay calm, Arlo. And try to keep up."

Without giving him another opportunity to respond,

she wrapped her arms around his shoulders, shifting them just enough so he had a view across the room.

Then she pulled down his head, their lips a fraction of a breath apart, and gave herself up to the moment.

Chapter 7

Need.

Sharp, sweet, all-consuming need swamped him as Kerrigan's mouth met his.

He knew his role. Knew the part he was playing and why she was even kissing him in the first place, but damn it, he wanted a taste of this.

He wanted it as badly as he wanted his next breath.

It was the only reason he could think of that he kissed her back, his eyes closing instead of focusing sharply on his quarry.

Soft, plump lips pressed against his, a veritable feast for the taking. Lost in the moment, he pushed for more, his tongue pressing past her lips to tangle with hers.

It was madness. Utterly. Totally.

And he was a drowning man who simply wanted *more*.

"What have we here?"

The interruption, the high-pitched voice, and the

sudden acknowledgment that he had completely abandoned his responsibility to support his partner had Arlo pulling back.

"Look at you two lovebirds on a date!"

The voice was cloyingly sweet, nearly as much as the bottle blonde who stood beside their table.

"Wendy?" Kerrigan spoke first, that calm he'd complimented her on settling the moment she put on a smile for their interloper. "Wendy Parker?"

"Yes! I can't believe it's you. I'd heard you'd moved to Brooklyn from the old neighborhood."

"Word travels fast. I only moved a couple months ago."

Wendy waved a hand. "You know how it is. Forest Hills only thinks it's a big place but it's as small-town as anywhere else."

"I suppose it is," Kerrigan agreed.

Wendy eyed him, her stare just barely proper, before she extended her hand. "I'm Wendy."

"Arlo," he said, taking her hand. Cool, slim fingers remained in his grip just a fraction longer than they should. "It's nice to meet you. Do you live here in the neighborhood?"

"Nearby. But there's so much action in Sunset Bay, it's hard to stay away. Especially on a Friday night."

"We were just saying that very thing on the drive over," Kerrigan said, neatly picking up the conversational ball. "Brooklyn feels like another world sometimes."

"About time, too. We spent so many years playing second fiddle to Manhattan. It's nice that the boroughs are finally getting some attention."

It was a familiar lament among his parents' generation, but Arlo found it funny coming from someone so young. Although the changes he and Kerrigan had discussed about Brooklyn were true, they'd been in progress for a while. Real estate and neighborhood growth didn't happen overnight. And it certainly had been happening longer than the time this woman had been an adult.

New York City was made up of five boroughs. From Manhattan, which so many thought of as "the city," to Queens, Brooklyn, the Bronx and Staten Island, it was a vast, vibrant place. That was only truer when you looked at the distinct and often individual neighborhoods within.

So, yeah, maybe he was getting old, but he hadn't heard a lot of young people frustrated about their counterparts over the bridges and tunnels to Manhattan.

Since he was veering dangerously close to bad-conversation territory—admittedly brought on by the interruption of that kiss—he plastered on a smile and tried to engage with their new visitor.

"What brought you to Brooklyn from Queens?"

Wendy's gaze dipped slightly, her smile taking on a distinct edge. "I guess I'm not a big fan of second fiddles anywhere in my life. I wasn't interested in going into the family business, so I struck out on my own. I have two clothing boutiques and am about to open a third."

"That's great!" Kerrigan's eyes widened. "Are you Wendy's Closet?"

"Yep."

"Speaking of keeping up with the old neighborhood, I did hear some good news about you. My mom was talking about your stores recently. Said she'd heard you were starting your own clothing line, too."

"I am. Fast fashion trend is all the rage, and it felt like the right next step for me, you know."

Although he had zero knowledge of the fashion industry, even Arlo was well aware that the "fast fashion" industry hadn't made friends with anyone. With its heavy toll on the environment and its labor practices in foreign countries, it was a difficult business.

Yet this woman had obviously seen it as part of building her empire and pushing even farther away from her hometown roots.

"Listen, I didn't mean to interrupt your date, but since I saw you over here, I couldn't resist coming to say hi." Wendy was already pressing a kiss to Kerrigan's cheek in farewell when it dawned on Arlo he hadn't seen the woman with anyone.

It was nearly out of his mouth to ask where her friends were when she laid a hand over his forearm. "It was lovely to meet you. Enjoy your evening."

And then she was gone.

"That was a blast from the past." Kerrigan picked up her wine, shaking her head. "And it's funny, but my mom *had* just mentioned her a few weeks ago. Sounds like she's making quite a name for herself."

"She certainly seems determined."

Kerrigan glanced up at that, her gaze sharp. "That's a bad thing?"

"No."

"Then?"

She left her question hanging there and Arlo wasn't exactly sure how to respond.

"Then good for her?"

"Somehow I don't get the sense you mean that."

"Nah, I mean it." When she only continued to stare at him, he added, "Really, I do."

To be fair, he had no real reason to be so immediately sharp or suspicious about the woman. It was his rotten luck Wendy had interrupted the kiss, but beyond that, she hadn't said much or stayed nearly long enough to have pulled this sort of reaction from him.

"I haven't known you very long, but I can tell you I'm not buying this attempt at Zen."

"Zen nothing. I think I just have too much on my mind."

Her eyes widened as her gaze darted to the door. "I totally forgot about the bouncer from before."

Since he'd forgotten, too, he scanned the area near the bar's entrance, subtlety be damned. "He was standing over there?"

"Yep, by the door. Maybe he's one of the bouncers and was just checking the room to make sure no one was getting out of hand."

"You believe that?"

"I—" She stopped, shook her head. "I want to believe it, but, no, not really. His attention felt way too personal."

That admission shot a hard spike into his chest and Arlo heard the flat notes in his own voice. "Then where did he go?"

"I got a bit too involved in my little hometown reunion to say."

Since he'd gotten far too involved in their kiss, Arlo could hardly chastise, but he still couldn't quite remove those hard edges from his tone. "Which reinforces that it's been a long evening for both of us, following a long day and an even longer week. Let's call it a night?"

"Alright."

She collected her purse, and it was only after they'd crossed the bar and gotten outside to wait for the valet to take his ticket that Arlo noted they were both scanning for the mystery bouncer.

"There's no sign of him. The guy I saw."

There were any number of reasons why the guy had disappeared, including everything from a shift break, if he was employed by the bar, to a patron opting to go home for the evening.

But possible reasons aside, it didn't sit well that Kerrigan had felt such a strong response to his presence.

"Maybe it really was nothing." Kerrigan slipped into the passenger side before he could open the door for her, so Arlo waited to respond until he was back inside the closed car.

"I never bet against a cop's intuition."

"Which takes me right back to Wendy. I know she's a lot and a little hard to take. She was a few years ahead of me in school and I remember that aspect of her personality even back then. To be honest, I don't think I even realized she knew me."

"She seemed to know you *and* have kept up with you."

Kerrigan shrugged. "We're from the same neighborhood. That's all it is."

"That small-town feel you're both insisting is alive and well here in New York City?"

"Remember I mentioned how close I was to my family?" When he only nodded, she continued, "My mother has her fingers, her toes and both her eyes on the pulse of Forest Hills. There's nothing that happens, and that includes someone sneezing in the park, that my mother doesn't manage to hear about."

"You do realize it's sort of funny that you both referred to Forest Hills as small-town. Especially when the population of Queens is over two million people."

"It's a neighborhood, Arlo. As long as people make walls and gardens and territories, it doesn't matter how big it gets, it'll always feel small."

Although he couldn't quite agree, as he drove away from the bar he had to admit the evening had taken more than a few odd turns. "So our evening was a serious bust in terms of cracking our case, but we did get a few unique moments out of it."

"Oh?"

"We now have one mysteriously threatening bouncer and one irritatingly perky high-school alumnus to show for our trip this evening."

"I guess we do."

She'd given him directions to her apartment building earlier and he headed that way after turning off the main thoroughfare of Sunset Bay.

And recognized how diligently both of them had avoided mentioning that kiss that, to his mind, was the most interesting moment of all.

Kerrigan laced up her sneakers and snagged her gym bag from the hallway on her way out. She'd already stowed her Murphy bed against the wall and tidied up her sleeping arrangements to maximize the space.

Her apartment was small, but it was hers, and not for the first time she was happy to have it all to herself. Both the physical aspects of living alone as well as the emotional ones.

She lived in her head and when she was deep in a case or working through a personal problem, she didn't want anyone around.

Because of that fact, she'd prioritized independent living at the expense of other amenities and took extra shifts when she could to help pay for it *and* add to her savings.

So, yeah, her oversized studio was small, but it was hers and that was all that mattered.

What it also meant was that she had a full Saturday stretching out before her with no plans beyond her workout and spending time with herself.

Not the best way to stop thinking about kissing Arlo Prescott.

It had been a foolish move on her part, dragging him close as a way to get a better look at that strange man by the front door of the bar. And yet…

What other choices did they have?

Whatever had been directed at her from that goon by the door had carried some seriously dark overtones.

Not that dark if one touch of Arlo's lips made me forget all about those bad vibes.

And hadn't that been the rub? The lone fact she kept coming back to, over and over. She might have felt threatened by that man at the door, but one kiss from Arlo and she'd been distracted.

More, she'd let her guard down.

And if those criminals Arlo was so determined to lure *were* out there, she'd put herself in a position of weakness by forgetting about the threat.

He'd complimented her levelheadedness and her ability to remain calm, but she didn't feel either this morning.

Which meant there was nothing to be done but to diligently focus all her attention and effort on getting it back.

Her move to the 86th Precinct had brought with it access to a new gym and she loved the facility. In addition to the indoor Olympic-size pool she and her fellow harbor-team members used regularly, there was a full suite of cardio machines and an impressive weight room. Several officers taught classes as additional options and she'd already enjoyed a regular Zumba session that was so popular they needed to manage the class size via a sign-up sheet.

The pool was pretty empty when she got there, and after changing into her suit, she easily found a lane and began her laps. Water sluiced over her in calming waves as she swam, one end to the other, her timed breaths coming in easy rhythm with her movements.

It should have relaxed her. That mix of movement, the comfort she always found in the water and the good, steady rhythm found in using her body were usually a balm for whatever she was dealing with.

But a half hour later all she'd managed to do was count off a solid fifty laps all while images of kissing Arlo swam in her head.

"Damn it."

She ripped off her swim cap as she headed for the locker room, irritated with herself and even more irritated with her racing thoughts, which were a solid match for racing hormones.

And that was going to be her excuse to herself later when she thought back on how she plowed into Arlo as he walked down the hall toward the men's locker room.

"Whoa! Where's the fire?"

"Oh! I'm sorry. I—" She glanced up, something discordant settling in her chest as the man who'd dominated her mental musings was suddenly standing before her and looking even better in person.

"You're here early."

"I wanted to get my laps in and I'm so sorry I barreled into you like that." She reached out, trying to wipe away the moisture that was already forming on the leather of his jacket. "And I got you wet, too."

"I'll dry."

"Sure. Of course. Well, I—"

"Look, I just got here but I can always come back later. I got a late workout in yesterday afternoon so I'm still feeling ready to tackle pancakes if you're up for breakfast."

Realistically she should say no.

It was the smart thing to do. And with the power of that kiss still humming through her body with more effect than her steady laps, it would be wise to just make an excuse and walk away.

Especially since something tickled hard against the back of her throat at the idea that she now knew something about him. Something more than the way he kissed.

He'd had pancakes at breakfast a few days ago and now he was offering them again. And something about that small fact tugged at her much harder than it probably should.

"I don't want to interrupt your workout plans."

"Since pancakes and breakfast with you sounds a lot more interesting than running a treadmill and doing bench presses, save me." When she hadn't yet answered, he added, "Please."

"Pancakes do sound good."

His smile was broad and it was silly to think about his personal situation. And yet...

Kerrigan couldn't stop thinking of his comments yesterday about his family. How all had left the area, claiming there was nothing left for them.

It was sad.

More, it seemed terribly lonely.

While she wasn't exactly in the same situation based on the strong bonds she had with her family, she did understand what it was to be alone.

Hadn't that dismal thought accompanied her as she'd headed over this morning?

Now she wouldn't be alone for part of her day.

And Arlo wouldn't be, either.

"Let me go get dried off and changed, and I'll meet you in the lobby."

Twenty minutes later they walked into a restaurant about two blocks from the precinct. Like the bars they'd visited the night before, this place was going for a bit more upscale and instead of the scarred Formica tables with booths of the local diner, they got aged wood and cane chairs. Within moments they were squeezed into a two-top in the midst of the brunch crowd.

A waiter got them coffee and took their orders for pancakes, then headed off back into the throng. "Thanks for joining me. I didn't realize I was quite this hungry until I caught a whiff of this place."

She'd already eyed several plates set down on tables around the restaurant and knew he'd selected well. "It's a great suggestion. And I'm going to enjoy every single bite of those pancakes."

His easy smile faded, and she caught the sense of

seriousness a heartbeat before he spoke. "I'm glad you came here with me for another reason. I owe you an apology."

An apology?

"Last night, you were dealing with whoever that goon was at the door and I got a bit carried away by that kiss. It was unprofessional and I'm sorry for it."

Since she'd spent the better part of twelve hours restless and upset with herself for initiating their kiss, there was no earthly reason she should be upset by his apology.

And yet…

"You're sorry for that? It was a ridiculous thing I initiated in a moment of panic. Don't give it another thought."

"It didn't feel ridiculous."

"Well, it was. You're my partner and it was a dumb impulse to make a scene at the bar instead of owning what was happening and just getting up myself and dealing with that jerk."

"That's not what I meant." Arlo shook his head, nearly sloshing the coffee in his mug as he set it down on the table with a hard thunk. "Why would you even think about instigating something with a man who gave you the creeps like that?"

"I'm a trained officer. I can handle a man who's acting like a problem."

"Unarmed in a bar where he could be carrying a weapon? Or possibly high on any number of things? No way."

"Are you suggesting I can't?"

"I'm suggesting you found a way to handle the situation without jumping into something rash. They're not the same."

"Yet here you are, apologizing for kissing me back."

"I'm not—"

"No, Arlo, what do you mean? Because you're suddenly offended at the idea I can take care of myself, yet you're equally offended at kissing me. You can't have it both ways."

That sense of calm he'd credited her for was nowhere in evidence, but she at least recognized the need to pull back.

Or, more to the point, to shut up and not make it worse.

"I wasn't offended. I was the opposite of offended." He toyed with the handle of his coffee mug before looking back up at her. "I enjoyed it."

Whatever impulse had him inviting Kerrigan to breakfast had then given way to some misbegotten need to discuss that kiss.

He should have let it lie.

Just like last night, when they'd both, by unspoken agreement, avoided discussing what had happened, he should have left things that way.

And instead, here he was apologizing? And, apparently, insulting her about her abilities to defend herself, which hadn't been in the cards, either.

Because no matter how well-trained and competent she was, the thought of her confronting the man who'd put such fear in her eyes had him seeing through a dark miasma of anger.

"I enjoyed it, too."

Her admission floated toward him across their small

table, kindling a level of satisfaction he had no business feeling yet was helpless to deny.

"So let's put it behind us. It's out in the open now and we can move on."

"Absolutely."

"Good." He took a sip of his coffee, trying to regain his equilibrium, but it had taken a serious vacation since the night before.

Hell, it had pretty much vanished the moment he'd seen her standing at the edge of the boat, stripping out of her wet suit.

"Can I ask you something?" Kerrigan's voice was quiet, her back arrow-straight as she sat opposite him. It was a jarring change from when they'd walked over to the restaurant, the two of them comfortable and relaxed.

He'd ruined that with his harebrained attempts to apologize. Or maybe, more to the point, to assuage his guilt?

"Of course."

"Is this going to change things between us?"

Until that moment, he hadn't considered his apology as anything more than something she deserved, but now that he considered it from her perspective, he got a sense of her worry. "If you mean will it change my respect for you and my belief you can do the work? Absolutely not."

"Okay."

"If you mean that it's going to be something we both have to live with? There's not much I can do about that."

Wow, Prescott, is this your first day talking to a woman?

He'd never considered himself clumsy with women,

but something about this exchange had put him on his back foot. First, his ill-advised apology for kissing her wasn't the best choice. But now he was rubbing salt in the wound?

Her jaw set into a hard line. "We're going to have to do something about it because it can't get in the way."

"I'm attracted to you, Kerrigan. It's already in the way. A kiss only cemented that fact even more."

Their waiter arrived with their pancakes, and Arlo used the break to simply look at her across the table.

The truth was out.

She was a beautiful, *interesting* woman and at least he'd finally admitted to his attraction for her. Which meant now was also the time to tell her about his dive into Big Will's background and his business because he had to get that report written up and added to the file.

"Kerrigan, I need to—"

"So what you're really saying is that things *will* change. Look, Arlo, I don't make it a habit to go around kissing my coworkers. In the line of duty or outside of it. I can't afford gossip or questions about my competence."

"There it is again. Why are you so convinced someone's going to question your abilities?" He gave her a beat, then two, before he pressed on. Because unlike last night in the car, he wasn't willing to wait and see if she might say something.

It was time to push.

"It's been the pervasive thread between us for the past week and I can't help but feel it all hinges on whatever happened at your first precinct. Get over it. Deal with it however you need to and then get it out of your head."

"Or what?"

"Or you're going to fall victim to it."

As pep talks went it was as poor as the bad apology for the kiss, but he was getting desperate. There were some very real ghosts in her past and it was long past time she exorcised them.

"I'm a professional. I'm past it."

"I don't think you are."

"So now you're playing armchair psychologist on top of telling me all the ways I can't go off and defend myself?"

"It's not armchair psychology to acknowledge that whatever happened at your last precinct is still affecting you."

"I'm fine."

"You say that, but no matter how good a cop you are, below *and* above the water, letting those demons in and allowing them to feed never ends well."

"Then how about this, Detective Prescott. I'm more than capable of handling this case and seeing it through to the end. Not only am I capable, I'm going to do that. And when it's over? When we have whoever these bastards are in custody? I'm going to remind you of this moment and all the reasons you thought I couldn't handle it."

"That's not what I said, Kerrigan."

"Save it."

She fumbled in her coat pocket for something and it took him a split second to realize it was a handful of cash. "This should cover my portion of breakfast. I have a dive Monday morning, but I'll be in the precinct after lunch. I'll see you then."

More than a few eyes followed her as she stood and

stalked from the restaurant and Arlo left them all to stare.

All he could focus on was the uneaten stack of pancakes on the opposite side of the table.

And the unmistakable lines of hurt he'd put on the face of the woman he wouldn't be sharing them with.

Chapter 8

Kerrigan finished checking the gauges on her oxygen tank and fought the roiling waves of exhaustion and sadness she'd managed for nearly forty-eight hours. She'd even feigned work overload to get out of Sunday dinner with her family.

If her mother had suspected something more was up, she didn't say, but Kerrigan knew she needed to get herself together. Because if she canceled for next week, her mother would be at her doorstep with a meat loaf, a vat of chicken soup and a box of tissues to talk it out.

And what, exactly, would she say?

I have the hots for my new partner, and he thinks I'm damaged goods from my first job.

Oh, but he's attracted to me, too, so there is that.

A lot of *that*, actually. Because no matter how upsetting their conversation had been, she was attracted too.

And wasn't that the rub?

She wasn't damaged but she did carry a hell of a lot of baggage with her from that Internal Affairs investigation. She'd believed it behind her. She'd kept her head down and had focused on her dive work, but here she was, with her first shot at working a high-profile case, and she was letting her past intrude.

Was Arlo right to question her?

Since every partner deserved to know they were heading straight into the fire with someone capable of handling the heat, yeah, she admitted to herself.

He did have a right to question.

Especially when that very baggage had driven every insecurity she had on this case.

"Yo, Kerr. You ready?"

Jayden had given her a wide berth this morning when she'd remained quiet through his chatter about his dinner date on Saturday night. Her automaton-like responses of "that's nice" and "sounds delicious" hadn't carried any heart and their friendship was solid enough that Jayden recognized she needed some space.

Even if she did owe him an apology for being a bad friend who couldn't even make a bit of Monday-morning small talk.

"You sure you're good to dive?"

"I'm fine. The quiet underwater will do me good." She stood up from where she'd crouched beside her equipment and put a hand on his arm. "And hopefully break my crappy mood this morning. I'm sorry."

"Save it." He grinned and she saw the partner she knew and loved behind that smile. "And since I'm going to be singing happy songs about that crème brûlée for at least another week you'll get my dinner story a few more times. You can ooh and aah later."

"It's a deal."

Jayden drifted toward the front of the cabin of the small police boat they were using today, and she took a seat on the deck with her tablet. She wanted to review the details one more time on their evidence recovery.

She scanned the report and figured this would be a quick drop down into the water. They had a lot of data since a beat team had chased a group of thugs across the Brooklyn Bridge the night before. The team had a good description of the weapons. Kerrigan already knew she was on the hunt for a sawed-off shotgun and two semi-automatic rifles that were a lot better off at the bottom of East River than in the hands of criminals.

Gavin gave the morning briefing and since the recovery was pretty straightforward, he was only sending her and Jayden down on the bridge dive. Once they had the evidence, their team would move on to whatever other duties awaited.

It was easy. Routine, even. And it was something she innately understood.

Since she had very little to prep for, her errant thoughts went straight back to the same place they'd been all weekend.

Is this going to change things between us?

If you mean will it change my respect for you and my belief you can do the work? Absolutely not.

If you mean that it's going to be something we both have to live with? There's not much I can do about that.

She'd played that exchange over and over and kept coming back to the sheer audacity of Arlo's words.

Live with it?

They'd have to live with kissing each other?

It infuriated her, both for his matter-of-fact attitude about the whole thing and—even more, she had to admit—because she couldn't let it go.

Live with it.

She'd kissed him in the line of duty and while she'd stand by that, there would have been other ways of handling the situation. Heck, she could have dropped something on the floor or just told him flat out to look at the thug by the bar door.

But no.

She'd used a kiss as an excuse to get him into the proper sight line.

It was selfishly motivated, and she could direct as much heat and anger in Arlo's direction as she wanted, but she needed to own her actions.

And maybe that was the root of the problem. She was angry at herself. For letting this attraction she had developed color her judgment, certainly in the moment, but overall, too.

Was she still raw over her exit from her last precinct? Yes, of course. That damage wasn't going away anytime soon and maybe it shouldn't. Experiences like that left a mark but they also prepared you for things to come.

She was tougher now and she no longer wore rose-colored glasses. Which also meant if feelings were getting in the way, then she wasn't doing her job well.

And since feelings *were* getting in the way it was time to get her head in the game.

She flipped over to her email while she waited for the boat operator to get them in position and scanned what had come in that morning.

Only to find an email from ten o'clock the night before.

The subject carried the case number and a very clear description of what was inside.

Report: Background check | Will Gentry, Dyson Gentry, Decker Gentry

She'd already written up the interview notes with Big Will after they'd gotten back to the precinct. Nowhere in that write-up was there a discussion of running a background check on Big Will or his family.

Which meant Arlo had taken it upon himself to do it.

She clicked into the report attached to the email, something dark and ugly greasing her stomach.

He hadn't told her.

And unless he'd gotten a wild hair yesterday to run the family—something he'd most certainly *not* discussed with her—it wasn't just something he'd been thinking about.

It was something he'd done.

Kerrigan read the date stamp on the report and had her answer.

Arlo had run the family the same day they'd visited Brooklyn Yacht.

He hadn't mentioned it then. Or in any of the numerous days or conversations they'd shared since.

As projects went, it wasn't completely out of the ordinary. It made sense to get a full picture of suspects or anyone who might have knowledge of a crime.

She'd believed Big Will was innocent, but she'd never suggest a cop's instincts weren't fair or valid or not worth pursuing.

Yet he'd deliberately kept her out.

And she had the date stamp to prove it.

* * *

"Arlo?" Captain Reed moved up beside Arlo's desk. "You have a minute?"

"Of course."

Arlo had been running through old case files all morning, trying to see if there was anything he'd missed on the drug-bust case he'd closed a few months ago.

So far nothing.

Just like he hadn't had anything from Kerrigan, either.

He'd left the restaurant shortly after she did, the pancakes he'd ordered like dust in his mouth. The minimal amount of food had made it easier to get through his workout without feeling weighted down and he'd processed, over and over, with each *thwap* of the treadmill belt how badly he'd messed up.

"I saw the report that you put in on the smuggling-boat case."

"The Gentry family?"

"That's the one. I know you've been busy, but it's not like you to be so late in your reports. Everything okay with that one?"

It was an example, yet again, that Dwayne Reed knew his team.

"I struggled with that one a bit."

"With reviewing potential suspects?" Dwayne's dark gaze sharpened. "They gave you a problem during your initial interview?"

"No, not at all. Kerrigan and the owner know each other, and he spoke easily with us about what he knew and how the boat business works."

"So he was more of a source than a potential perp?"

"More or less." Arlo felt the heat creep up his neck.

"Nonetheless, I felt it important to run him, but I did it without telling her."

He hated the way this one made him feel, that sense that he'd betrayed his partner, even though he knew full well he was doing his job.

"Why'd you keep it from her?"

"I was concerned her friendship with the owner would make it difficult to be objective."

"Did you tell her that?"

"No, sir."

"That sounds like a real problem here." Dwayne paused, obviously weighing his words, before continuing. "You know you have my full support on this. Kerrigan does, too. You brought her in, Arlo. She deserves to be all-in."

"I know that. And it's why it took me so long to write up the report."

Dwayne just nodded at that before he leaned forward, bracing his forearms on his knees. "Partnerships aren't easy. You've been doing this long enough to know that. But we support working in a partnered environment for a reason, Arlo."

"Yes, sir."

"Since I can see your face, I recognize you've been through this over and over in your mind. I suggest you start with your partner and apologize."

"I'm not exactly her favorite person right now."

"Oh?" There was a shocking depth of meaning in that lone word and Arlo quickly retrenched.

"She's eager. She wants to solve this case. I want to support that in her. That drive. That ambition. But I can't help feeling, just like you said last week, that there are some really dark overtones in this one."

"You get any new leads?"

"No, and that's part of the problem. We've been turning over every rock we can find. That look into the Gentry family was an example. I don't want them to be guilty, but nothing is popping. No one is talking. And when you add in two grisly murders on the boat, it makes you wonder."

"What lines are you tugging?"

Arlo filled in the captain on the theory they had been working, that somebody had stepped in and replaced the Papa. Dwayne keyed in on that, his attention sharp and reinforcing Arlo's gut that they had something with that. "It's a good angle and it makes a lot of sense. Switching leaders always causes havoc. Taking the Papa out of circulation? That's a lot of upheaval and a lot of room for new ambitious leaders to move in."

Not for the first time, Arlo acknowledged how much of human nature was wrapped into criminal activity. The hierarchies. The loyalties. Even the strange use of "family" as a way to bring people into the work together.

Although most of his friends were cops, he had some that worked in the corporate world. Hell, his brother was one of them. And the way they talked about their companies, referring to them as families and as teams. There was an odd match there.

Did it get people to fall in line? Make them feel more loyal? Or was it the simple human need to belong to something?

"I know it's frustrating when you don't have a lead, but you and Kerrigan are working some good angles. Keep at it. Keep pulling those lines." Dwayne stood. "And apologize to your partner."

"Yes, sir."

"Now I really know you're remorseful."

"What do you mean?"

"I haven't gotten a single 'Dwayne' out of you. It's all been 'yes, sir,' 'no, sir.'" A broad grin split Dwayne's face, his teeth flashing bright white. "It's your tell, Prescott."

At the idea he even had a tell, Arlo mentally bristled, but he still couldn't resist asking... "Respect is a problem?"

"It is when you hide behind it."

Dwayne left on that note, his ability to read his people and to know when to give them space on full display.

Which meant Arlo was left with all the thoughts racing through his head, his lingering guilt and the very real need to figure out his apology to Kerrigan.

He decided figuring out that apology was a good place to start.

Kerrigan moved through the dark, murky water, her gloved hands removing pile after pile of silt, and cursed her inability to come up with a weapon. Jayden had found the sawed-off shotgun quickly, but neither of them had had any luck finding the semi-automatics.

Gavin's voice echoed through her comm unit. "You guys have about twelve more minutes of air. Start wrapping it up down there and get going on your ascent. We'll do a second dive for the other pieces."

The water around the bridge was some of the deepest in the harbor and they had to manage their ascent slowly or risk adding in decompression stops. She knew the logistics, but damn, she'd worked out a rhythm for combing the harbor floor and she really wanted to find those guns.

Couldn't one thing go right?

Even as she thought it, she disregarded it. The specifics of her training were absolute. You followed protocol and you followed the instructions of your lead. Gavin was lead and he said to come up, so they'd get fresh tanks and start again.

Jayden sent back his affirmation, and Kerrigan was about to do the same when she heard a shout through her comm unit.

"Kerrigan. Jayden. Start that ascent now." Gavin's voice brooked no argument through the headset. "We got a jumper on the bridge."

The instructions were clear, delivered as an order, but her reaction was in immediate violation of her training.

Her single biggest goal under water was to remain calm.

To control her breathing.

And at those four words—*we've got a jumper*—it all shot to hell.

Desperate, Kerrigan focused on her breathing first. She *had* to get this under control.

Breath stuttered in her lungs, and she put a hand over her breathing apparatus, struggling to find a calmer way to handle the news of the jumper, to no avail. Especially when Gavin's voice came through their now-open comm line, apprising her and Jayden of the situation, confirming the jumper was getting closer to the edge of the bridge.

Additional cops on scene.

Second police boat en route.

Coast Guard notified and moving in as well.

She listened to it all, her breath still coming in sharp, spiky gasps as Gavin relayed what was happening. The waters that had felt calm and welcoming even a few moments before as she'd worked now felt cloying and thick.

A distinct sensation of being trapped filled her, a match for the deep despair triggered by the thought of the jumper.

Kerrigan fought through the natural reactions of her body, cataloging her way through the mental checklist that was as much protocol as her lifeline.

Manage your air.

Control your ascent.

Slow and steady on both.

She made it another few feet, her gaze focused on her depth gauge, even as she fought her adrenaline for every single foot.

Breathe, damn it. You know the way. Slow and steady.

Slow.

Steady.

Her training was expansive, and the harbor team was fully prepared to support bridge suicides. The unpredictability of it was a challenge, but the goal was always to minimize loss of life. She'd been fortunate to have a high rate of success so far, but she'd also never been involved in one while working another dive.

Nor had she been involved in one since the events at her last precinct.

The chatter continued through her comm unit, Gavin doing his best to keep her and Jayden aware of what was happening. His voice helped settle her, even as she felt the hitch in her breathing as the memories of what had come before continued to swamp her.

"Patrol's on the bridge. They're keeping their distance, but they made contact with the jumper."

It's a civilian, Kerrigan reminded herself as she stared diligently at her depth gauge, carefully moving steadily upward. *It's not the same.*

But it was the same.

Somewhere deep inside she knew that. Taking one's life, no matter the reason, was the same.

"Kerrigan! What's your depth?"

Gavin's voice echoed through her comm unit, and she held tight to it, using it as a lodestone to keep her moving steadily upward. "Forty-two."

"Keep it steady."

Steady.

She upbraided herself for letting the past into her head and tried to clear her mind of everything else. Under the water, her problems at the surface had to take a back seat. Her breath, her equipment and her work could be her only focus down here.

Yet she'd let all she was dealing with up above color her judgment.

Breathe.

She kicked slowly, keeping her ascent properly paced to avoid decompression issues, and finally felt her breathing slow.

Finally felt her world right itself.

The hull of the police boat became visible above her and she kicked the last few feet to the surface. Breaking through the water, she swam the remaining distance to the police boat, Jayden visible at the top of the deck, waiting for her.

The quiet beneath the water, with only her comm unit for sound, had vanished. In its place was the cacophony of the boat engine, the whipping of the wind and the shouts coming from the bridge.

She looked up to see the commotion surrounding the jumper and was surprised to realize the situation was happening almost directly above their boat.

"Finally!" Jayden hollered from the edge of the ladder, his hand extended to pull her up.

She grabbed the bottom rung, carefully navigating the steps, when the shouting got louder, echoing off the comm unit in her ear. Jayden twisted to look up at the bridge and Kerrigan's gaze followed his. The already loud shouts exploded as a large form fell over the edge, flailing as it headed for the water.

Without conscious thought, she pushed off the ladder, falling back into the water. Her only goal was to get to the fallen man.

"Kerrigan! No!" Jayden's scream from above her faded out as soon as she sunk beneath the water. She moved on blind instinct, pushing herself as fast as she could in the direction she saw the man fall.

Gavin's voice echoed in her ear, loud and firm. "Kerrigan. Stop your dive immediately. We've got a crew ready."

She ignored the summons, focused on the churned-up water in front of her.

She was close. So, so close. And she could *save* him.

It wasn't like last time. She wasn't responsible for this, but she could help him. She could make sure that he got help.

That was her only thought as she swam closer.

Not the steady shouts in her ear, ordering her back.

Not the roiling water as she swam ever closer to the body she could see sinking in the murky darkness.

Not the underlying knowledge that she had no more than three minutes of air in her tank.

Still, the man fell, and she reached out, trying to grab the hands that were, even now, raised above the body as he sunk. Kicking out, she pushed herself downward to try and get to him. Pressure exploded in her ears as her fingertips caught the edge of his jacket sleeve and she gripped as hard as she could, grasping that thick material and pulling hard to stop his descent.

It wasn't much, but she held on tight, using her other hand to grip the man's fingers.

Kerrigan had no idea if he was alive, but she'd stopped his descent and now she had to get him to the surface. Keeping tight hold on her prize, her forearms strained at the minimal grip she had, centered in the flex of her fingers and wrists.

And still, she refused to let go.

Vaguely, she keyed back into the shouts in her ear. The steady orders to surface had given way to new shouts from Gavin.

"Wyatt's on his way. You are ordered to ascend, Kerrigan. Now! You don't have any air."

That reality—one she'd known but had deliberately ignored in favor of action—became clear as her tank gauge read one percent. She had her bailout cylinder, and she could use that, but the only way she could get to it was to let go of her tenuous hold on the jumper.

But he'd need it, too.

So she tightened her grip, her wrists straining as her fingers cramped. But there was no way she was letting go.

No way she'd fail now.

Kicking upward, she pushed her body to its limits, dragging the man and working her fingers, small movements that gave way inch by inch, to get a better grip. She had to get a hand free to get him air from her bailout cylinder. He'd been under too long at this point and he needed air.

Stopping the ascent to focus on her grip, she managed to secure his wrist in one tight grip, then used her free hand to reach for her cylinder.

She just had it in her hand when the man's eyes popped open, his movements suddenly jerky. She saw a world of hurt in those eyes a split second before he began waving his free hand, knocking the bailout bottle from her grip.

She scrambled for the cylinder, but it fell beyond her reach, the tip of her gloves just brushing the edge of it as it descended into the murky depths of the river.

Her gaze darted back to her oxygen gauge and she was determined to do something to help him, even if it was to share her breathing apparatus, when she registered the readout.

Her oxygen was gone.

Chapter 9

"Kerr!"

Wyatt's voice echoed in her ear a moment before she registered his form descending above her. She still had a grip on the fallen man, but his continued flailing was straining her wrist to the point of breaking.

Did she let go?

She *had* to surface for air.

Wyatt took in the situation immediately and she used her free hand to make the signal for "no air." In moments, he had his own bailout cylinder off his belt and in her hand while his dive partner secured the jumper.

Kerrigan took a steady pull on the bailout tube, the air welcome as she fought to calm herself and her breathing for the second time in five minutes.

In.

Out.

Slow and steady.

Satisfied she was taken care of, Wyatt gestured her to start to the surface as he and his dive partner secured the jumper. His partner, Connor, was holding his own bailout cylinder to the man's lips to get him oxygen.

Whether it was the innate self-preservation humans were hardwired for, or an unwillingness to fight three of them, Kerrigan saw the man take the breather between his lips, nodding as Wyatt's partner gestured him to take breaths.

They had no idea what injuries the man might have sustained, but he seemed to have the wherewithal to hold the cylinder and keep breathing.

With a small push against her shoulder, Wyatt pointed up in their understood gesture for the surface. "Go."

She knew she'd already broken several regulations and put herself in serious danger by going after the jumper, so she just nodded and started her ascent.

And surfaced to find a boat full of concerned faces.

Jayden was already at the base of the boat ladder, his hand extended toward her. She took it and felt the hard strength of him as he half pulled, half dragged her into his chest.

"God, you took five years off my life." He whispered it against her ear the moment he had his arms around her. "What were you thinking?"

"I—"

Adrenaline had emotion cratering her stomach and she suddenly feared she'd start crying if she answered him.

It was only his knowing stare as he pulled back that

kept her in the moment. There'd be time for tears and admonishment later.

But she'd be a fool to think she'd escape, either.

Arlo glanced at his watch for what had to be the tenth time in as many minutes and wondered where Kerrigan was. She'd said she had a morning dive but would be in after lunch. It was nearly two and he still hadn't seen any sign of her.

She'd said those words in anger before leaving him to two plates of pancakes. Before he'd sent the report on the Gentry family. Had she reconsidered and wasn't coming in at all?

Could he blame her?

Wyatt waved at him from the entrance to the squad room. Arlo lifted a hand in greeting, curious to see his friend at this time of day. Although Wyatt was a fixture around the 86th, he was out on dives on most weekdays.

"To what do I owe the visit?" Arlo eyed the white paper bag his friend set down on the desk, the garlicky scent of a meatball sub wafting from it. "With lunch, too?"

"I need to talk to you. Mind if we go snag a conference room?"

For the first time, he registered the weariness in Wyatt's gaze and the haggard lines that creased his forehead.

"Sure."

He followed his friend to a small room off the main corridor and found his curiosity spiking even higher when Wyatt closed the door.

"What's going on?"

"Kerrigan had a bad dive today. I wanted you to hear it from me."

"Is she okay?"

"She's fine. Shaken up and taking a few days off from her dive work, but she's alright."

Whatever else he was expecting, the news that Kerrigan had almost been hurt had him reeling.

"I need to go see her."

"I need you to talk to me first. Let me tell you what's going on."

He didn't just consider Wyatt a colleague, but he was also a valued friend, so the serious tone shot something damn near frigid straight through Arlo's midsection.

"What is going on, Wyatt?"

"Kerrigan ran out of air today on her dive."

It felt like his stomach curdled at that news. "She what? But that's not possible. You dive in pairs. And don't you have extra air? That backup you carry?"

"We have all those things, and she still ran out of air. I found her in time and was able to give her my backup."

"It doesn't make sense. She's a good diver. An experienced one, too."

"She's all those things."

He heard the pause in Wyatt's voice as clearly as a gunshot.

"But what?"

His friend's eyebrows narrowed over blue eyes that missed nothing. "But I'm worried she's taken on a bit too much."

"She's assured me repeatedly she can handle it. That she could juggle the case, and her dive work. And from what I've seen that's true."

"I thought so, too. Even as late as Friday, talking

with her, it seemed she was handling it all. But the woman I saw today on that dive? She is not handling things."

His heated discussion with Kerrigan on Saturday morning filled his mind once again. It hadn't been far from his thoughts, but standing here, facing Wyatt, Arlo had to admit there was something there.

"She and I had a tough discussion the other day. Maybe it's on her mind."

"Tough discussion? Something so tough she wouldn't know how to manage a dive?"

"You keep saying that. What actually happened?"

Wyatt filled him in on the recovery work that Kerrigan and Jayden were responsible for this morning. It all sounded straightforward until Wyatt explained how she'd gone after a man who had jumped from the bridge.

"Kerrigan saved that man?"

"Yes, she did. People can survive a jump from the Brooklyn Bridge, but it's tenuous at best. She saved him because she was right there, and she acted quickly."

"And that's what you think is a problem? She acted with compassion and saved somebody?"

"She broke protocol, Arlo. She knows better. She put herself in direct danger."

The rules and regulations they all lived with were a part of the job. Necessary ones, yes, and they were drilled into everyone from the first day at the academy.

It didn't change the fact that sometimes gut instinct overrode the most specific training.

"She saved someone, Wyatt. And at obvious personal risk to herself. That's pretty amazing."

Even as he complimented her, pride swelling in his

chest, Arlo wasn't fully immune to Wyatt's accusations. Whether it was the cause or just an underlying symptom, his fight with Kerrigan on Saturday likely hadn't helped. But he also wasn't ready to write her off for doing something so heroic.

"Amazing, my ass. She nearly killed herself in the process."

"Look. I'm not disregarding your concerns. But tell me honestly. Would she have gone after him, anyway? Regardless of working a case alongside her dive work?"

Wyatt ran a frustrated hand through his hair. "I don't know."

"Would you?"

"Hell." Wyatt let out a few more curses before dropping into a seat at the small round conference-room table. "That's what's killing me about this. She had her bailout cylinder, and she was right there."

"What do you mean *right there*?"

"The jumper was nearly on top of her boat when he jumped. I'd have gone after him, too. Especially if I thought I could reach him."

"She did reach him."

"Yeah, I know. And she'd have been okay if the guy hadn't accidentally knocked the cylinder out of her hand."

That wash of ice was back—had he ever felt this cold?—as Arlo pictured all that had happened on the dive.

But she was alive. And so was the poor soul who'd believed jumping to his death was a preferable alternative. Now the man could get help. Now he had a chance.

It was minimal solace as he thought about all the

ways this could have gone very wrong, yet at the same time, Arlo couldn't shake that solid burst of pride.

Kerrigan had saved someone.

And she was okay.

Captain Reed's admonishment earlier to apologize still rang in his ears. He was going to do just that.

Kerrigan filled her teakettle with water and considered all the possible outcomes of telling her parents about her dive. There was no question she'd tell them—it was a solid promise she'd made when she'd entered the harbor program—but it was the "how" she was struggling with.

They deserved to know. Just as she'd expect to know about them and their safety, for any reason, in return. But letting them know she'd gone after a potential suicide victim with three minutes of air left in her tank wasn't going to sit well.

Hell, it hadn't sat well with her, either.

But what was she supposed to do? She was the closest to him. And she had a duty to help.

You have a duty to yourself, too.

That lone thought had remained steady each time she considered how to explain what had happened.

She set the kettle on the stovetop but didn't turn on the burner, instead grabbing her phone off the counter to call her parents. She'd nearly pressed the call button when she heard a heavy knock on her door.

"Saved by the bell," she whispered as she laid the phone back down and headed for her front door. A look through the peephole showed Arlo on the other side.

A quick glance down at her ratty old NYPD gym

shorts and torn navy blue sweatshirt had her cringing, but there wasn't anything to be done for it now.

Besides, if he was here, it meant Wyatt had already gotten to him and he knew about the dive.

And she might be mad at him, but after the danger in the water this morning, all that anger seemed inconsequential. It *was* valid—she reassured herself—but it didn't seem quite as important as it initially had.

She pulled open the door and drank her fill of him, standing on the other side. He had on dark slacks and a blue button-down shirt that should have looked staid and somehow just appeared solid stretched across his broad chest.

Reassuring.

And the place she'd like to bury herself for a few hours.

"Arlo."

"Kerrigan."

And then there were no words as her vision came to life in a near-perfect rush. One minute he was standing there and the next he had her in his arms, his cheek pressed to the top of her head while that strong chest cradled her close.

"I heard what happened."

"Arlo, I—" She tried to lift her head, but he simply lifted one hand and pressed it against her neck, keeping her flush against him.

"Please." He let out a hard exhale and she felt the tremors slide through his body. "Please just give me this for one minute."

So she did.

And they stood there like that in her doorway for a lot longer. She knew she should pull away—it wouldn't do to get so much warmth and comfort and physical support from this man—but she couldn't do it.

When his arms finally loosened, he still held on to her but took a small step back. "Can I come in?"

"Sure."

She gestured him into the large room that served as her living and sleeping area and was glad she'd cleaned up that morning before leaving. He moved to the love seat and armchair that dominated the corner of the room and she remained standing where she was.

"Can I, ah, get you anything? I was about to put on some water for tea."

"Don't go to any trouble, but if you're having some, I'll join you."

"Okay."

The kettle was already on the stove, so it was a quick task to turn on the burner. And then she slipped back into the room and took the seat beside the love seat.

"Wyatt told you what happened?"

"He did. He's pretty upset about it."

She laughed at that, but the sound came out harsher and more brittle than she'd intended. "I'm a bit upset about it, too."

"He thinks you've taken on too much."

Although she should have been prepared for that, the words still felt like a blow. One that cut her off at the knees, all while knocking her breath fully from her lungs.

Arlo must have seen it all brewing on her face because he quickly held up a hand.

"I think we do need to talk about the workload, but I told him I didn't agree with his assessment."

"You don't?"

"Not about today. You saved that man, at great personal expense to yourself. But you did the job, and I don't think you should be castigated for that."

The sweetest relief flooded her veins and Kerrigan had the oddest sensation of floating.

Not the feeling she had in the water, but something far lighter and airier than mere buoyancy in the water.

For the first time in a lot longer than she could remember, she felt free.

"You told him that?"

"I did."

"Is it truly how you feel? And why are you suddenly protecting me for this job?"

He shook his head, an odd mix of humor and something deeply serious filling his gaze.

"There you go again. First you were convinced I was hunting for some reason to get rid of you or believed your performance was flawed. Now you think I'm protecting you."

"I'm sorry." She waved a hand. She was aware her reactions were tied to her own concerns that her competency would be questioned.

Not that it actually *was* being questioned.

"Why do I keep getting the feeling that I'm being judged? Or worse, that I'm judging you for whatever came before."

"I—" She stopped, his words making a certain sort of sense.

And then the kettle went off, the loud whistle interrupting them. She realized it was her chance to not only get her thoughts together, but also to stand and take a few deep breaths and tell him the truth.

To stand tall and tell him *her* truth.

"Let me get our tea. Then I have something I need to tell you. About my last precinct. About the man I testified against to Internal Affairs. The one who committed suicide."

Arlo waited for her to make the tea, a mix of dread and relief flooding his veins.

She was okay.

He hadn't realized just how important it was to look at her with his own eyes until she'd opened the door.

But to hold her? To feel the press of her body against his and know that she was alright?

It had meant everything.

How had she come to mean so much to him in such a short time?

Yes, it was attraction—the lure and that deep tug of desire—but it was so much more. He knew he should fight his feelings, but it was hard to argue against something so real.

Kerrigan came back into the room with two steaming mugs and settled them on the end table that cornered the love seat and chair. Her apartment was small but cozy, and he could see her here. Could picture her deep in the oversized chair reading a book or sitting on the love seat as she watched TV.

What caught him off guard was how easily he pictured himself here, too.

Whoa, Prescott. A hug at the door is one thing. Something more permanent…

He let the thought taper off, unwilling to go too far down that rabbit hole.

They were still colleagues and partners. To assume anything more was a fool's game.

"So Wyatt told you all about what happened this morning on my dive?"

"He did. Although I'd like to hear your version."

"It was stupid and against protocol and—"

"*And* incredibly brave and heroic." He stressed those points again. Somewhere in Wyatt's recounting and the obvious self-recrimination she'd spent the past few hours marinating in, the message had gotten lost.

"I hope you don't do it again. Or maybe do it again but not in quite that way. You know. With air in your tank."

"Trust me, that's not an experience I ever want to repeat. It's a diver's worst nightmare and one my parents regularly have. Your arrival just helped me delay the inevitable phone call to tell them about it."

"I can be here for moral support if you'd like."

Exhaustion rimmed the delicate skin around her eyes, but he didn't miss how they softened at his offer. "I appreciate that. But I can tell them later. What I really need to do is tell you about what happened before."

"At your old precinct?"

She nodded, then reached for her mug of tea, wrapping her hands tight around the ceramic.

"I joined my precinct in Queens right out of the academy. I'm from Forest Hills and I wanted to go back to the community. I hadn't made the harbor team yet and while I was already working toward it, I had to put in my time on street patrol, too."

"And you wanted to go back to your neighborhood and be the face of the NYPD to the community."

He remembered those days. When all of your training and ambition were finally let loose and you had to learn the job from the ground up, step by step on the streets of New York.

"I did. And for the first year I was so busy I couldn't see beyond it all. I was working my shifts, and on top of that I was swimming several days a week, pushing myself to meet the requirements of the test. One morning, early, I headed in for a swim at the precinct's gym facility."

"So your Saturday pool visits have a history?"

A vague smile ghosted her lips. "Something like that."

Although he'd intended to lighten the mood a bit, he knew he needed to give her time to tell the story. He picked up his own mug and leveled his full attention on her.

"As I was changing into my suit, I heard this muffled crying from the far side of the lockers. I went to see what was going on and found a woman from my academy class. She'd been beaten pretty bad, and one eye was nearly swollen shut."

"Was she responsive to you?"

"Not at first. She told me she had trouble with an arrest the night before and was still dealing with the adrenaline rush. I would have believed her, but she slipped up on a few details."

"Enough that you realized she wasn't telling the truth. Or not the whole truth."

Kerrigan shook her head. "In the end, there was barely any truth at all. She was partnered with an older cop who'd just lost custody of his kids. He was already on the decline, dealing with the twin demons of gambling and drugs, and he was pretty out of control. He dragged her into a scam he was running on the side for extra money. The thugs he was meeting with didn't like the look of the new young partner and they took quite a few shots at her to gauge his loyalty."

"And he let them?"

She nodded her head, almost in slow motion, her gaze on a time and place only she could see. But it was obvious how it still affected her.

And how determined she'd been to stop such an awful wrong.

Her gaze cleared as she looked his way. "It's such a sad story it's almost cliché."

"They exist for a reason."

"I guess they do."

"How'd you get her to tell you what really happened?"

"She didn't tell me much, but I followed them a few days later. The whole situation didn't sit well with me. Especially because here I was, a recent academy graduate, all bright and shiny and excited about being a cop. And maybe she was, too, or maybe the job ultimately wouldn't have been for her, but no one would ever know because of how she started out."

"Media and entertainment love to make a big deal about cops going bad or rogue. It makes for good storytelling."

"But it's a heartbreaking reality in every way."

He'd been fortunate not to see a whole lot of it in his career, but Arlo had heard the stories. The cops who burned out or who were lured to criminal pursuits for the right payout.

Hell, wasn't that a bit of what they were all still reeling with from the news of Anderson McCoy's betrayal? Marlowe's grandfather had been protecting his son, but it was still a betrayal of the badge to look the other way at a crime so his son could stay safe.

"How'd it end?"

"I saw enough to take it to Internal Affairs. They already had a dossier on him and were keeping notes. His decline was evident to a lot of people, and he'd had a few cases that had some suspicious details to them. Add on the fact they paired a rookie with him and IA was quick to get as many details from me as they could."

"I believe I used the words *brave* and *heroic* before. Clearly, it's a pattern with you, Doyle."

"There's nothing heroic about tattling."

He could acknowledge that it was a bad experience in every way, but to stand up to a bad cop to ensure he couldn't continue his destructive ways was the very opposite of *tattling*.

It was necessary.

"There's everything heroic about it when it means standing up for what's right. This isn't the second-grade playground or a kids' pool party. He had a responsibility to his new partner and he sure as hell had one to the job. He failed on all aspects of that."

"He then deliberately waited until I was on shift one night. He followed me close enough to know where I was patrolling. Even now, I suspect he had someone help him goose my schedule so he could plan it all."

"You were there when he jumped?"

"He made sure of it."

Once again, her gaze had drifted to a memory only she could see. And as he watched her, Arlo understood a bit better why she was so determined to make a good impression on their case. Why she wanted to learn and grow and earn everything on her own merits.

And why she was so afraid of messing something up.

"I'm sorry this was your experience. And I can't change what came before, but I can feel regret that was a side of the job you had to experience. And there's something else I'm truly sorry for that I want to own up to. I kept you out of my review of Big Will and his boys."

"You did it deliberately?"

"At first, yes. When we left Brooklyn Yacht, I wanted to do a bit more nosing around about the family and I didn't want to alarm you. That was wrong. In every way."

"And then you sat on the report."

"Because I knew you'd see it and I wasn't ready to face the inevitable."

Her gaze never wavered as she looked at him across the small expanse between the chair and the love seat. The dark brown depths of her eyes were sharp, reading him as she seemed to weigh her words.

"I don't like it and I'm going to reserve the right to be mad about it later, but not today, Arlo."

"No?"

"No. Today's a day for focusing on the good, and what is good is being your partner and learning from you." She stared into her tea before continuing. "I was holding back from you, too. My last job and how it was coloring my reactions to things. Our relationship has changed since we went to see Big Will, and you've had a chance to see me work. But…"

She shook her head, seeming to shift gears. He was still curious what she was about to say, but as he stared at her, a picture of strength and vulnerability as she sat in that chair, Arlo had to admit the truth.

It didn't matter anymore in the face of almost losing her.

"It's time to move forward, Kerrigan."

"Water under the bridge." She grinned at her own words, the cliché not lost on either of them. "You know me now, and I'm going to move forward and trust that there aren't any more secrets between me and my partner."

Chapter 10

No more secrets.

The idea settled deep in her core, spreading outward. It was a satisfying thought, and with respect to their partnership, Kerrigan had every confidence they were over the hump.

Arlo had willingly addressed the background check he'd done on Big Will and his sons and she'd shared her past. Their partnership was back on solid ground.

But what else was between the two of them?

That was another matter entirely.

She had feelings for him. She'd been hard-pressed to deny them from the first, but the way he'd pulled her into his arms?

It had meant everything.

And that was something she needed to play close to the vest.

Which meant—as always—it was much easier to focus on work.

"Why did you run Big Will and his family?"

"I can't fully say. Something about our visit struck me as worth digging into. But part of why I didn't say anything was I couldn't put my finger on why."

"You can work a hunch without any reason other than it's an angle. I wouldn't have been upset."

"I know that now. But at the time the captain's words were still ringing in my ears about the dark, violent overtones of this case and then seeing you with someone you knew so well." Arlo tapped his fingers on the arm of the love seat. "I let it cloud my judgment. I didn't want to cast aspersions on your friend if I could help it."

"The captain's worried?"

"He's trying not to be, but, yeah, he is. The sheer viciousness of those kills on the boat has him engaged on this case. A bit of that rubbed off in my approach, I'm afraid."

"Because I'm a woman."

"Because you're new and eager and learning, and I overrotated a bit too much on the protection angle." Something distinctly mischievous lit his blue gaze. "I won't do it again."

She was helpless against that hint of mischief. "See that you don't."

"Besides. Not every hunch pays off and I'm glad this one didn't."

Although she had a fondness for Big Will and certainly didn't want to think anything problematic was running through his business, she didn't think Arlo was off base, either.

"Let's play this out. The Gentry family has a lot of

history in the boat business and a lot of access to a variety of stakeholders in that industry."

"You think something's there?"

"I'm saying let's not be too hasty and write it all the way off. Part of why we visited Brooklyn Yacht in the first place was because Big Will knows everyone. He knows the business forward and backward, and it stands to reason he'd have some knowledge of that unregistered boat that went down."

Kerrigan almost laughed at the look of pure, unmitigated relief on Arlo's face.

"You're really into this line of questioning."

"It makes sense. And while I'm not saying Will lied to us, he's running a big business with a lot of tentacles. Wholesalers. Mechanics. Parts. It's equally as likely he knows something as it's happening underneath his radar. But it's worth poking there a bit more."

"I think you're on to something with the associated aspects of the business. The search I ran focused specifically on Will's company, but I never thought about the other people who work with them. Especially other people who make a living with an adjacent business."

"The mechanic and parts aspect is definitely something we should run down. The boat that went down had no serial numbers on anything the evidence team has recovered." Kerrigan paused, thinking about the last report she'd read that detailed every recovered part, with photos. Not a single one had traceable provenance. "Someone who can do that?"

"They're running quite a racket."

"Which means we have a place to start." She was out of her chair before Arlo grabbed her hand, gently holding her in place.

"Tomorrow, Kerrigan. We can look into it tomorrow. You need to rest today."

"I'm good. I can do this."

He shook his head. "Nope. We'll start tomorrow and I promise not to start without you. But you've got a phone call to make and then get some rest."

"I'm fine."

"Then you'll enjoy an afternoon off and to yourself."

He got up so they were standing side by side. Once again, that same delicious sensation of his height advantage over her kicked in and she stared up at him. "Clever."

"Necessary."

His focus on her was absolute, the vivid blue of his eyes drawing her in.

Those eyes that were so mesmerizing.

Enticing.

And once again, she was reminded of the emotional secrets between them. Of what she wanted deep down but knew she couldn't have.

They stood there for more than a few extra heartbeats before Arlo seemed to come to some conclusion. With it, he stepped back and away, putting space between them.

"I'll see you in the morning."

Before she could say anything else, he bent down, pressing his lips to her cheek. He cheated the kiss a little, the edge of his lips pressing to the edge of hers. If it had been anyone else, she'd have said they missed the mark, but she knew full well Arlo Prescott didn't miss anything.

Which was likely why she still felt the brand of his lips—just there, at the edge of hers—long after he'd left.

* * *

Arlo scanned the digital board he'd created on his laptop and considered the information on the case. They'd been focused on how few leads they had and, as he looked at all the details they'd assembled so far, he had to admit perhaps they'd been too focused on the obvious.

Yeah, it would be great to close this quickly. Find the bastard responsible for such a nasty deed and get them off the streets.

But his gut, as well as Kerrigan's and the captain's, recognized something more was going on here.

What was beneath the surface?

It wasn't until he'd written those words on the legal pad beside his computer that he had to stop and laugh.

Clearly, he'd been spending too much time in the company of a diver.

"I'm not so sure what's funny about a murder board, but I'm sure you'll tell me."

Arlo glanced up to see Kerrigan, looking bright and fresh with four boxes of doughnuts piled high in her hands.

"You brought doughnuts?"

"I brought doughnuts *and* a challenge."

When he looked again, he could see the boxes were two different colors. Two from Sunset Bakery and two from Cake Brothers.

"Taste test?"

"Of sorts. I figure we can lure whoever's not heavily focused on something into the conference room I reserved for the taste test, sugar them up and then get their creative juices flowing by looking at the murder board we'll already have projected. There's something in those files we keep overlooking. It's time to bring in some other experienced eyes and ask what they see."

"Great minds."

"You brought doughnuts, too?"

"I didn't think that far ahead. But I was thinking we needed to look at everything all together again and see what we've got."

Kerrigan tapped the edge of his computer screen. "Something's in there. We just need to find it."

Twenty minutes later, ideas were flying as fast as the doughnuts. The four boxes Kerrigan had brought in had been rapidly emptied, leaving nothing but a conference room full of coffee and doughnut-fueled souls anxious to take down a killer.

"The gunshots bother me." Andrea Wainwright, a twenty-year detective sitting near the screen, spoke up as she studied the evidence Arlo and Kerrigan had laid out.

"Bother you how?" Kerrigan was sitting next to the woman and turned to face her.

"I agree with the assessment of the order of the shootings. They were a surprise and the first victim had no idea, while the second victim at least moved in some attempt at defending himself."

"The ME's office concurs on that as well," Arlo added.

"What I don't get is the killings at all. They were henchmen, so why take them down? The evidence suggests they were there to support and that is further proven by the fact they were dousing the boat with gasoline to make the escape. If there was going to be this big effort to make them take the fall, find another way to kill them. One that isn't so obviously murder."

Andrea's observations got a lot of chatter going and one of their newly minted detectives, Devante Johnson, spoke up. "There's something to that. I'm not saying the ME's office wouldn't have found it if they were poisoned, but the vics also spent time under the water and were already in decomp. But gunshots to the head? That's a bad, bad end they couldn't have done themselves. It's, I don't know—"

"It's vindictive," Andrea said, with a firm nod of her head. "You failed me and I'm taking you down. Which shows anger and impulse and a lack of self-control."

"Torching a boat that had to cost a fortune reinforces that, too," Kerrigan added, tapping the side of her coffee cup. "That boat's not cheap on the regular market. But to get it unmarked like that? Someone paid premium dollars to just set it on fire and sink it."

Arlo took in all the good feedback, pleased they'd pulled in the broader team. The ideas were good, but even more, coming together was a sign of their camaraderie and work as a unit at the 86th.

With Kerrigan's story from the day before it was even more important to him that she see what a good unit looked like. Dwayne Reed's leadership was important, and the training of his people was an obvious reflection of him. But their hard work and devotion to the work and to each other was on them, too.

And the 86th was someplace special.

With that pride at the forefront of his mind, he tossed out one more theory. "We have another angle we've been playing.

"With the takedown of the Papa, room's opened up for a new kingpin. What if this was either a loyalty test or a way to set the tone from the beginning? It's cruel and impulsive, but there could be more calculation there than we're giving credit to."

"Hell of a way to assert power," Dwayne said from where he was standing in the doorway.

Arlo welcomed in their captain, and everyone sat up a bit straighter as he moved into the room.

Dwayne's dark brown face creased into a broad smile. "I heard a rumor there were doughnuts in here."

"It was a taste test, sir," Kerrigan said. "Between Cake Brothers and Sunset Bakery. We figured it would be a bit easier to talk gruesome murder on a full stomach."

"A wise choice, Officer Doyle." Dwayne snagged the last cruller from Cake Brothers left in the box. "And on a personal note, I'm not picky on where my doughnut comes from, just that the sugar and dough ratio is correct." He took a large bite to punctuate his point, nodding his head as he swallowed. "And this one fits the bill."

"Would you like us to take you through what we've been working on, Cap?" Arlo asked.

Dwayne nodded, reaching for a napkin. "I heard the ideas about the Papa as I walked in. Take me through the others."

Since Dwayne's warm manner and open mind immediately put his team at ease, everyone was more than willing to share their theories. Their captain listened and nodded, giving everyone the runway to puzzle through the problem.

He waited until everyone had shared before offering his own theory. "I think there's something with the boat and the new-management-in-town angle you're playing with. Find the boat and you get a sense of who that might be. Alternatively, get a lead on the new king of the hill and you get some clues on what lines to tug about the boat. Who provided it and what they might be running."

"The boat has a lot of possibilities. Sellers, mechanics, even someone who gives out bank loans could know contacts," Kerrigan said, ticking off a list. "There are a lot of associated businesses wrapped up in the boat business."

"That's good, Doyle. And all those facets?" Dwayne added. "Somebody somewhere's going to talk."

Arlo considered the board one more time, recognizing Dwayne's words as truth. What thread could they pull that would finally give them that one person who gossiped about what went down in the harbor?

"We just need to find them."

"That you do, Detective. Based on what I've seen and heard this morning," Dwayne said, "I think you're close."

"The captain really supports us." Kerrigan followed Arlo out of the precinct as they headed for his car. "His leadership drives the whole team."

"Dwayne's special. He's one of the best cops I've ever known and one of the best men as well. He believes in the work, and he believes in the people who do it."

"Yet one more reason I'm glad I'm at the 86th."

One of many reasons.

Kerrigan pulled up the locations of the businesses she and Arlo had discussed after the meeting broke up. She was anxious to look into the mechanic angle. The boat itself could have been scrubbed clean in a chop shop that was anywhere along the eastern seaboard, but the owner would need someone local for maintenance.

The longstanding joke that the two best days of a boat owner's life were the day they bought their boat and the day they sold it rang with a specific sort of truth. Boat ownership required a willingness to do maintenance, either on your own or because you paid someone.

That would be even more important for a boat that had to be in fighting shape, able to move quickly at a moment's notice.

"Let's go to Waverly's first." Kerrigan read off the address in Brooklyn Heights.

"Why pick them first?"

"I met Buck Waverly a few times—he supports our mechanics on the NYPD boats. He's a good guy and I think he can give us a sense of the market and what we might be looking for."

"You think whoever owned the boat was working with a mechanic?"

"They had to have someone. I guess you could keep someone directly on the payroll who only works for you, but it's probably easier to just give the work to someone with a business front who's willing to take a cut of the action."

"And you're not worried Buck could be that person?"

"I hope not. And feel free to call me naive, but I also think a mechanic supporting chop-shopped boats wouldn't also try to work contracts for the NYPD." She shrugged. "But people are an endless surprise."

"That they are."

Sunlight glinted on his hair, the blond strands glowing gold. He slipped a pair of sunglasses out of his pocket and Kerrigan had the briefest thought that he looked like an honest-to-God movie star. She was almost tempted to look around, expecting to see a film camera capturing the shot.

"What's that look for?"

Arlo caught her staring and Kerrigan nearly shrugged it off, that lingering need to hide her feelings for him rising. But then she thought better of it.

They were partners and instead of dancing around every personal thing, maybe it would be easier to give in to some of it, make it feel less all-consuming.

"You pulled out those sunglasses and all I could think was how much you looked like someone who just stepped off a Hollywood soundstage. The quintessential cop, moving out on a big case."

"All flash, no substance?"

"Hardly." She considered, once again, the spirit of partnership she felt in that conference room this morning and knew that he was so much more to him than flash. "It was just an impression as you slipped on those shades."

"I'm not complaining." His grin was irresistibly sweet, and her heart did a hard double thump in her chest.

And again, she had to admit how compelling he was. Yes, he was handsome, in a way that was overwhelmingly the first thing you noticed when you looked at him. But with time, what came through even more clearly—and with even greater impact—was what a good man he was.

It was something so innate and he showed it, over and over.

The way he spoke with his colleagues. The way he'd mentored her and willingly listened to her ideas. And today, the way he'd led the meeting yet was able to support a wide variety of ideas and opinions.

It mattered.

And it was an example…

"Arlo."

She came to a hard stop about ten feet from the car.

"What is it?" he asked as recognition dawned in his eyes. "Light bulb?"

"I think so. This angle about the killings on the boat. Whoever did this took out two obviously trusted henchmen."

He nodded, waving a hand in a come-on gesture. "You've got something. Keep on."

"It's like I said about this morning. There's real support and camaraderie at the 86th. And here's a situation, moving those drugs on the boat, where you have, by nature, a small circle of trusted individuals. It might be criminal pursuits, but there should be a fair amount of camaraderie in that circle, too. Like us, they're dependent on each other.

"Plus," she added as the idea whirled faster and faster in her mind, "if they were high enough in the organization to be on the boat, they were likely part of the inner circle."

When he only waited, she continued. "Why kill people who'd obviously moved up the ranks? That sends a message, not necessarily a good one, that you can be removed, even if you're loyal."

"And what else do these organizations have besides loyalty?"

"Exactly. So maybe it *was* a test. Someone's trying to replace the Papa and they're marking their territory as they go."

"I'm following, but what if it was another henchman? Someone at the same level or maybe a lieutenant in the organization?"

"To what outcome? If you kill the others on the boat and still let it and all the drugs sink, you've got nothing. And you took out a few operatives when it wasn't your purview to do so."

"Good." His smile grew. "This is good."

"Whoever it is, they're trying to break those bonds. Whether it's a tactic to break down what the Papa had before or a way of testing loyalties, there's so much here that's about breaking down to the bone. Culling people and making them feel alone, forcing them to act aggressively to keep their place or, even more, to stay alive."

Arlo gestured them to the car. "This makes a violent, sort of vicious, sense. But it's an angle and it works. And it explains why we're not hearing any gossip. No chatter or anyone running their mouths. They're all afraid and no one knows who to trust."

"It's standard manipulative behavior. I saw it with that cop at my old precinct. In a matter of weeks, he'd taken that rookie and methodically separated her from the team. He cut her off and made her feel alone. And once you achieve that, you leave people thinking they have nowhere to go and no one to turn to."

As upsetting as her experience had been at her former precinct, it was fascinating, Kerrigan realized, to see how practically she could use that knowledge.

Especially because the theory fit. Almost too well.

Isolation did terrible things to people and in a world where the stakes were already high, it would be an especially torturous tactic.

Yet a highly effective one.

Arlo pulled out of the precinct lot after she'd set Buck Waverly's address in the GPS. She was still musing on the possibilities of the case when she noticed Arlo's demeanor.

"What is it?"

"Behind us. I think we've got a tail."

"You think?"

Arlo pulled hard on the wheel, quickly turning off the main thoroughfare through Sunset Bay. When he let out a long, low curse, Kerrigan recognized the truth.

"We do have a tail."

"Yep." He gritted his teeth as he navigated the lighter, late-morning traffic, instructing her to call it in. "Let's get some marked patrol cars to bring up the rear. We'll see what they're made of and how serious they are."

She called in the ask of all available patrols and responses rapidly came in, affirming positions and engagement of the vehicle.

"Officers Kohler and Peachtree responding," a voice said through the dash radio system. "In pursuit, but keeping our distance. Officer Peachtree is running the plates."

A second car responded, giving similar coordinates, and Kerrigan waited for further direction from Arlo.

"He's not bugging out," Arlo muttered as he kept watch on the rearview mirror.

"Can you see who's in the car?"

"No, visor's low and there's something else on the dash limiting visibility. All the other windows are tinted."

Arlo continued through the neighborhood, moving them deftly toward the warehouse district on the edge of town. Although the neighborhood had been slowly reviving a few of the places as clubs or entertainment areas, most were still used for the needed warehousing of goods for retail.

"What's the endgame here, Arlo?"

He shook his head as they moved along, block after block. "No idea, but it feels like a taunt of some sort."

"More tests?"

"Of the cops? Or the rank and file pursuing the criminal arts?"

As jokes went it was a poor one, yet it had an odd sort of truth, too.

Especially if half of Brooklyn's criminals were currently trying out for a new puppet master. Kerrigan swirled that around in her mind, her eyes going wide just as she caught sight of a shooter perched on the roof of a warehouse on the next corner.

Arlo had already pulled through the intersection and all she could do was scream.

"Shooter with a gun!"

Chapter 11

Arlo slammed on the gas, rushing past the warehouse as fast as he could, helpless to do anything in the moment but hope they escaped any gunfire. He'd already mentally braced for the sound of shattering glass, when nothing appeared at all.

But then he heard a barrage of shooting a few moments later.

"Kerrigan! Down!"

He fought to understand where the noise was coming from, even as his senses processed there was no damage to the car, no shattering glass and no blown-out tires.

They were still moving forward.

But one glance in the rearview mirror and he could see all hell had broken lose.

Kerrigan was bent low, as he'd instructed, but remained on the car radio, communicating with the other patrol cars behind them. It was their collective shouts coming back through the radio that brought everything into clarity.

"Shooter on the roof! Shots fired into the car we're pursuing."

"In pursuit of car now out of control. Driver appears shot as car is veering wildly."

Arlo did a quick check of traffic and did a U-turn back in the direction of his colleagues and the out-of-control car.

"What in the ever-loving hell is going on?"

"They were shot, Arlo." Kerrigan remained calm. Level. Yet he heard the quaver under her words. "The car following us was shot."

"Why? What the hell is going on here? Why were they following cops only to get shot sniper-style? And how were they the target?"

The questions were rhetorical because he was already piecing together an answer. One that had a surprising amount in common with Kerrigan's theories in the precinct parking lot.

Not only was someone pulling the strings, but they'd also created a scenario where no one knew if they were safe.

Which only added a deeper dimension of darkness to this case.

She wasted no time, calling for emergency services even as shouts of "Officers in pursuit" echoed from the car radio as the second squad car to join them had already taken off after the shooter.

"We need to get to that car."

Just as their fellow officers had relayed, after the gunshots, the car that had been following them ran straight into a business storefront. Smoke streamed from the front of the hood as Arlo came to a hard stop beside the other squad car. The two officers who'd stayed on scene were already approaching the smoking vehicle slowly, weapons drawn.

Arlo and Kerrigan jumped out as soon as he put the car in Park, their weapons at the ready. They started in on their approach when Arlo realized the risks.

"We need protection behind, too. Someone has to keep watch for the shooter while we investigate the damage here."

"On it, Detective." Officer Peachtree was already moving into position at the back of the car, sweeping the perimeter.

Arlo was torn between following the other team headed after the shooter and dealing with the victims. But even at risk of losing the shooter, this was their most immediate need.

"Arlo." Kerrigan's tone was urgent. "This is bad."

"Yeah, it's bad." He took in the two men in the car, blood spreading across their chests and smeared on what was left of the windows.

Peachtree's partner raced back to the squad car for a field kit and returned with a box of rubber gloves.

"Officer Doyle's already called for emergency services, but we need to check for signs of life."

Arlo and Kerrigan slipped on gloves while the other officers kept watch on the car and checked for an external shooter, then they quickly changed places as the other two officers slipped on gloves.

By unspoken agreement, Kohler took the driver side while Arlo and Kerrigan took the passenger. Kohler reported back almost immediately that the driver was dead. And it was Kerrigan who leaped toward the passenger-side door when they heard a dark groan through the window.

"He's alive!"

She was already working on the door, pulling hard on it around the damage it had sustained from the crash. Arlo kept his sights on the victim, covering her from behind.

The door came open with one final creak of metal and Kerrigan moved up beside the man.

Peachtree came around the back of the car. "Officers in pursuit radioed back the warehouse is clear."

Even as he asked it, Arlo knew what the answer would be. "Any luck on the shooter?"

"Nope. None. But I'll back you up here. You help Officer Doyle."

Arlo stepped up beside her to help, the two of them working to disengage the man from his seat belt, then pulling him from the car. Although the EMTs would likely have handled it differently, using a board to brace the guy, he and Kerrigan didn't have the time. They needed to assess his injuries as quickly as they could.

And as they got him flat, Arlo recognized one more stark truth. This guy wasn't going to make it long enough for the EMTs to get there.

As pain-filled gray eyes stared up at him and Kerrigan, it was obvious the guy knew it, too.

"Fight for power," the guy hissed out before reaching up to grab Kerrigan's hand. She held tight to it, her innate compassion evident as she crouched beside the man.

"What's a fight for power?" Her voice was gentle as she tried to coax something more from him.

"The streets... Brook... Brooklyn... The drugs."

"Who?"

"Hidden." The man licked his lips, his breathing labored. "Rumors. New empire." He gasped, hard, before his head lolled to the side. "The street's saying she—"

The man took one last hard breath and then there was nothing.

Kerrigan settled the man's hand back by his side and sat back on her haunches. "She?"

Arlo was still processing it all, but the vic's words went a long way toward reinforcing their developing theory that everything was tied to the new turf war in Brooklyn.

But *she*?

They'd run it as soon as they got back to the precinct, but he couldn't immediately summon up any high-level women in any of the local crime organizations. That didn't mean they were absent, he acknowledged.

But it was still a development he hadn't expected.

"Arlo. The gunshots."

His gaze traveled over the man's chest before Kerrigan interrupted him. "On the boat. The gunshots. We theorized they were done by someone a lot shorter. A woman would likely be shorter."

"Of course." He nodded, her assessment spot-on. "That fits."

The screaming cry of the ambulance filled the air as it got closer. Two more patrol cars had already arrived to manage the scene, as well as the small crowd that had formed on the block.

The fact they were in a less-populated area worked in their favor, but the noise of gunshots and the crash had pulled people who were close by out of various businesses and into the street in curiosity.

He and Kerrigan made room for the EMTs and then moved to stand with Officers Kohler and Peachtree. It was Kohler who spoke first.

"They didn't get the shooter. There were shell casings on the roof of the warehouse they've taken into evidence, but the shooter's long gone."

Arlo knew it had been a longshot, too much time elapsing from the gunshots to the pursuit, but he was still frustrated. Even as the dying victim's words filled his mind once more.

Fight for power.

New empire.

The street's saying she—

Captain Reed had pegged it from the first. That they were dealing with something dark and vicious.

And it was escalating.

Wendy Parker reviewed the footage of the rooftop shooter and assessed his technique as she wondered if she had time for a quick manicure. They'd opened a new place on Sixth she wanted to try, and her tips desperately needed a touch-up.

Thoughts of her nails vanished as she watched the shooter run from the roof and she let out a harsh, quick curse.

"Don't tell me you were that big an idiot," she muttered even as she rewound the video.

The camera she'd placed on the warehouse rooftop opposite had caught everything clearly and she fixated once more on the casings dropping from the bottom of his gun.

Casings he never picked up before he ran.

Incompetent ass.

Did anyone know how to do their job?

That had been the biggest frustration she'd had since starting this project. The ability to think quickly, on their feet and with strategic focus, was sorely absent from the thugs she was stuck working with.

Crime, like any other matter in life, was a business.

Her mother had taught her that young and she'd used it as a mantra. Loyalty was an illusion and power without control was meaningless.

It was why she was so determined to do this right. The Papa had his day, but he'd been weak.

He'd gotten caught, hadn't he?

And all because his lower-level drones had big mouths and his higher-level lieutenants didn't know how to keep them in line.

It was how she'd been able to make her move in the first place. She was the one who'd drip-fed the clues to the cops about the Papa's organization. Her mother had been one of Queens' wealthiest madams for a long time and there were few secrets she wasn't privy to. Wendy had used that cache of information to put the pieces together.

And then she'd triangulated all the weak spots in the Papa's organization.

It had been a simple matter of strategy, and once all the elements were in place, she'd made her move.

Incompetent criminals aside, today's exercise was a risk. It was one she'd put into motion when she'd realized Kerrigan Doyle was assigned to the boat case.

For all her attempts to build the right connections and loyalties, layered over a base of fear, she hadn't spent much time trying to ingratiate herself with the cops. Her mother had always had a few on the take who were willing to look the other way with respect to her business, but Wendy needed bigger allies.

Could Kerrigan be one?

They were a few years apart in school and she'd always gotten a sense of the kid as well-liked but not part of the in crowd. Kerrigan had managed to stay off the radar of high-school politics, which was a feat in and of itself.

It also suggested a high likelihood that she'd be a problem.

There was no way of knowing, so it was time to play the angles. They'd gotten reacquainted again, so she had a good excuse to reach out. She'd make up some crap about news traveling fast in the old neighborhood and ask how was Kerrigan doing. Was she surviving such a difficult time on the force?

Wendy pictured the cop she'd met along with Kerrigan in the bar Friday night. *The hot cop*, she amended to herself. Hot or not, *that* one was a straight arrow. He'd led the big bust at McNulty's, and he had a reputation for getting the job done.

Various approaches flashed through her mind as she closed the video from the rooftop. She'd already killed the uplink connection so no one could trace the camera back to her.

It was necessary, but her expenses had been mounting and her mother was getting a bit pissed about continuing to front her. The drugs dropped in the Hudson hadn't helped. That supply was going to fund her enterprise for a few more months until she pulled in a really big score, but there was nothing to be done for it now.

Jordan and Dallas had been good partners, setting up the pickup down in Baltimore and working with her to bring it all up the coast. Dallas had made the connection with the Gentry boys, too. But he was itching for a promotion and thought her approach to the takeover of the Papa's territory unnecessary.

And then the arrival of the Coast Guard was serious bad luck. Dallas had argued with her as the Coast Guard was closing in that they needed to open the throttle and make a run for it on the boat.

Men.

She admired limitless thinking as much as the next person but hauling ass through a near hurricane wasn't the answer. Thinking a bigger gun or a faster car would do the trick wasn't the answer.

Brains.

Strategy.

Focus and vision.

Those were the pathways to the top.

So, yeah, she missed Dallas, and she missed sleeping with him even more, but it was a split-second decision on the boat and she'd made it.

This was *her* job. She wanted complete loyalty and if someone couldn't give it to her then they were of no use to her.

Focus and vision.

They were her stock in trade.

Kerrigan took a sip of coffee as she entered notes on the digital murder book they were keeping on the boat case. She closed her eyes and tried to remember all the things the victim had said as he lay dying in front of her.

The power struggle she and Arlo had theorized was spot-on. So was the fear factor that seemed to have spread through Brooklyn's criminal class.

And then that part at the end.

The street's saying she—

She.

A woman was behind this brutality?

As a woman who performed in a challenging profession, she'd never gone in for the gender distinctions often thrown around. People chose who they wanted to be and the life they wanted to live.

But in this case, it was worth considering.

The boat victims had been shot at close range, from behind. It was brutal, yet as they'd surmised in the assessment in the conference room this morning, there was an impulsiveness to it, too.

And then the shootings today.

Another hardcore, brutal act, to set up your own people for a job and then take them out.

It wasn't the first time she'd seen someone die on the job, but today was one of the most unexpected. The moment she'd seen that shooter on the roof, she'd fully expected the guy was aiming for her and Arlo.

A series of horrifying thoughts had raced through her mind, including not getting to say goodbye to her family and how sad it would be to never know who was behind the boat murders.

But there had been that other, lone thought that had threaded through all those deeply important ones, and it had felt extra weighted somehow.

Was it because she and Arlo were together, both their lives at risk?

Or because it was simply the way she felt?

But pounding in time with the thud of her pulse had been the insistent reality that she'd never get to kiss Arlo again.

Their kiss in the bar had been designed to manage the moment and the need to get a bead on the guy at the door. It had morphed quickly into something more, but it was still the sheer work of a moment.

But what would it be like to kiss Arlo because she wanted to? Or to be on the receiving end of a kiss simply because *he* wanted to?

It was heady, yet it left her feeling oddly bereft, too.

Regardless of how she felt about him—and his visit to her home yesterday had reinforced that he wasn't immune to the attraction that sparked between them—Kerrigan knew there was nowhere for it all to go.

They were working together.

When this case wrapped, she'd go back to her focus on the harbor team.

So why did she keep coming back to how much she wanted to try for something with him, anyway?

A light knock on the conference-room door pulled her from her errant thoughts and she looked up to find the subject of her musings and their captain. She immediately stood, placing her hands behind her back. "Captain."

"No need to stand, Officer. Arlo was just filling me in on today's events and I wanted to get your take on things as well." Captain Reed took a seat as Kerrigan projected the digital board onto a screen.

"I've added the events of today. The car that followed Detective Prescott and myself. The as-yet-captured shooter on the roof and the details we have so far on the victims."

"Anything strike you as you wrote it up?"

"The shooting overall. What was the enticement to

follow cops? And then to be shot at like that. I'd say turf war, but it doesn't feel like it's escalating like that."

"Like what?" Captain Reed asked.

"There's no sense of a gang war going on. This feels far more calculated. It has me circling back to the working theory Arlo and I have about someone replacing the Papa. And it's further reinforced by our victim's dying words."

"Which was a lucky break for us." Arlo pushed himself off the doorjamb and walked into the room. "I'm trying not to be a cynic and think we're too lucky. Or that we're not being deliberately pushed in a new direction by a dying man's words."

It wasn't an approach she'd thought about yet, but it was one worth considering. "You think him telling us those things was a setup?"

"I'm not ready to say that, either. Especially since the guy *was* dying. But what I keep coming back to, with whomever is behind this, is why take out your team? What's the possible endgame?"

"There's an endless supply of criminals waiting to step up and take their place," Dwayne pointed out.

"Maybe yes, maybe no. There's still time, training, dependability and some degree of trust built over time. That doesn't happen overnight."

"There's also the woman angle." Kerrigan returned to where she'd been before Arlo and Dwayne walked in. "There's an innate desire to push back on that and believe it's not possible. That a woman wouldn't commit such dark acts of malice. And yet—"

"And yet, it fits." Arlo moved closer to the screen, pointing to a few of the notes she'd added to the file.

"The angle of the gunshots on the boat victims provides a strong reinforcement to a dying man's reference of a woman trying to take the reins."

Kerrigan tapped lightly on the table as a new dimension opened in her evaluation. "If it is a woman as well, working in a man's world, she's likely sweetening the conversation and playing these men up."

The captain's attention was caught with that one. "Give me a sense of what you mean with that?"

How did she articulate it?

Yet, with the captain's kind gaze on her, she realized she had to try.

"While there are certainly women who commit crimes, if we move forward with the theory this is a woman looking to ascend to the top, she's battling a glass ceiling. I know it was coined for boardrooms, but the principles are the same. You're pushing to take over the leadership of a large number of people, most of whom are male."

"And there are men who don't want to work for a woman."

Kerrigan shrugged at Captain Reed's statement. "It's a sad fact. And I don't say it to paint every man with that brush."

Arlo held up a hand. "We're playing a theory and you're the woman in the room who has experience. Keep going."

"Take feminine wiles, for instance. It's an outward play. Fawning and flirting and smiling and laughing. It's sending cues beneath that fawning and flirting."

"Like what sort of cues?"

"Like 'I hear you.' 'You're important.' 'Tell me more.'

It's a way to captivate but it's got a layer of manipulation in it, too."

"And it would be a powerful way to motivate a group that's predominantly men," Dwayne said.

"Even more, though, it's second nature to all of us. Sort of how babies smile to get attention or dogs put on big eyes to get treats. These nonverbal patterns we fall into aren't always manipulation in a cold-blooded way."

Arlo picked up the thread. Easily. "But if you honed it and perfected it and found a way to use it—"

"No, to *wield* it," Kerrigan argued.

"There you go. To wield it. It could be a deeply powerful approach."

"Of course, it still doesn't explain why a woman would go to all that trouble to build herself up in the organization only to kill the men she was using to gain support."

"Loyalty test?" Arlo asked.

"Possibly. And I might have agreed up until today. But why send that pair out to tail us in an obvious way and then kill them?"

Dwayne looked at them both as they came to a halt in their theories, today's events still stumping them all.

"You need to get out there. Something's going on under the surface and you need to put yourself in a place to find out what's going on. Ask questions. Talk about how shocking it is that this happened at all."

Kerrigan thought about the thug at McNulty's who'd bothered her on such a visceral level. She had no idea why, but something in his attention had seemed too sharp. Too focused.

Too specific.

"Should we head back to McNulty's?"

"It's where my last case centered. It's as good a place to start as any."

Captain Reed stood at that. "The overtime's approved. Get out there and see what you can find."

Chapter 12

Arlo pulled up in front of Kerrigan's building at exactly eight o'clock. They'd batted a few ideas back and forth as to how they wanted to approach the evening, including inviting Wyatt and Marlowe out with them, but ended up deciding it was better to go alone. They were playing the affectionate couple tonight and he already knew they risked discovery as cops.

Bringing yet another cop into the mix might tip off someone and shut down any opportunity they'd have to get answers.

And if going it alone meant he needed to ignore the strange knot that had settled beneath his breastbone, then so be it.

Yeah, he was attracted to her. But he'd been attracted to other women in the past, none of whom managed to stay a part of his life for any length of time.

He wasn't cut out for relationships.

It would be easy to blame his family but, in the end, he'd realized that *he* was a part of that family, too. He did well with surface relationships, his DNA ensuring he was a congenial and fun date. The where-are-you-from? and what-do-you-do-for-a-living? stage of dating was where he shined.

Only the deeper it went, the more uncomfortable he got, as he ultimately checked out before things got too serious.

Whatever reasons he gave himself up to now about Kerrigan and the case—he was functioning as her mentor, they needed to keep their focus, even the fact that he didn't want to do anything to make others question her reputation—were all excuses.

What he really didn't want was to ruin the genuine relationship and camaraderie they had with his inevitable departure if he pursued something romantic with her.

Even if he hadn't gotten that kiss in the bar out of his mind for more than a few hours at a stretch.

Or the way she'd felt in his arms after her bad dive.

Or the desperate need he had to protect her earlier today as they realized there was a shooter potentially aiming for them.

None of it could matter.

Even as a very large part of him wished that it did.

He was just about to turn off the car when there was a knock on the passenger window. Hitting the button for the locks, he smiled as Kerrigan got into the car.

"I could have come up to get you."

She waved a hand, a couple of gold bangles sparkling and clanking at her wrist. "No need. This isn't a real date."

Although the comment had a breezy quality to it, so

much so that she probably thought nothing of it, something about it needled him.

This isn't a real date.

No, it wasn't. Hadn't he just been giving himself all the reasons why it wasn't?

So why had her words crawled under his skin?

"You still want to go to McNulty's first?" Kerrigan asked.

"I think it's a good place to start."

"Good. That will give me a chance to see if that guy's in there again. See if we might be able to figure out who he is, or if we can get him to react a little."

"Are we back to that?"

"Back to what?"

Even with the subtle hints of confusion, her light, easy tone was really poking at him. She was already in cop mode—undercover-cop mode—and he…*wasn't.*

She looked good.

She smelled good.

Here she was casually talking about wanting to draw thugs seemingly out of the ether.

And his brain had short-circuited the moment he took in the long length of her legs, where they stretched out in tanned glory from beneath her skirt.

What was she thinking?

What was *he* thinking?

"Arlo? Is something wrong?"

"No."

"Why don't you reel it back and try again?"

He glanced over as he put the car into Drive and put it right back into Park to turn and face her.

"I thought we'd settled the matter of the thug in McNulty's. No approaching him or trying to draw him out."

Makeup artfully highlighted the contours of her face, from the delicate bones around her eyes—a rich chocolate tonight beneath mocha-colored eyelids—to the sweeping arch of high cheekbones.

None of it could hide the brewing storm or the way that gorgeous mouth dropped down into a frown.

"Funny, that's not how I remembered it."

"We talked about the risks."

"It's all a risk. The only reason we're going out tonight is to figure out what is going on and why every criminal in Brooklyn is running scared. And there's something about that guy. The way that he looked at me the other night wasn't right. There was a sharpness and a sort of knowledge to it I can't shake, and I know in my gut something is off."

"Sharp how?"

"Sharp like he was focused on me."

"You're a beautiful woman. He was probably thinking of any number of nefarious things to do with you."

This isn't a real date.

"Arlo. What is going on here? I'm a cop. I need to do my job. Figuring out who that guy is and why he was so focused on me is something we need to try and determine."

"You *are* doing the job." He stretched a hand out between them. "Undercover clothes and all."

She looked momentarily stymied by his reference to her outfit but regrouped quickly.

"No, I need to do the job the captain approved overtime for. Scouting the bars and nightclubs in Brooklyn to figure out what is seething under the surface. People know things and we need to find someone willing to talk to us. That person knows something. I feel it."

"Which further reinforces my point. If that guy means you harm, baiting him and having him make you as a cop the moment you pull your gun doesn't make sense." He focused on the small bag in her lap. "You do have your gun?"

"Yes, I do. I have a rather wicked blade strapped to my thigh, too. I'm prepared. And I can handle myself.

"But I'm starting to question if *you* can. What is going on with you tonight? And if you need time to get your head in the game, we'll go tomorrow night instead. We had a big day today."

This isn't a real date.

"I don't need time." The words came out through gritted teeth, harsh enough to have her eyes widening as she stared at him across the small expanse of the front seat.

"Then what do you need?"

"*You*, damn it." He reached out even as everything inside was screaming at him to stop.

To not just ignore this path but to actively avoid it.

But for reasons he couldn't figure out, he'd lost the ability to focus.

To reason.

To say no.

Her eyes widened a bit more as his mouth closed the distance to hers, his arms going around her shoulders as he pulled her close.

And then he feasted.

Kerrigan had feared earlier that she'd never kiss Arlo again. That there'd never be another moment between them to know those lips, to explore that mouth.

Oh, how gloriously shortsighted she'd been.

That thought filled her mind, over and over, as Arlo's lips plundered hers.

She *should* stop him. Not because she wanted him to stop, but because she wanted him to continue far too much.

Yet each time she thought she had gathered enough willpower to break the kiss, he tilted his head just so, or artfully stroked his tongue against hers, or moved his thumb in a glorious stroking motion across her collarbone.

She might've told him this wasn't a date, but she had dressed like she was going on one.

Partly because it was a necessity, the two of them playing a couple this evening. And partly because she'd wanted to.

He'd told her she was beautiful.

A sigh slipped from the back of her throat as he nibbled lightly on her bottom lip, like an escape valve for the heat that continued to ratchet up between them, degree by exciting degree.

And then it all came to an abrupt end as Arlo pulled back.

The enticing blue of his gaze had gone dark, his pupils wide in the darkened interior of the car.

"I'm sorry."

She struggled to regroup at the quick change of pace. And while her words might have held a breathy tone she couldn't fully erase, she felt quite confident her meaning was clear.

"If you're apologizing for kissing me, please stop right now. If you're apologizing for underestimating my ability to take care if I have a potential problem in the bar, lean right on into that."

"Why do I have to apologize for worrying about you?"

"Why do you *have* to worry about me doing my job?"

And why did they continue to circle around the same argument? She understood why her family carried concern for her safety and well-being. Civilians didn't understand the job and, often, all they could see were those risks to their loved ones.

But a partner?

They understood those risks because they took them, too.

Which meant he had no right to question her decision. Nor did he have any right to try and alter their op out of some misguided sense of protection for a well-trained, damn fine cop.

"I can see the fight brewing. It's in your eyes loud and clear."

"Damn straight, it's in my eyes. I'm an NYPD officer. I work in one of the finest, if not *the* finest, police departments in all the world. I'm a good cop and I know how to do my job. And you questioning that undermines me in every way. It isn't just a waste of time, it's destructive. Are you trying to shake my confidence in my work?"

It felt like repetitive territory and whatever Kerrigan had expected for this night, this wasn't it. So why were they here?

Again?

"You took me on for this job. You worked with my captain and my shift lead to bring me on the case. You've encouraged me. You keep telling me I can do this, and I should be focused on growing and learning and—"

"I want you."

The head of steam she had going tapered off at his interruption.

"You what?"

"I want you. Against my better judgment. Against my own horrible history with dating. Against every feckless, unreliable trait likely passed to me by my family when it comes to interpersonal relationships."

His words were weighted in the darkened interior of the car, heavy with promise and potential and a layer of sadness she'd never expected.

When he'd told her about his family, she'd innately understood his experiences hadn't been the same, idyllic childhood as her own.

What she hadn't understood was how those experiences influenced what he believed about himself.

"You aren't your family, Arlo."

"Of course I am. Just like you are your family. They're the people who made us. Who influence us. To suggest we can turn those aspects on or off is silly."

He'd already started driving, heading off her street in the direction of McNulty's. Kerrigan wanted to argue, but she also recognized the no-trespassing signals.

And maybe they were warranted.

Hadn't she also questioned the viability of a relationship? Perhaps for different reasons, but the fact was they both kept turning away, despite the interest and attraction between them.

If she added on that incendiary kiss, the answer became even more clear.

Desire arced between the two of them on a damnnear visceral level.

Was it possible all that heat and need was causing her to lose perspective?

She could still feel the way her heart had slammed in her chest. Could easily conjure the memory of the touch of his fingers against the exposed skin of her collarbone. And even now, she could still sense the hard press of his lips like a brand against hers.

There *was* something between them. It was a point she came back to, over and over. But there was also a shocking amount keeping them apart.

She wanted to lean into the first but would be doing herself a disservice to dismiss the latter one.

Relationships—even the really good ones—took a tremendous amount of work. One like theirs, that was fraught with so much baggage before it even got off the ground?

Well, it would be damn near impossible to make work.

She might not have a lot of experience with her own romantic entanglements, but she understood the basics of relationships. And she also understood that the feelings she'd developed for Arlo Prescott had a depth to them she'd never felt before.

Was she really willing to put her whole self into something that had *disaster* written all over it?

She'd never considered herself a woman of half measure, but the situations she went all-in on were ones she could control. Because she only had to depend on herself.

A relationship with Arlo was the very definition of something she couldn't control.

Arlo pulled up to the valet stand at McNulty's and she allowed one of the attendants to open her door for her. As she slipped out, she saw Arlo coming around the front.

With a deep breath, she pasted on a smile she didn't feel and prepared to spend the evening playing the enamored girlfriend to his besotted boyfriend.

If it struck too close to home, she'd have to live with it.

The only sort of romantic relationship she could have with him was one where they both acted like they could have a happily-ever-after.

Because real life wasn't going to give them one.

Wendy knew the moment Kerrigan Doyle walked into McNulty's. She saw it on the bar cameras in her office and she briefly considered putting her plan into motion early.

And then opted to hold back.

It wouldn't do for Kerrigan to see her so quickly. She knew the woman went to her parents' home every weekend for dinner. She'd have to come up with a way to accidentally run into her next time she headed to the old neighborhood.

Which meant this evening, she'd watch and refine her strategy instead.

The warehouse shooter had finally reported in, apologizing profusely for the left-behind shell casings, but promising her they were untraceable. He bought them from a supplier in the Midwest and there was no way the cops would make him here.

Wendy doubted that, but she'd allow him his illusions for now. Plus, it was hard to find someone with his skills.

So she'd overlook the evidence he left behind and focus instead on what she wanted out of him next.

Her new boat would be ready on Friday, and she

was already lining up a quick score that wouldn't fully make up for what went down in the harbor, but it would ease some of the financial pressure in the short term. She needed to get product on the streets or risk losing ground to local mafia and a particularly ambitious supplier out of Philadelphia.

She'd come way too far to let that happen.

His sharpshooter skills would come in handy as extra eyes and gun power on the op.

The knock on her door was brisk as Mark "the Tank" Holman walked in.

The dude fit the role of bouncer to a *T* with broad shoulders and thickly muscled arms, ink up and down the length of them. He also sported an IQ of 180 and an ability to read people that was impressive.

"That woman from the other night. She's back."

"Did she see you yet?"

"Nah. I saw her at the valet stand and moved out of her line of sight until she got inside."

"She with that guy again?"

"Oh, yeah. Rumor has it they're partners."

"Which explains why they were together today when we had them followed out of the precinct. Do you think they're together, too, or casing us tonight?"

"I'm getting vibes on both."

Hmm. That was interesting. And if she was being fair, she definitely felt the relationship vibes the other night herself. She'd put down a bet they hadn't had sex yet, but working together was getting them both hot and bothered.

"You told me you thought you scared her the other night."

"She didn't like me looking at her."

"Then do it again. Let's see if we can get him riled up enough to act."

Arlo handed over his credit card to their waitress after she laid down a beer for him and a glass of wine for Kerrigan. The bar had a rollicking crowd, those who'd come in after work still here a few hours later.

Their decibel level had increased with their alcohol consumption and he and Kerrigan had to sit close to talk to each other.

A feat he wasn't sure was possible after their fight in the car, yet she'd kept up her side of the bargain with steady conversation and the physical cues of someone happily out on a date.

Even if she was still seething inside.

It was scorched earth, so why he kept marching back over it, he had no idea.

Which was a bold-faced lie to the one person he never lied to.

Himself.

He knew damn well why.

Kerrigan Doyle tripped his protector switch, a wildly unsubtle reaction to the bone-deep desire that kept catching him off guard.

He hadn't once questioned Officer Doyle's ability to deal with whatever was tossed her way.

But what was happening *to* Kerrigan?

Hell, *those* fears clouded his words with unhelpful sentiments and admonitions that she step back from the risks.

"I haven't seen him yet."

Her comment had been spoken in a low tone, even

though anyone's ability to hear her from even five feet away was unlikely given the noise level.

"I haven't, either, but we'll keep watch for him. In the meantime, who do we think looks like they have information to share? The waitress didn't even blink when you asked her about how business had been since the drug bust in here."

"Which was odd, don't you think? She didn't even try to shut it down. She just ignored the question outright."

"I'd say she couldn't hear you," he said with a wry smile and a glance at the happy revelers around them, "but I saw it, too. She checked out and she glanced back over here when she got to the bar."

"She knows something."

"That's my guess."

Even with the fraught moments in the car, they really had rebounded well into their respective roles once inside the bar. It was a trait he admired in her—that ability to keep focus on the work, even if she was dealing with other things.

It was professional and showed a seasoning well beyond her years. It also had him wondering more about the organization now being built from the ground up. What would it take to assess talent? To harness it and grow it and—

"You look like you have an idea."

"Talent and professionalism. They're the two biggest things we keep circling around."

Kerrigan ran her finger around the edge of her glass, stopping a small drop from running down the side. "Crime as a job."

"For lack of a better description, yes, that exactly."

"And how's it relevant here?"

"We keep looking at what's going on as a talent assessment. Someone's being groomed and evaluated for their abilities."

"You have another angle?" She was clearly intrigued, her hand falling away from her glass.

"What if it's actually a matter of cutting down?"

"Removing the poor performers?"

"Exactly. If you can't keep up, you're out. If you don't follow my rules, you're out."

Kerrigan picked up on his point, that seamless give-and-take they had keeping the idea moving. "If you can't run a successful op in the harbor, you're out."

"Exactly."

"You know, it makes sense. Especially if you think about it from a woman's perspective. If you're trying to build loyalty and keep yourself safe, you're going to test those around you.

"Can I trust you? Are you going to support me? Are you here for me?"

"It's another dimension."

They exchanged theories, their conversation moving back and forth, the time passing easily and quickly. Although they were technically on duty, they needed to make a show of doing the social things a couple did for an evening out. With that, Arlo eyed their half-empty glasses. "Should I ask our waitress to bring us a new round?"

"Sounds good. I've flagged the guy refilling water glasses so many times I need to excuse myself. But we don't want to draw attention by not drinking, either."

"Then I'll order some potato skins while I'm at it."

She slapped a hand over her breasts. "A man after my own heart."

Since the move did nothing to hide the attractive curves currently resting beneath her fingers, Arlo counted himself the toughest of men when he managed to pull his gaze away and just nod his affirmation on the food.

And then watched her wend a path all the way across the bar, the beautiful shape of her ass drawing more than a few glances as she walked.

He wanted to be mad.

Hell, he was irate and feeling rather vengeful that any man would dare look at her, even as he understood that beautiful women drew attention.

And goodness, she was gorgeous.

It wasn't just her body, even though the physicality of her work and her athletic grace were evident. Nor was it just that stunning face.

No, it really was the entire picture.

She was the most determined woman he'd ever met. She wanted to be the best and she pushed herself and competed every single day to do that.

But what he also hadn't been able to get out of his mind was how she'd helped their victim today. The man later identified as Christos Jenkins had been a full person to her. One whose hand she'd held as he passed from this world. It had showcased a level of compassion that had left him in absolute awe of her.

"Can I get you another round?"

Their waitress had returned, her smile bright, if perfunctory. Arlo quickly ordered them another round as well as the potato skins, then he opted to try once more.

"I know I said it before, but this bar really is something. When I'd heard about the cops shutting this place down for a while, I was sure I wouldn't get to come back here anymore."

Her gaze was sharp—overly so—as she made a show of picking up his empty glass and placing it on her tray. It was only as she stepped to the side and reached for Kerrigan's water glass, that she spoke.

Low.

Insistent.

And with a quaver in the voice that didn't just happen.

"I'd stop making those sorts of comments if I were you."

Arlo didn't make any move at all to suggest he'd heard her, but he did slip a card out of his pocket in a smooth move that was likely hidden from view by her body.

He tucked it beneath the napkin where his beer was sitting. "I'll just leave this here for you to pick up later, then."

She made no move to touch the card, or to even acknowledge it was there. "Wise up, pal, and do what I said. Stop. Asking. Questions."

He watched her go, her attention on weaving her way back through the crowd that had only gotten louder and more packed, a sea of bodies enjoying the evening.

It was only as his gaze shifted away from her that he caught sight of the man by the door.

Big. Burly. And while Arlo would ensure Kerrigan made the final ID, the man's attention was far too sharp to make him think it was anyone else but the thug who was watching her the other night.

Chapter 13

Kerrigan dried her hands and stared at herself in the mirror. Despite their dismal start to the evening, she and Arlo had managed to settle into a rhythm over the past hour sitting there at the table. She mentally congratulated herself on keeping her cool, even as a very large part of her felt like she was overheating every time she looked at the man.

Because, wow, could he kiss.

It hadn't been like the other night, when they'd spontaneously come together out of a place of distraction and subterfuge.

Those tender moments had been wild enough.

But tonight?

That kiss was all electricity and wild combustion, not to mention basically every single fantasy she'd ever had.

A fantasy she'd spent her life dreaming about and waiting for.

And, yeah, she admitted to herself as she leaned forward, lightly wiping away a small bit of mascara that had stuck on her lower eyelash, it could be as much about the lack of exciting kisses in her life as it was about the sexy guy she'd shared it with.

But…

She stepped back and assessed herself frankly in the mirror. It would be an easy brush-off to say she didn't know any better because she didn't have an extensive history of boyfriends. But a small, still-rational part of her brain didn't think so.

No man she'd dated before had made her feel quite like Arlo.

And no one had drawn such an immediate and all-consuming response to a simple kiss.

I want you.

Against my better judgment.

Against my own horrible history with dating.

Against every feckless, unreliable trait likely passed to me by my family when it comes to interpersonal relationships.

The mere idea of him wanting her was heady, but it was all the disqualifications that came after that had had her wondering.

Did he really believe those things about himself?

Or was it more of a defense mechanism to warn her off?

She wasn't a woman who'd ever bought in to the idea she could "save" the other person in a relationship. People came to their relationships with—hopefully—every intention of wanting to be in them. It would hardly do to think about Arlo's words as something she could conquer or overcome with her will and sheer determination.

That way lay folly and, frankly, it showed disrespect for the other person's words and feelings.

Yet even with that deep-seated belief, she couldn't fully dismiss the feeling that he was trying to convince himself as much as he was convincing her.

Kerrigan was so lost in thought she nearly missed their waitress step out of a stall. The bathroom had been loud when she'd walked in, but the large crowd dissipated as she waited her turn for the sink, and it was quiet and empty for the moment.

"Hello." She smiled and nodded at their waitress and made a show of pulling out her lipstick to reapply.

The young woman beside her mumbled a hello and focused on washing her hands.

She took in the skinny frame nearly gaunt beside her in the mirror and considered various conversation starters. The brush-off earlier hadn't been a simple act of not hearing Arlo's question and Kerrigan wanted to find out why.

Which made it that much more surprising when the woman reached over and turned on Kerrigan's sink tap at full blast, a match for her own, which was still running. She leaned in, her voice urgent beneath the noise of the sink.

"I told your boyfriend this but figure you've probably got more brains than he does. Stop asking questions."

The woman made a show of washing her hands, her gaze on the soap filling her palms.

Kerrigan got the sense the woman believed in the

warning she was giving, but what really bothered her was the clear shake in those soapy hands. "Why?"

"No one around here likes it."

The tart, edgy response reinforced all the reasons she and Arlo were here tonight. Their undercover efforts weren't misplaced.

But she kept her tone even, the slightest edge of her own winging back at the woman. "It was a simple question. A big bust went down in this bar. People are curious."

"Curiosity helps no one. And the people who are still here are just trying to keep their heads down, live their lives and make enough to get by. You get it?"

The waitress finished rinsing her hands, and in addition to that light shaking, Kerrigan could see the haggard lines of her face in the light of the overheads. Wide, scared eyes further reinforced all she was trying to warn Kerrigan away from.

"Yeah, I get it. Even if I don't agree."

"People who don't agree in here don't last very long." The woman reached over and turned off the taps in quick, harsh motions, her agitation clear.

"Then let me help you."

She snagged a handful of paper towels, quickly drying her hands. "There's no such thing as help."

With that she turned on her heel and marched out of the bathroom. A few women tumbled drunkenly through the door, blocking any attempt Kerrigan might make to quickly go after the waitress and pull her back.

Remorse permeated the space where the woman had stood. In that moment, Kerrigan finally understood exactly what she and Arlo were up against.

Whoever was running things and working toward

making a name for themselves had effectively scared everyone in their orbit. The turf war they'd imagined might still be a possibility, but Kerrigan would lay odds their discussion earlier was more on point.

Whoever was trying to take over was thinning the herd, paring away anyone they thought wasn't up to snuff.

In a world where there was minimal security, anyway, that sort of unrelenting "justice" would be hard to escape.

And what could people really do?

Go to the cops? Not with a rap sheet and a reputation.

Try to go up against someone amassing power? Not when you needed a fair amount of your own personal power to make the play.

She didn't think their waitress was a power player, but the woman was a reflection of the bigger problem. The criminals in Brooklyn were running scared, along with everyone in their orbit.

And if the fear she just saw reflected in the mirror was any indication, she and Arlo didn't have a lot of time left to figure out who was the cause of it all.

Arlo moved into the alley behind the bar, the large, fenced parking lot where the valets parked cars stretching out before him. He'd sent Kerrigan a quick text that he was heading outside and that he wouldn't be long.

But you didn't tell her why.

The thought taunted him, and he almost pulled out his phone and texted her again, but he didn't have time.

He needed to get a bead on the thug who was at the center of this.

If it meant he kept Kerrigan far away from the guy, then, yeah, that worked, too.

He'd pay for it later. By rights, he understood that. They were partners out on the job. She not only deserved to know where he was, but department protocol also insisted they work together.

And still, he wasn't turning back.

He kept his back to the wall and moved closer to the valet stand. The various young men who were responsible for parking cars were in a variety of places and by Arlo's quick count he thought there were four on duty tonight.

One had just come around with a car, another was running back across the parking lot, having just parked one, and one was on his phone at the valet station. The guy who'd taken Arlo's keys was nowhere in sight so he must be on point out in front of the bar.

It was a tough job but one that could pay well if you were working a hot spot and could pull in decent tips.

It was also a job rife with information about the community.

The guy with his cell phone had just lit a cigarette and Arlo walked over, his intention to bum one as his cover. A quick glance at the ground offered him the additional boon of an empty cigarette pack and he grabbed it and shoved it into his breast pocket.

Patting his pocket as he walked up to the guy, he pasted on a congenial smile. "I'm fresh out. You got an extra?"

The guy glanced up, his eyes narrowed, even as he took in the empty pack Arlo crunched in his hand.

"There's a machine in the back of the bar near the johns."

"I know but my girlfriend hates it when I smoke. I figured I'd just get one more and avoid the riot act. I've got a fresh pack at home."

The lie did the trick, and the valet extended his pack, tapping the box so Arlo could take a dislodged cigarette.

He realized his additional mistake when he had no lighter on him but played it off by snagging the small blue plastic one sitting on the edge of the valet stand. He made quick work of lighting up and cupping his hands around the flame.

The valet seemed uninterested in conversation, so Arlo took over.

"Big crowd tonight."

The guy shrugged. "Big crowds most nights."

Arlo let it go, keeping his gaze on the parking lot, when the guy inadvertently gave him the perfect opening.

"You'd better get out of here. Boss hates it when people come back here."

"Hates it why?"

"They don't like it." The guy turned to face Arlo. "Look, I gave you a smoke. You want me to lose my job?"

Arlo held up his hands and took a few steps back. "No, man. No way. I'll leave." He shook his head, putting on a solemn air. "This place sure has changed since the cops came down on it a few months ago."

The valet removed his cigarette from his mouth and spit to the side, disgust lining his face. "You're not kidding about that. I'd've quit if the money wasn't so good."

"I thought they caught the thugs running the drugs. You'd think it would make things better."

"It hasn't." The valet side-eyed him as he lifted his cigarette back to his mouth. "So get out of here."

"Yeah." Arlo lifted his hands once more. "I got it."

He considered pushing the situation once more but figured a hasty retreat was better. They might be in a rush to solve this case but blowing their cover a few hours in wasn't the best course of action, either.

With one last glance around the parking lot, Arlo turned to head back into the bar, only to find the thug they'd been after blocking the entrance.

Despite the snap of cold weather fall had brought, the man's broad frame was set off by the tats visible up and down his exposed arms.

It was a cultivated look, Arlo realized, designed to instill fear and obedience.

Fortunate for him, he wasn't impressed.

When something that looked a lot like anticipation filled the man's face, Arlo felt his own spiking in response and considered his next move.

The guy recognized him, that was obvious. Had he made him as a cop? Or was it tied to the fact he'd been escorting Kerrigan around?

Was she a target somehow?

But why?

Arlo made a show of leaning against the wall, bringing the pilfered cigarette to his lips. He had an excuse to be out there, whether the man liked it or not. His instincts told him to wait the guy out and see how he handled things.

He didn't have to wait long.

"You've been asking questions around my bar."

"Your bar?" Arlo took another drag on the cigarette but made a point not to exhale a stream of smoke directly at the guy. "You own it?"

"I'm responsible for it."

"Still not the same."

"You and your very pretty cop girlfriend need to stop asking questions."

Ice coated his stomach at the dual reference—to Kerrigan's looks *and* her status as a cop—and pushed himself up off the wall.

"My girlfriend and I came in to have a good time."

"Yet you both look like you're waiting for root canals." The guy stood where he was, still as a statue, but his entire demeanor grew harsher. Meaner. "It's interesting to watch. And your half-finished drinks only reinforce the fact."

Even without the guy moving an inch, Arlo felt him loom closer.

His attention was laser-sharp and it had obviously been focused on them.

He quickly cycled through the past few hours, trying to assess where they'd gone wrong. They'd laughed and talked at the table, but the guy had made them on the drinks, which was a bad move on their part.

But the questions?

Arlo knew the guy hadn't been anywhere near him when he'd questioned the waitress.

So how had he known?

"Seems to me you'd like questions. It's good for business when people get a cheap thrill knowing something big went down here."

"People have short memories and thirsty mouths. No one cares anymore. Except the cops."

There it was again. That direct challenge that the guy knew they weren't casual daters out for the evening.

But it was the distinct click of the switchblade he pulled out of his pocket—one that suddenly pressed firmly between two ribs—that had Arlo going still.

Killing a cop took gang warfare and criminal politics to a whole new level. There wasn't a cop in New York who wouldn't be out for revenge if the guy slipped that knife a few inches deeper into Arlo's skin.

But as he felt the sharp press of that knife, he recognized the truth.

If he didn't act quickly, that scenario was a frightening possibility.

Tia Lutz walked the three blocks to her car, cursing herself all the way. She'd had the lunch shift and agreed to help through happy hour and on into the early evening to help with the after-work crowd. She had nearly completed her shift, willing to take on one more table, and she'd gone and gotten *them*.

The happy couple with sharp eyes and pointed questions. Why the *hell* were they asking questions?

And why did she always get the shaft?

She knew some bad crap went on in the back office. She'd known it before, when the drugs were flowing out the back door. She knew now, despite the we're-good-neighbors-and-the-heart-of-Brooklyn routine the owners were peddling, bad crap was still going on.

But, damn it, she needed this job.

Getting into the hot spots around town wasn't easy and she needed the tips. Needed *something* to make the long shifts worthwhile, with her aching legs and the roaming hands and the suggestive come-ons.

And she knew she had a good thing. She kept her head down and her eyes on the prize. A growing bank account, which was her pathway out of this hellhole. She wanted a new life, maybe in the Carolinas or down in the Gulf Coast. Somewhere warm and nice, and a place where she could start over.

She'd been running on fumes too long and this was her meal ticket out of New York.

It might be the city of dreams for some, but it had been her nightmare with the expensive rents, neighbors who lived on top of you and the ever-increasing cost of just getting by.

She was getting out.

Tia fumbled for her keys, her hand brushing over the business card she'd swiped out of the guy's napkin. She didn't want to get caught with it but she also didn't want it left anywhere near her station.

She glanced down at it and just like she'd figured, the dude was a cop.

Truth be told, she was actually surprised he'd left the card. Not a great way to go undercover, was it? Handing off your business card to whoever was handy?

Did he think she was an easy mark?

Did it really matter?

She wasn't ratting him out and she wasn't ratting out her bosses, either. And all she really wanted to do was keep her head down, get another few thousand saved and get out.

Even now, she could picture the warm Carolina breezes waving over her face. She'd find a small apartment and a good, solid waitressing job and she'd have a new life.

A nice life.

Pretty blue skies filled her thoughts as she walked up to her car, unlocked the door and slipped in. She quickly locked the doors once she was seated and put her key in the ignition.

"Damn it!" She cursed as the car sputtered, trying to turn over.

Tears welled up, an image of whatever repair was needed taking a chunk out of her moving fund and firmly replacing her thoughts of blue skies.

Wasn't it always the way? Two steps forward and ten freaking ones back?

Taking in a heavy breath, she tried again, turning the key and willing the engine to catch.

That heavy grinding sound of the engine whirling filled the car, the lightest whiff of gasoline accompanying it. One lone tear fell just as the engine caught, turning over.

"Yes!"

Swiping at her tears, she reached for the gearshift as she depressed the clutch, a strange creaking noise filling the car.

That was a new one.

And as visions of heading to the auto-body shop consumed her once more, a loud popping noise filled the air as the car exploded around her.

Kerrigan fought the waves of anger as she stalked out the back of the bar toward the rear entrance. She ignored all the signs saying Employees Only and stayed her course as she knew exactly where Arlo was.

The spot he had avoided actually telling her about or suggesting they go to and handle whatever was out there. *Together.*

Like partners.

Which made her slam through that back door a surprise when she nearly plowed into a very large form standing in her way.

She sidestepped quickly, but as she caught sight of Arlo on the other side of the large, hulking form, she immediately moved into action.

She quickly followed with another sidestep when Arlo used her surprise arrival to go on the attack with the man. She couldn't see one, but she assumed there was a weapon and used Arlo's quick attack and her position from behind to lock her arms in the man's bent elbows.

The position was awkward and unsustainable, but it was just enough to give Arlo additional leverage and he plowed a fist into the guy's gut, then thrust outward with his right hand, dislodging a blade that went flying to the ground.

The thick form she was hanging on to like a monkey back-stepped—*hard*—slamming her into the door. She saw stars as her head hit the thick wood and Kerrigan felt her grip slipping as the pain took over.

Determined, she knew she needed to fight through it, but felt her grip giving way all the same.

And then it didn't matter because Arlo was barreling forward into the man like a bull, the two men quickly descending into full body fighting.

Abstractly, Kerrigan heard a shout from the direction of the parking lot, and she inched her way back, struggling to get herself to a sitting position and clear the swirly, raging lines staggering through her vision.

Two younger men came rushing over, one she remembered because he'd taken their car earlier when

Arlo had pulled up to the valet stand. They went to work pulling Arlo and the bruiser apart and Kerrigan debated how to play this.

Did they give up their date-night ploy and pull out their badges?

Even though she was mad at him for going off on his own, she was willing to let Arlo see it through and watch how he played it.

But if the thug attacked again, all bets were off.

The skirt she had on didn't allow for particularly decorous movement, but it did give her quite good range of motion, so she braced her feet apart, prepared to leap back in, if needed.

The back of her head still throbbed but the squiggles had cleared from her vision, and she was able to take in the scene.

Arlo wiped blood from his lip off the back of his hand, but he'd stopped fighting and the valet holding him had dropped his arms. The thug was still struggling, and Kerrigan saw the man holding him whisper something in his ear, but she couldn't make out the words.

Whatever it was, they had a calming effect, because the big guy stopped, even if his body still braced like a mad animal ready to strike.

He spit a stream of blood before speaking. "You want to tell me what you're doing back here?"

"Came out to bum a smoke." Arlo stood at his full height, layers of menace telegraphing out of his gaze. That fathomless blue, normally bright with humor or alert with ideas, had gone a flat, cold, icy color that made a shiver run down Kerrigan's spine.

This was Arlo?

It was a side of him she hadn't seen. She should have expected it. He was a cop—an excellent one—but even with that knowledge, she hadn't ever envisioned such a bleak, unyielding visage.

"A cigarette? Yeah, right." The thug's hands were clenched at his side but he made no move to strike again. "You've been asking questions you have no business asking."

"And you've been eyeing my girlfriend and I want to know why."

"I've been eyeing a cop." The guy looked over his shoulder, his slimy gaze settling on her. "Two cops."

Kerrigan feigned surprise at the accusations, but it was Arlo's quiet, steady presence that never wavered. "Prove it."

Those words—part challenge, all threat—hung in the air and Kerrigan nearly pulled out her badge, willing to end it all there, when a loud noise rent the air.

Everyone glanced in the direction of the noise, and in the distance, visible beyond the chain-link fence surrounding the parking lot, a few more blocks down the street, a ball of fire rose up toward the sky.

Chapter 14

Arlo grabbed Kerrigan's hand and the two of them raced back into the building, then out into the street. Whatever had happened, someone needed help, and he and Kerrigan would be the first on scene.

Their cover was already blown so they might as well do something useful.

Not that he'd expected they'd last long nosing around the bars in Brooklyn, but he had estimated they'd get through at least an evening before being fully made as cops.

It wasn't to be.

They'd worry about it later, in the debrief. Right now, someone needed help.

He reached for his phone to call in whatever had happened, but Kerrigan had beat him to it.

"Downtown Sunset Bay," she said into her phone.

"Intersection of Fourth and Bay. Apparent car explosion of some sort."

She matched his quick pace next to him, her long legs eating up the sidewalk, in heels no less. He'd also seen her take that hit when the bar jerk was trying to throw her off and she had to be hurting right now.

"You okay?"

"We'll worry about it later."

And then she put on a burst of speed in the last block as they saw the smoking car, still burning from the front, its hood blown off.

A crowd had already started to form, and Arlo pushed his way through it, his badge in hand. The sound of sirens filled the air, but it was Kerrigan's soft cry that held his attention.

"Arlo! It's our waitress."

The woman was lying oddly positioned in the front seat and he and Kerrigan immediately went to work. He hauled open the driver-side door, using his sport coat to protect his hands from the heated metal, while Kerrigan reached in and unbuckled the woman's seat belt.

"Hello! Can you hear me? We're going to get you out of here."

Blood ran freely from a wound at the woman's hairline and her face was covered in dirt and debris. Shattered glass from the windshield covered the car and lay over her in a scattered pattern that refracted the overhead light shining in, and Kerrigan brushed some of it away as she reached for the woman.

"We're going to get you out of here."

Arlo helped Kerrigan pull the woman fully out of the seat, careful to take her weight into his arms as Kerrigan made sure the lower part of her body didn't hit the ground as they pulled her free.

He'd already assessed her as painfully thin when she'd waited on their table, but as Arlo cradled the woman's body in his arms, he felt how small and slight she really was.

Who had done this to her?

And what, exactly, was going on? He and Kerrigan had asked a few questions, nothing more. Suddenly there were knife-wielding thugs in the back parking lot behind the bar, scared valets and one of McNulty's waitresses had been attacked.

He and Kerrigan had been there a few hours. Who the hell had the wherewithal to put this together?

And this fast?

After verifying she still had a pulse, Kerrigan kept up a steady chatter to the woman. She wasn't getting any response, but blue-veined eyelids did waver and flutter a few times as Kerrigan continued a soft conversation, coaxing her to talk to them.

Just like the sniper's victim, he thought.

It was oddly similar, people in a position to know what was going on suddenly facing death because of it.

The sirens screamed closer and closer, and a few uniforms had already been dispatched to the area as well and were helping with crowd control while also creating a lane for the EMTs to get in.

"What's your name?"

Kerrigan stroked the woman's hand, speaking to her softly. Those eyelids fluttered open. "Tia."

"Tia, we're here to help. You need to hang on."

"Blue skies," Tia murmured, the words slurred and uneven. "Was going to go... Was saving...up."

"I know. We all dream of vacation."

"No." Tia's voice was firm on that. "Moving away. Just—just needed enough...money."

"Why were you moving away?"

"Far away. Want to get away from here. From all of it."

"From all of what?"

"Away." The woman's voice drifted off and Arlo knew they'd lost her.

Kerrigan seemingly did, too, as she looked over at him.

"Another one." Kerrigan said, her voice strained and choked. "All we did was ask a few questions. It's a terror campaign."

"It is."

"But *we* asked the questions. She's on us, Arlo."

He wanted to stop that train of thought immediately, but the EMTs rushed over, inserting themselves between the two of them and taking over with Tia.

"She's gone." Kerrigan moved into full cop mode. "We removed her from the car, laid her down. She was speaking to us."

One of the EMTs barked out a series of questions as they worked over her, and Kerrigan answered them all.

And as he stood there, watching her work, Arlo recognized the truth.

There were cases in a cop's life that left an irrevocable mark.

He'd sensed from the start—so had Captain Reed—that this case was bigger than they expected.

Darker, too.

But as he watched Kerrigan's face and the near-robotic responses she relayed to the medics, he knew this would be a case that would forever leave its mark on Kerrigan Doyle.

Kerrigan stared at the form lying under a sheet on the EMT gurney and replayed the night in her mind. They shouldn't be here.

There shouldn't have been what was inevitably a car bomb in the middle of Sunset Bay.

And the woman under that sheet shouldn't be dead.

Tia Lutz.

They'd identified her prints from a possession charge she'd faced just after turning eighteen. It hadn't necessarily defined her—the ME would confirm, but Kerrigan hadn't gotten the sense the woman was using—but it had likely set her on a course.

One she was looking to escape.

Blue skies.

Was going to go... Was saving...up.

Just—just needed enough...money.

Would those words ever not haunt her?

And why had this woman been targeted?

Kerrigan sat perched on the edge of the EMT's back fender, submitting to various tests to see if she had a concussion. The dull throb of a headache hadn't subsided but it sort of faded in and out of her consciousness as they'd worked the crime scene. She would have forgotten about it altogether if Arlo hadn't insisted the EMTs look her over.

The raw look in his eyes brooked no argument and she knew a checkup was inevitable if she wanted to do her next dive, so she submitted to the quick series of tests.

"You're lucky, Officer. It looks like you're going to have a bad headache that you should baby for a few days is about it. I'm not seeing immediate signs of concussion, but you should be checked again in a couple of days to be absolutely sure."

"Thank you."

And just like that, there went her next dive. The protocols were inarguable and she'd be manning the Zodiac boat or riding a desk until being fully cleared.

She thanked them and headed back to the car and the bomb squad that had been called in to handle the scene. She was just in time to catch the end of the lead's summation to Arlo.

She'd met Lieutenant Rhodes before, when he and his team worked a device she'd brought up off the harbor floor. His dark skin bore the stress and pressure of a big job, with lines around his eyes and across his forehead, but the dark brown gaze that took in the sight before them was rich with empathy and care.

"Crude car bomb but effective. It was placed on the undercarriage and designed to go off once the engine caught."

"Who has the knowledge to do this?" Kerrigan struggled to understand how someone did this on a busy street, full of people at any moment.

"Far too many people, I'm afraid. It's pretty straightforward and can be done with household items."

"We can start checking exterior cameras on the businesses and homes around here," Arlo affirmed.

"Do that. It's a quick job and if someone remained low enough it's not hard to stay unobtrusive." Rhodes dropped into a crouch and pointed out a few points on the car. "They'd be in and out in under thirty seconds if they knew what they were doing. They'd need to stay low and wedge themselves under the front left tire to make the connection."

Rhodes moved off to handle the rest of the cleanup and Arlo turned to Kerrigan. "What did the medics say?"

"They don't think it's a concussion. I need to get checked out in another forty-eight hours but I think I'm fine."

"The doctor will confirm that."

"Yes, Arlo. Others can certainly make the final decision."

The response snapped out, as surly and nasty as she felt, and she knew she'd hit the right chord. His own ire flared, his eyes going dark, before he seemed to catch himself.

"See that you do."

"I'm going to get started on the video footage. I'll see you later."

"Kerrigan—"

He broke off as she turned back to face him. "What, Arlo? We need to get to it as fast as we can. I'll take this side of the block. You take the other. We'll have it done in no time."

Whatever he was about to say, he seemed to think better of it.

And without saying another word, Arlo turned on his heel and headed off across the street.

Kerrigan stripped off the clothes she'd be very happy to never see again and climbed into the shower. She already had a hot mug of tea steeping on the bathroom counter, and she figured it would be the perfect temperature by the time she scrubbed the night off her skin.

Even if there was no scrubbing off the shame and guilt she felt over Tia Lutz's death.

As she'd agreed with Arlo, she'd hit all the businesses on the north side of the street while he'd taken the south. A bodega, a dry cleaner and a national bank branch ATM were the businesses in likely view of Tia's car. The bodega owner was quick to comply, and she'd made notes on the dry cleaner and the bank.

She'd swing by in the morning to get the cleaner's footage and had already left a message for them that she would be coming in. The bank would go through standard information-request protocols, so she hoped like hell that wasn't the lucky shot because it would be another three days, minimum, before they saw any footage.

Who would do this to Tia?

The question haunted her as she scrubbed her hair and then lathered in conditioner before rinsing it all out. The water might have sluiced away the soap of her shampoo, but it did nothing for the guilt that continued to pound beneath her skin.

Had this really happened because of the questions she and Arlo asked?

Even now, she could remember the haunted look in the woman's eyes as she warned Kerrigan away from nosing around when they stood side by side in the bathroom.

What still didn't play for her was the speed with which it all happened. Arlo made one lightly probing ask of the woman as she took their drink order. A question she roundly ignored.

And then there was the conversation in the bathroom, the running water obscuring their words.

Had someone heard, anyway? Was the bathroom bugged? Clearly, Tia had thought so if she'd run the water in two sinks.

Although there was a big part of her that just wanted to curl up and forget the night, she was anxious to look at the footage from the bodega owner. After drying off and giving herself a few minutes to let her tea do its work, she sat down at her computer and loaded up the footage.

The owner had given her a full day's worth of footage and she started in the morning, moving through quickly until she saw Tia park in that space. The footage was grainy and it was hard to make out specific details, but she did have a clear view of the car and Tia as she climbed out of it.

Other cars surrounded Tia's parking spot and the view of the ground wasn't great. Based on Lieutenant Rhodes's description of what they were looking for—someone who had to get down on the ground and go under the front driver-side wheel—Kerrigan figured she was unlikely to get a view to whoever set the bomb. But...

She kept scrolling the footage and realized she might get enough of a view of people walking by or approaching the car to narrow in the data they needed off another camera.

The work was tedious and she kept it on double speed to ensure she didn't miss fine details, but the daytime showed nothing of interest. She was working off the theory that Tia didn't become a victim until she'd spoken with her and Arlo, and it meant the money shot was likely later. Still, she was determined to watch it all.

The timing still bothered her.

They simply hadn't had enough contact with the woman to make her a target that quickly. Right?

Even as she asked herself the question, she knew it was possibly a foolish thought. Whoever was running this deal behind the scenes wanted absolute obedience and compliance. The only way to do that was to make quick decisions.

Impulsive.

That idea flashed back in her mind, one of the assessments the team Arlo had assembled in the conference room a few days ago had landed on.

There was a reckless nature to what was going on that continued to pervade each crime. And it kept coming back to the lack of impulse control.

Own a fancy, unregistered boat? Kill your henchmen, then burn and sink it all?

Set up some guys to follow the cops, then set up a sniper to take them out?

See a waitress handling a standard evening crowd of curious, misplaced questions? Kill her with a bomb?

They were all outsized reactions to the situation. Reactions that kept screaming "look at me" and "see what I can do" and "don't you dare mess with me."

The knock on her door pulled her from her thoughts and her heart leaped in her chest. She knew it was Arlo, despite the anger that still remained over his actions.

He went out to the back lot of the bar on purpose with nothing more than a deliberately vague text.

It hadn't taken her long to piece it together and she'd tossed money on the table to pay their bill, somehow intuitively knowing they weren't coming back inside.

But it had all left her with the sinking feeling that no

matter what she did or how hard she worked, he didn't see her as an equal on this case.

He only focused on the risks to her.

What he didn't seem to understand was that as partners, not trusting her to go through the door with him meant he was putting himself at risk, too.

They had to face this together.

Or she might as well ask for reassignment.

It pained her to think that way, but what other choice did she have? He didn't trust her to have his back and because of it that thug in the bar had gotten the jump on him.

She crossed to the door, looking through the peephole, confirming it was her partner on the other side. She opened the door and stared at him across the threshold.

"What do you want, Arlo?"

What did he want?

That question had haunted him on the drive over to her place. Hell, it had haunted him since that first moment he'd seen her stripping out of her wet suit in the pouring rain on the police boat.

He wanted her.

And it had messed with his head, his logic and, most of all, it had messed with *her.*

Her career and her safety, yes. But on top of it all, her trust.

He'd been a bad partner tonight. Worse, he'd violated her faith in him because he couldn't get out of his head or out of his own way.

"Can I come in?"

She stepped aside and let him into her apartment, and he waited until she'd closed the door behind him.

"I need to talk to you."

"Oh? You need to talk to me now? That's rich. After you've done your lying deeds without informing your partner and avoided me and put yourself in terrible danger? *Now* you need to talk to me?"

"I made a mistake."

"No, Arlo. You keep making the same mistake. Which means it's not a mistake at all. It's deliberate action against me."

"It's not against you."

"Then who the hell is it against? The poor dead woman we pulled out of a car? The thug who tried to shiv you? Who, Arlo?"

She was right.

In every single thing she said, she was right. He'd put them both in danger and he'd betrayed her horribly in the process.

"I wanted to keep you safe."

"That's not your job."

"I'm your partner!"

"Yes. Just like Jayden or Gavin or any number of individuals are my partner when we go down on a dive. We trust each other and we follow the rules set up to keep us both safe. *Both* of us. One of us doesn't go rogue to satisfy some urge to play cowboy."

"It's not about playing cowboy or going rogue."

"Then what's it about?"

"I don't want anything to happen to you!" He ran a hand through his hair, tugging hard on the strands as the old memories rose up, swamping him and nearly stealing his breath. "I've been you, okay? I know the risks to you because I took them."

"Took what risks? And what do you mean *to* me? I'm

a cop, Arlo. The job comes with inherent risk." Her gaze had narrowed but her voice had softened. "So what, exactly, are you talking about?"

"Early on. My first case."

Even now, he could still conjure it up. The cold warehouse. The feel of the duct tape on his wrists. The belief he'd walked into something he wouldn't walk out of.

He'd spent a lot of time over the years putting it behind him. He'd extensively analyzed where he'd gone wrong and had worked methodically to ensure he didn't make the same mistakes again.

It was why he was so good at his job.

Why he'd closed the cases he had and how he kept it all by the book.

He worked harder and smarter than anyone else because there'd been a time, once, when he'd done neither.

"Arlo, what's this about?"

Although he usually avoided alcohol as a way to handle the memories or the nightmares that came with them, it had been a long day.

Too long.

"Do you have anything to drink?"

"Wine or whiskey?"

"Whiskey would be good."

She nodded and went into the kitchen, puttering around in the cabinets before coming back with a glass of amber-colored liquid. She'd seemingly understood his need, the glass not holding much more than about two fingers, but it was enough to wet his throat and give him the extra boost to get through this as they crossed to sit on the couch.

She deserves it.

The thought whispered through his mind, and he

knew it for truth. She deserved it as his partner and as his friend. And even more, in this very room where she'd shared her past. The career problems that had hurt her, but not broken her.

Didn't he owe her the same honesty?

He took a sip of his drink, warm fire coating his throat, and he leaned into that as he launched into his story.

"My first big case was working with Vice to bring down a prostitution and trafficking ring."

"That's quite a case to start on."

"I earned my way onto it with several proactive late nights and some additional questions I managed to ask some of the working girls when I was a beat cop."

"They trusted you? That says a lot."

"A few of them did. They knew I was looking out for them. I'd protected a few when I was off duty and gained some trust."

"That's not exactly protocol, Arlo."

It wasn't. In fact, it was the opposite of proper protocol, using his off duty time to pursue cop work. To look the other way when crimes were being committed just because he wasn't in uniform.

"I know. And I thought it was in service to the bigger cause, so I did it."

"What happened?"

"One of the girls I befriended and offered some protection to. Her name was Gabrielle. She gave me some feedback and details on a new shipment of trafficked women coming in. She didn't have a lot of details, but what she did know matched chatter the lead detective on the case already had and she was able to give us the date. So we set up the op and promised to keep her safe."

Even now, he could see it so clearly in his mind. The hopeful eyes in a face whose beauty had long worn thin. Her belief that he really was working to help her and her friends. And that he would help save those other girls before this horrible phase of their lives even started.

He'd believed it, too.

And in the end had been too confident of the intel and not nearly focused enough on the pimp who'd gotten wind one of his girls was giving out information to the cops.

"Only we didn't keep her safe. I walked straight into a setup. She was already dead after being tortured for information and the traffickers who managed her pimp were waiting for me."

She'd remained quiet through his retelling, her eyes big, solemn oceans of empathy in her face. Despite her anger—fair, righteous fury she was fully entitled to— she leaned forward and laid a hand over his where he still held his glass with both hands.

"How'd you get out?"

"There was enough chatter on what was going down that it got back to someone working undercover at Vice. They weren't directly on the case, but they knew the op we were preparing for and knew enough to call in backup. I figure I had about two hours left."

She nodded at that, her hand tightening over his. "I'm sorry."

"I can still see her. Gabrielle."

He'd long stopped thinking he'd forget what she looked like, splayed out like a piece of discarded garbage on the floor of the warehouse he was held hostage in. He saw her in his dreams, and he saw her on every op he went out on.

"Some cases are harder than others. They take more out of you. They're the ones that haunt us."

"I was responsible for her. I got her to trust me so I could get the big score. Win the big case."

"You didn't do that to her, Arlo."

"You can sit here and tell me you don't feel the same way about Tia?"

It was a low blow, especially knowing how fresh their waitress's death was, but Arlo pushed it anyway.

Because, yeah, there were cases that were harder than others. The ones that haunted you long after they should.

And then there were the ones you felt responsible for.

"Are you weaponizing what happened tonight?"

"I'm making a point. You feel responsible for her."

"I am responsible for her. You are, too."

"No, Kerrigan. The people who did that to her? They're responsible for her. Don't forget it or lose that perspective."

She sat back then, her hands falling away from where she'd held his.

"And here you go, once more, protecting me."

"I'm telling you the truth."

"No, you're not. You're telling me a version of the truth to get me to back off. To get me to stop feeling what I feel when I do this job. To my earlier point, you're weaponizing your pain to make me step away."

She stood at that, whirling on him.

The woman who'd opened the door to him, fresh-faced from a shower with wet hair piled atop her head, had changed. Morphed, really, into an avenging goddess. Color rode high on her cheeks and the hair that had begun to dry as they spoke framed her face in soft, curly waves.

"I haven't weaponized anything."

"Sure you have. You've done it from the start. Protecting me. Hiding the run you did on the Gentry family business. Going out tonight to confront the thug from the bar. You keep doing it, over and over."

She was right.

Arlo knew she was right, to the depths of his soul he knew it. And damn it, he hadn't been able to stop himself.

"I don't want you hurt."

"So what's better? Sabotaging me? Putting me in a position where I'm unaware of danger and walking into it without protection? Without knowing it's happening? How's that protecting me?"

"I was going to handle it. You were never going to be in danger."

"News flash, Arlo! We're both in danger. Each time we put on the badge and go out to do the work, we're targets. The only protection we've got is our training and our minds and our partnership."

He sat there, his empty glass in hand, and could do nothing but stare at her.

Could only look his fill and finally—*finally*—acknowledge what he'd been doing all along. Why he'd been so upside down and why he'd been so insistent on acting in a way that he not only knew was wrong, but also deeply believed was wrong.

"I love you."

Kerrigan had already stalked off toward the fridge

and turned at his words, two bottles of water in her hand. "You what?"

"I'm falling in love with you."

She stared at him for several long moments, the light from the fridge highlighting her features in the dim overhead she had on in her kitchen area.

He got the distinct sense she was working through something, but try as he might, he couldn't pinpoint what it was.

Had he surprised her?

Pissed her off?

Or hurt her because every single one of his actions flew in the face of how you loved someone?

"That's your excuse?"

"Yes. It's a damn poor one, too, for all the reasons you named. If I cared, keeping you in the dark is the worst thing I can do."

"So why have you done it? Worse, why have you continued to do it?"

"This is new territory for me."

"And sabotaging me is the answer?"

"No! It's not like that." How did he make her understand? This bone-jarring fear for her that he'd never felt for anyone. It clouded his judgment and had been doing so from the start of the case.

From the very first moment he'd asked Wyatt if he could take her on as his partner to solve the harbor crime.

Which meant he had to try and explain himself.

Love was a powerful word, but it meant nothing without action. And it meant even less if you weren't willing to speak truth behind it.

He'd spent his entire life living that reality with his family.

Was he really interested in staying on that same path? Worse, was he determined to hurt someone he cared for—truly, deeply cared for—because he refused to chart a new course?

Chapter 15

Kerrigan's head spun from the argument with Arlo.
And she didn't think it had anything to do with the
knock she'd taken against the back door at McNulty's.

He loved her?

Was *in* love with her?

Why was it those few simple words had lodged
like a boulder in the middle of her chest, generating
wild flutters throughout her body even as she felt their
weight like being encased in concrete?

She couldn't let it matter. Not now. Not in this moment, when she was not only entitled to her point of
view, but also where he had to realize that telling her
he loved her wasn't a substitute for his actions.

Even though it did matter.

That he loved her.

"It's not sabotage, Kerrigan."

He'd stood and crossed to her in the kitchen, taking the cold water bottles from her hand and setting them down on her counter space. She knew her studio was small, but it had never felt quite as crowded as it did right now. And that included the time her immediate family, as well as cousins, aunts and uncles, had come over after she'd first moved in.

Arlo crowded her.

It was both delicious and overwhelming and it only served to heighten her anger once more.

"Don't play with my emotions."

"I'm not. I'm trying to get my own under control. I've—"

Just like earlier, when he'd fought the man at the bar, Kerrigan saw yet another facet of Arlo.

Raw emotion limned his face, the small light over the sink reflecting all the heat and need and true confusion in his deep blue eyes.

"I don't know what I'm doing," he finally said.

"I don't know, either."

"But I can promise you, it's not to undermine you. Or make you feel less than. Or to put you in harm's way. It's just that I couldn't see past myself when that guy looked your way. And when he hurt you—"

Arlo reached up, brushing her hair away from her temple before painting the tips of his fingers over the crown of her head. "He hurt you."

"Yes, he did." She reached up, putting a hand on his chest. "And I'm fine. He also nearly hurt you. If I hadn't shown up when I did... I shudder to think what would have happened to you."

"I was working on that."

"Yeah, well, from my view it looked like you were

stuck in the middle of a blade and bad decision." She stopped then, willing him to understand. "I can handle myself. In that situation and in any other my training calls me to."

"I know you can. And I know you do. Hell, you dive the depths of New York Harbor. If that doesn't take a serious amount of mettle and courage, I'm not sure what does."

"Then you'll get out of my way?"

"Yes."

"And you'll stop with this ridiculous need to protect me?"

"I—" He stopped, his hand drifting to cup her shoulder. "I will stop leaving you out of things. I'm not going to apologize for wanting to see you remain safe. It's not ridiculous."

"But you won't stand in my way."

"No."

They stood like that for long moments, wrapped up in each other yet wary to move forward or to move away.

And in the space of a few heartbeats, she knew she loved him, too. It wasn't something she could put to words—she needed time and she needed to process what had happened—but to keep pretending she didn't have feelings or could will away the ones she had was no longer possible.

"Stay."

The request slipped out, as powerful as a bomb detonating in her small apartment.

His eyebrows slashed over those gorgeous eyes, even as she saw the distinct notes of desire in the deep blue. "I didn't come here to sleep with you."

"I know that."

"And I have a lot of bad behavior to make up for."

"You do."

"Then why—" He broke off even as she heard the questions stamped so clearly in the husky timbre of his voice.

"I want you. It has nothing to do with being partners or being mad at you or expecting more from you. I want to be with you and after all we've experienced today, I can't see any reason to keep denying that simple, life-affirming fact."

In the end, Kerrigan acknowledged to herself, it really was that simple.

As she lifted her lips to his, finally meeting in the one place they could wholly agree, she gave in to all that she wanted.

And all the promise that stretched before them.

Arlo wasn't sure how he'd gone from rightfully being taken to task to kissing a beautiful woman, but he was nothing if not an opportunistic bastard and he wasn't letting this moment pass.

He wanted her, with a desperate yearning he'd never felt before in his life.

Never had he met a woman who could make him feel on top of the world and wildly taken to task in a span of moments.

Yet somehow, with Kerrigan, it was all part of the same.

He loved her, that he knew.

But he also respected her. Who she was. Her opinions. And her unwillingness to let him skate by without owning his actions.

He'd done her wrong earlier this evening. He'd put them both in danger with his solo stunt at the bar and he'd nearly paid for it with a knife to the ribs. And still, she could separate her anger at him with her feelings for him. It was a level of generosity he'd never experienced before and it took the base desire that had throbbed between them from the start and moved it to something rare.

Special.

And oh, so sweet.

With their mouths still fused together he moved them into her living room. The love seat where he'd confessed his feelings beckoned, but she stopped him. "I have a Murphy bed. Help me pull it down. It's way more comfortable than a love seat."

He couldn't hold back the smile. "It doesn't look so bad."

"You're not exactly short and neither am I." She nipped a quick kiss at the base of his jaw. "I'd rather have room to spread out."

"When you say it like that…"

She gave him one more quick kiss before directing him to the handles that pulled the bed from the wall. The process was seamless, and in moments she was smoothing the sheets over the bed and placing already-plump pillows at the head.

"That's a nifty trick."

"You've never seen a Murphy bed?"

"Admittedly, not in real life."

"So glad I could offer an education."

She gave him the perfect opening and he wrapped his arms around her waist, pulling her close. "One of many tonight."

A small moan drifted from the back of her throat as he kissed her again, settling one hand at the base of her spine while the other roamed over her body. The thin robe she was wearing, wrapped over a small tank and pajama shorts, was removed in short order and he stepped back to look at her.

He knew what she looked like and knew the innate strength in her lean, lithe body.

And still, staring at those high, firm breasts, nipped-in waist and the long, long legs clad in only those thin shorts had his breath catching. Hard.

"God, you're beautiful."

"I feel beautiful." She leaned in, her fingers seeking the buttons of his shirt. "You make me feel beautiful."

Moment after moment spun out, just the two of them, with the entire world outside the door kept at bay. Arlo felt her hands glide over his chest after she finished with his buttons before dipping lower, over his stomach.

His muscles quivered under her touch, but it was her deft movements, one hand slipping lower beneath his belt, that had him drawing coarse, uneven breaths at her touch.

"Temptress."

"Why, thank you." Her eyes glittered beneath her lashes. "You're quite tempting yourself."

Although he was desperate for her, his body responding with aching need to every single one of her touches, he was determined to make the moments last. To not only make this memorable, but also to know that they'd managed to brand one another before the night was over.

It was nearly feral, this wild, untamed need for her,

and he leaned into that ferocity, allowing himself to feel it all.

To give in to the deep desire instead of holding himself back.

With that foremost in his thoughts, he slipped his hands over her hip before grabbing the material of her tank top, pulling it up her body and over her uplifted arms. He then worked down the thin material of her shorts, dispensing with them equally quickly.

He filled his hands with her breasts, his thumbs caressing each firm nipple. Another deep, low moan drifted from the back of her throat, and he bent his head, trailing kisses over the column of her neck.

A light sheen of sweat coated her skin, and he savored the slightly salty taste of her. A taste that was at subtle odds with the sweet floral notes of her soap.

It was a sensory feast, Arlo realized, as he pushed her down onto the bed, replacing his hands with his mouth. And as he slipped one taut nipple into his mouth, tracing his tongue over the thick, distended tip, he knew a deep satisfaction.

One that filled him wholly, even as there was so much left to explore between them.

Kerrigan writhed beneath him, so responsive, and it spurred him on, continuing a path down her body. He painted his tongue in the dips of her stomach, over the small cavern of her belly button, before moving on. And felt his own body tighten several more degrees in response when he heard her gasps, his mouth closing over the most intimate part of her.

Her thighs tightened slightly against him in subtle resistance before she seemed to go slack as her body simply indulged the pleasure.

And Arlo drank his fill.

This greedy need for her was all-consuming and the sheer openness of her sensuality awed him beyond measure. She was wholly in the moment, her body rising, up, up, up with the increasing pleasure, and he felt the moment she crested, her deep cries the sweetest response.

"Arlo!"

His name was a hard cry on her lips, and he moved up, traveling the return trip over her skin, before wrapping her up in his arms and pulling her close.

And as she smiled up at him, her dark eyes now a fathomless black, he felt a special sort of triumph.

Shared pleasure. And a sort of liquid desire that flowed between them with fiery need.

"I believe you're overdressed, Detective."

He glanced down, where his shirt hung haphazardly off his shoulder, the slacks he'd worn that evening open at the waist. "We'll get to it."

"We most certainly will."

Something sparked in those dark depths, and she rose up beside him, tossing a leg over his waist. "And I believe we'll start now."

Kerrigan was amazed her vision had cleared enough to see Arlo, let alone be able to climb onto his body and begin the delicious act of stripping off his clothes.

But she considered herself an enterprising gal and there was no way she was ready to stop what had started between them with all the power of a tornado.

Even if the man had simply shattered her with that clever, artful mouth.

He sat up beneath her, helping her with the sleeves of his dress shirt, before lying back. She worked her way farther down his body, pulling his slacks the rest of the way off his legs, allowing the heavy material to drop to the floor beside the bed.

The same awe and reverence he'd held as he looked at her hit her in spades as she took in the hard lines of his body. The thick muscles of his chest that tapered into those firm ridges over his stomach.

She was a woman who worked a physical job with nearly all male colleagues. She'd seen them in various states of undress, their chests exposed to the air after a dive or in the practice pool as they swam laps and ran drills.

But none of those physiques she'd seen up close had prepared her for Arlo.

He was magnificent. Hard lines and broad shoulders, a tapered waist and an impressive erection she was doing her level best not to stare at.

But a woman was only so strong, she admitted to herself as she allowed her gaze to roam over him.

Fully.

"Kerrigan." His voice was strained, strangled even, and it had a smile breaking out despite her best efforts to keep her cool.

"Yes, Arlo?"

"You keep looking at me like that and this will be an awfully quick ending."

"Hmm." She flicked a glance up at him before returning her gaze to the delectable lines of his very impressive body. "That would be something to see."

"Honestly, woman." His voice tightened another notch. "I wish I was teasing you."

"I wish you were, too." She reached down and ran the tip of her finger over that length. "But a woman's got to test boundaries, you know. See if she can take a man just to the edge—" She added her palm to the next stroke. "And over it."

He reached up and pulled her down on top of him, crushing his mouth to hers. She wanted to laugh from the sheer joy of the moment, but he captured her mouth, occupying her with far more interesting pursuits than simple laughter. And as their bodies pressed to each other, the increasing urgency of the moment took over.

Hot kisses that electrified matched the glide of hands over sweat-slicked skin.

Tongues that teased and stroked pushed want and need to ever higher heights.

"Give me one minute."

She slipped from his arms, edging off the bed.

"Where are you going?"

"Just need to get something."

She scampered off to the bathroom to get the box of condoms she'd purchased a million years ago. It had been her intention to enjoy what her friends were calling a "hot girl summer" a few years back, but all she'd managed to do was go on a few uninspiring dates from Memorial Day to Labor Day.

And those poor little condoms had remained snug in their box.

She was suddenly grateful she hadn't touched one of them. Especially with the evidence still warm in her bed that the right man was worth waiting for.

And the uninspiring ones…well, they hadn't been worth her time.

"What's this?" Arlo smiled at her as she climbed back into bed.

"A box that promises us both a sexual feast, assuming I haven't had them past their expiration date." She held the box up to the light, breathing a hard sigh of relief. "More than a year to go."

Arlo reached for the box in her hand. "Nothing like a ticking clock to push a man into high gear."

She couldn't help but glance back down at his naked form. "I think you're already in high gear."

His harsh bark of laughter was infectious, and she fell into his arms, their lips meeting in an effortless kiss. It was sweet and funny and more than a little odd to be talking about expiration dates on condoms and yet…perfectly normal.

And wasn't that just the oddest—and most wonderful—thing?

Arlo already had the box open and a small foil packet in hand, but she took over before he could get it open. "I'll do the honors."

"And what was that I was saying about you being a temptress?"

"You ain't seen nothing yet," she whispered in his ear as she unrolled the condom over his length.

Slowly.

She took great joy from the hard exhale that whispered the hair over her face.

And then the foreplay was over and his hands were at her waist, guiding her down over his hard length. Kerrigan took him in, that delicious, aching stretch of bodies a precursor to the most beautiful movement.

They quickly found a rhythm and as their bodies met, again and again, pleasure building with each stroke, Kerrigan felt herself rising again. A seeming impossibility after the heights he'd already taken her to, but the pleasure was even more powerful than before.

It was all *more*.

More intense.

More feeling.

More *love*.

She might not be ready to say it, but as the wave broke over her once again, Arlo following immediately on her heels, Kerrigan knew it with all that she was.

She loved him.

In fact, the real question wasn't whether she loved him.

It was whether it would be enough.

Dyson Gentry walked the perimeter of the boat, delivered just that night, inspecting each piece as he walked along the dock. He looked up at his brother, who was standing on the other side of the boat slip. "You think she'll be satisfied?"

"She'll have to be."

"It's not as big as the other one."

"But it's faster. And how much room does she really need?"

Dyson wasn't sure his brother's casual response was quite the right one, but he kept it to himself. Decker had grown increasingly distant and it had taken everything in him not to go to their father.

But what would he say?

Gee, Pop, we've been running some off-market parts?

His father and his grandfather before that had run Brooklyn Yacht with pride, passion and the deepest sense of honor. Was he really thinking of breaking the old man's heart that way?

Especially since they'd run a hell of a lot more than parts.

Which was why he was now resolved. All they had to do was get through this. Give the bitch her boat and move on.

He certainly was ready to.

Because in the end, Dyson had come to realize he wasn't cut out for running off-market and under the table.

And if Decker didn't agree, he'd find a way to convince him.

His brother might have grown oddly distant these past few months, but he needed to see reason. After the favors they'd called in to get this boat delivered, he had to know it was time to cut bait and get out of whatever this all was.

The sound of heels broke him out of his thoughts, and he turned to see Wendy Parker confidently clipping her way down the dock.

"I see you have my boat, gentlemen."

"As agreed. Early, even."

She eyed Dyson, her disdain evident. Despite the fact he'd spoken, she turned toward his brother. "You have delivered."

"In full."

Decker's cool facade never changed, but Dyson didn't miss the way his gaze roamed over the woman.

He was fascinated.

Dyson was fascinated, too, like a person watching a cobra exposing its full hood. But Decker...

In that moment, realization after realization filled him.

Decker didn't want out of this. In fact, he'd built a

program and a supply chain specifically because he wanted *in* on the criminal game.

And he'd pulled Dyson in, too.

He'd preyed on the desire Dyson had to grow the business. To grow his skills and his influence and go beyond the staid, boring business their father ran.

Why hadn't he seen it before? He'd been a pawn, following along like an eager puppy who saw a new toy and not the cliff he had to leap into to get it.

Damn it.

Decker walked up to Wendy, his hands extended to hers. "I'm sure you'll be pleased."

She wrapped her hands in his and pressed a warm kiss to Decker's cheek, lingering there a few extra beats, then pulling back. "You did deliver."

Then she stepped back, and those heels *tap-tap-tapped* as she walked the perimeter of the boat, just as he and Decker had, before she came to stand back beside his brother.

"This is smaller than my last boat."

"Faster, too. This will get you down the coast and back at a speedy seventy-five knots per hour."

"Hmm." Wendy's smile remained in place, but Dyson could see, even from this distance, she wasn't happy.

"I wanted a replacement for my old boat."

"And you have one." Decker kept his smile in place, too, his chest puffed out. "A better one. A faster one."

"A smaller one."

"I appreciate you're growing your business, but this has more than enough space for what you need."

"Yes, but I was clear I wanted a replacement."

No matter how enamored, Decker held his ground. "Which we delivered on."

Dyson thought of the cobra again, its hood extended as it presented itself to its opponent.

Who would blink?

And who would fold up and back down first?

Since it looked like something was needed to break the tension, Dyson stepped forward again. The woman might not have much time for him, but she'd hardly walk away from the celebratory champagne he'd bought for the occasion.

"I think you're going to be quite pleased with the boat. And to celebrate, I've got two bottles of champagne. One to christen the boat and one to toast your new, sweet ride."

Wendy turned to him then, her smile broad. "A lovely idea."

Satisfied the showdown had ended, Dyson crossed over to the small ledge that rimmed the boat dock. They often used the shelf for the same ceremony, with paying customers, of course. But it was a matter of honor and hospitality at Brooklyn Yacht that a new owner got one bottle of champagne to christen their boat and a second to toast it.

For tonight, he'd pulled out the big guns, the green-and-gold label winking in the overhead lights on the dock for the champagne they'd sip. The second was the sort used for this purpose, with a scored bottle in a fine mesh bag.

He'd initially thought the impulse silly, but realized this was just the ice-breaker they needed to get the woman happy with the boat and, frankly, out of their lives.

Then he'd go to work talking some sense into Decker. Assuming, of course, it wasn't too late.

"Thank you, Dyson." Wendy took the bottle he held out to her, her long, slender fingers closing around the neck of the christening bottle. "Where do you want me to stand?"

Dyson picked up the other bottle, then walked her back down the dock. "Right there on the edge of the bow. That should make the perfect spot to officially make the boat yours."

It was a good idea on a few fronts, Dyson admitted to himself as he helped Wendy get into position. The small ceremony defused the current situation. And they hadn't christened her first boat. He was just superstitious enough to believe the troubles that had followed had been because of that fact.

Decker looked vaguely amused by the whole thing, but he crossed around to stand beside Dyson for the ceremony.

"What do you need me to do?" she asked.

"Have you named the boat?" Dyson asked.

"*Speedy Money,*" Wendy answered without missing a beat.

It was just the level of crassness Dyson had expected, but he kept his smile in place and nodded all the same. "Then hold up the bottle and as you smash it against the bow, say 'I christen thee the *Speedy Money.*'"

Wendy lifted the bottle, doing as he asked, the distinct sound of breaking glass echoing off the bow of the boat.

Dyson placed the other bottle in the crook of his arm as he clapped, before moving forward to take the now-broken bottle in the mesh bag from her. "Why don't we switch?"

"Yes. Let's."

He took the broken glass and walked to the small trash can they kept for the ceremony. It was only as the glass made a satisfying thunk as it hit the bottom of the can that he heard his brother's shouts. They echoed into the darkened night, followed by a heavy blast of gunfire.

"What?" Dyson whirled around, shock and a slimy layer of panic crowding his throat…

Only to find Wendy standing over the body of his brother, a gun now pointed at him.

"We delivered." The words felt like they were coming from a million miles away as the thick sound of the gun firing still throbbed in his ears.

"I know you did." He read her lips as much as heard the faint sound of her voice through the ringing.

But it was the lift of her gun that had him shrinking back, even as he knew there was nowhere to run.

There was no getting out of this. Not now.

Nor was there going to be another chance.

Dyson briefly eyed the water, thinking he could slip into the cold depths and take his shot, but another gunshot ripped through the air, effectively ending his plans.

The shot had him staggering into the same railing where he'd left the champagne.

It was only as he looked over, the woman's cat eyes narrowed on his, that Dyson felt his knees give way. The last thing he saw was her lift the champagne high.

"Thank you, Mr. Gentry."

Chapter 16

Kerrigan rolled into a hard, warm body and burrowed in, vaguely questioning when her bed had gotten so hot and why she felt so loose and comfortable.

And then she remembered.

Her eyes popped open, right into Arlo's amused blue ones. "Good morning."

"Hi." The word came out in a squeak, so she swallowed hard and tried again. "I mean, good morning. Have you been up long?"

"A few minutes. Did I wake you?"

"I'm an early riser."

"How does your head feel today?"

Since she hadn't given her head a single thought since last night, she almost needed to ask why when her ill-advised monkey-cling-on-a-determined-criminal move came winging back into her thoughts.

"Okay, actually. I feel good."

Good sex must be even more restorative than she'd imagined was all she could come up with. Especially since her monkey-cling move had likely landed her a few more days off the harbor team until she cleared the possible concussion protocols. By all rights, she should be taking it easy, but she and Arlo had done nothing of the sort last night.

And she felt amazing.

"What time is it?"

Arlo reached for his phone on the small end table she kept near the couch. "Just after seven."

"We didn't get much sleep."

"I consider that the highest compliment, Doyle." He punctuated his point by leaning in and nibbling kisses down her neck and into the crook that led to her shoulder, and Kerrigan had the abstract thought that it would be incredible to wake up like this every day.

Which was a dangerous thought to be having after one night of good sex. And yet…

He said he loved her.

The thought didn't fill her with dread, especially knowing she felt the same, but even after sleeping on it, she wasn't entirely sure it was the answer, either.

They still had a lot to work through. And while she appreciated his apology the night before, they also had an open case to solve. One he kept maneuvering her out of.

Yes, he'd apologized.

Would he also change his behavior to match?

Because much as she wanted to believe they were close to solving this, they still had precious few clues. Wrapping it all up felt like a distant milestone.

Who was trying to take over the drug trade?

And there was still the matter of taking care of the thug at McNulty's. A man whose name they didn't know and who'd proven himself to be more than problematic. Arlo hadn't formally addressed himself as a cop last night out behind the bar, but there had to be enough in the man's unprovoked behavior to pick him up for questioning. Especially with Tia Lutz's death.

"Your ambition is spiking."

"Sorry?" She whispered it against his ear. "Because I really would love to stay just like this."

"And I can hear you thinking about all we need to do." Arlo lifted his head, his gaze eminently understanding. "There's a dead body of a young woman in the morgue and a brute keeping watch at a bar who knows far more than he's letting on."

"And don't forget someone who's behind it all."

"That, too."

Arlo rolled over, his impressive back and very naked ass catching her attention. "You really are built, Prescott."

He glanced over his shoulder, his gaze appreciative as he reached behind himself to tug the sheet down her naked body. "Lady, I've got nothing on you."

She lifted herself up on an elbow to kiss him, the moment quickly taking both their good intentions and scattering them to the wind. It was only the ring of one of their cell phones that pulled them apart.

"Yours or mine?"

He glanced at the end table. "Mine."

Arlo disengaged himself and snatched the phone. She'd nearly fallen back onto the pillow, prepared to admire his delectable backside, when she keyed into his side of the conversation.

"What? When?"

Kerrigan sat up, unsure what could possibly have happened but sensing by the immediate stiffening of his back it wasn't good.

"I'll inform my partner and we'll be there within the hour."

He disconnected the call, a string of curses spewing into the air.

"What is it?"

"Dyson and Decker Gentry. They were found about a half hour ago by one of the people who has a boat slip at Brooklyn Yacht."

"Found how?"

"With bullets in their chests."

The words were harsh but the sheer anger and shock in Arlo's gaze mitigated the unforgiving language.

"No way."

"I'm afraid so."

They dressed quickly and within fifteen minutes were in Arlo's car and heading toward Sheepshead Bay.

Although she didn't know Big Will's sons well, she had a clear picture of them in her mind. They'd been part of Brooklyn Yacht for a long time, and she'd talked to them over the years at various events.

"Everyone we've touched. It's uncanny, Arlo."

He glanced over at her as he navigated the morning traffic. "You're not responsible for this and neither am I. The person killing people is responsible for this."

"I know. I do. But hear me out."

When he remained quiet, no obvious arguments, she pressed on. "Each person we've talked to. Each person we questioned. Even those guys who were sent out to follow us. Someone's getting ahead of our investigation. How?"

"You think we're being targeted?"

"I think we're being watched. And taunted." She played it through her mind, that steady impression of impulsiveness continuing to feel like an answer.

Or part of one.

"The waitress certainly feels like a taunt."

"She's sort of solidified the idea for me. There's no way she was targeted until she got our table. Yet, as soon as she did and we ask a few innocuous questions, she's hurt."

"Those aren't innocuous questions to the person who wants to keep this all under wraps."

It might not have been but a few nosy people weren't reason enough to kill someone, either. The fact was a big neighborhood drug bust did go down at the bar. There was no way in hell they were the first people to ask about it or make a comment.

"We still need to go through that footage, too," he added.

"Which reminds me. I started looking last night at what I was able to get from the bodega across the street. There were good clean shots of Tia parking but not much at ground level, where we could see someone tinkering with the undercarriage."

"Something else should come through from the other businesses."

She agreed with that, even as her thoughts about Tia kept spinning out. "Here's the thing. Someone had to have eyes on her talking to us."

"I tried to slip her my card when you went to the ladies' room."

"Did she take it?"

"Nope. Didn't even look at where I had placed it on the table beneath my napkin."

"She tried to warn me off in the bathroom, too."

"Cameras in the bathroom?" Arlo asked. "They certainly have them in the bar."

"Could be. Or they've got it bugged, at minimum. Which takes us back to the ownership of McNulty's."

Arlo shook his head. "We'll run him again. The guy was clean, though. And we looked at him for the drug bust. Over and over we ran him and the financial forensics on his business."

"Is he still there?"

"What do you mean?"

"He didn't know what was going on the first time around. Is he a figurehead somehow?"

"He seemed involved. Knew his business and talked knowledgably to the cops." Arlo zipped in between a few cars. "Who the hell knows anymore? Because something's going on in that place. Again."

Arlo took the exit and traveled the now-familiar path to Brooklyn Yacht. There were several police cars already there when they arrived, as well as the coroner's van, and Kerrigan braced herself for what they would find.

Fifteen minutes later she was still shaken by all they'd discovered.

The bodies of Dyson and Decker Gentry had been covered but they were still in the same position in which they'd been found, shot dead on the deck that surrounded an empty boat slip.

"No video footage at all?" Kerrigan asked the first uniform on scene.

"Nothing. We've spoken to the office manager and

were given access to enter the business office to review the tapes. Nothing was there."

"No footage?"

"Nothing. It stopped around nine o'clock and wasn't started again."

Kerrigan filed that away as the booming voice of Big Will Gentry filled the air. "Where are they?"

The man raced down toward the boat slip, his gaze lasered in tight on the two bodies covered in white tarps, with several officials working around them.

"My boys!"

Kerrigan was already moving in to intercept Big Will, Arlo intent on doing the same.

"What happened?" Will's face was filled with an impossible level of anguish, his movements nearly frantic. "Who did this to my boys?"

Arlo already moved in. Though his own sizable form was dwarfed by Will's, he stood tall, authoritative in the moment.

"Will. Please give us a few minutes. They're being cared for, and we'll take you to them, but we need to talk to you first."

Kerrigan put a hand on Will's arm. "Will, it's me. Kerrigan Doyle. I'm here to help."

"Kerrigan?" Will's gaze brightened as he looked at her. "You came."

"Of course. I'm here to help. We all are."

She and Arlo walked Will through what they knew so far, gently probing him on the business and what he'd believed were his sons' plans the evening before.

"Decker had a date and Dyson had tickets to a concert. Both were heading out straight from here and I said good-night to them around six."

The man's face crumpled at that. "I just said good-night. Didn't even hug them or spend time with them or—" He broke off as the tears came. "I didn't really say goodbye."

"You had no way of knowing, Will. No one could have known."

"Why were they here?"

"Mr. Gentry. Do you keep your security cameras on?"

The vague, disoriented look in Will's eyes faded at the question. "Twenty-four-seven. It's a promise we make to everyone who rents a slip from us."

"The cameras were turned off around nine o'clock last night."

"Impossible. The cameras are never off. We have a backup generator to ensure it."

"They were off last night." Kerrigan kept her voice gentle, but firm. "Which means someone turned them off."

"I don't understand."

"We think it's possible one of your sons turned the cameras off."

"But I—" Will shook his head. "It's impossible. They know the rules. Know how much we focus on a secure environment."

Arlo gave her a quick nod and tilted his head toward the bodies.

She understood his point. Whatever Will might or might not know, his only thought right now was for his sons.

Sons whose deaths had broken his heart.

And sons who would break it again when he realized they were the ones most likely to have shut down the cameras.

* * *

Two hours later, Arlo walked back into the precinct and headed straight for the captain's office. He'd texted Dwayne from Brooklyn Yacht and quickly got the request to check in as soon as he was back at the 86th.

Kerrigan had opted to join the uniforms who'd been first on scene to try and canvass the area after seeing Will got safely home to his wife. She was also keeping watch on the various employees as they arrived at Brooklyn Yacht, gauging their behavior and anyone who seemed to be out of the ordinary.

Or who didn't show up at all.

Although the idea of splitting up to handle the case left him ill at ease, he knew they needed to divide their efforts in hopes of getting to the bottom of the situation quickly.

You have to stop protecting her.

The night before had been beyond anything he'd have ever expected. Because it wasn't like anything he'd ever experienced before.

She was responsive in bed, yes, but she'd artfully separated the attraction between them from the work frustrations that brewed between them. It was a rare skill and more than twelve hours later he was still awed by her emotional generosity.

Even if she hadn't responded to every aspect of last night.

She didn't say she loved you back.

That had been the lone sticking point of an otherwise perfect evening and he wasn't sure how he felt about it.

He'd never said those words to a woman before. Hell,

he was still trying to process why they'd come out so easily with Kerrigan.

And yet they had.

Because he *did* love her.

In the bright light of day, a small part of him wanted to run from it. All while another part wanted to run to her and beg her to tell him she felt the same.

Which left him stuck in the strangest reality.

He had to wait and give her time. She'd certainly been generous and responsive the night before. They'd been in the moment together and he knew she felt something.

But love?

Especially after the way he'd acted, she had every right to be wary.

Had his actions ruined the chance for something more with her?

He wanted to believe they could work through it, but he had a lot to overcome. He'd betrayed her more than once and if the positions were reversed, would he be so quick to leap to declarations?

Resolving to talk to her about it later, he knocked on Dwayne's door.

"Come in, Detective." Dwayne had gotten an early start. His jacket was hanging on a coatrack in the corner and his shirtsleeves were already rolled up. "I looked at the file. Nice, detailed job there, by the way."

"There's a bit more to include after this morning."

"Fill me in."

He walked Dwayne through the events at the bar, the car bomb that killed Tia Lutz and the news of the Gentry brothers.

"What the ever-loving hell, Arlo? We've got three bodies in a matter of hours?"

"Yes."

"You've got more than enough for a warrant at Mc-Nulty's."

"First on my list this morning."

"And you need to get a handle on who the bouncer at the bar is."

He'd gone over that one in his mind and still cursed the fact that he didn't have Kerrigan go check on the car bomb while he dealt with the guy. "I should have dealt with him last night."

Dwayne's tone was grim. "You were a little busy. And saving the woman's life took priority."

"We were a little busy." As the idea hung in his mind, Arlo's thoughts racing through last night, something clicked. "That's it, Dwayne. There's a lot going on. Murders and bombs and snipers. One thing after another, with the wind constantly changing direction. Kerrigan keeps going back to impulse."

"Impulse, how?"

"On the part of the mastermind behind this. Nothing's predictable and we barely have time to catch our breath before the next problem erupts."

"It's erratic, that's for sure. Nothing methodical other than the sheer willingness to cause chaos and loss of life."

"We've been working off the theory that the chaos is designed to keep the criminals in Brooklyn on their back foot. But what if it's also a strategy for the cops? Kerrigan and I have been chasing our tails since we started this case. No time to breathe and certainly no time to sit back and consider all the pieces."

"Then maybe it's time to sit back. You set the pace."

"We need to catch this killer before they hurt someone else."

That reality was sharp and oh-so stark in his mind.

But Dwayne had a point, too.

Right now, all they were doing was bumbling around. If they didn't slow down and get some direction to follow, they weren't of any use to anyone.

And keeping them running in circles only gave the killer more time to hide in the shadows.

Kerrigan accepted a ride back to the 86th with one of the uniforms at Brooklyn Yacht and she'd bought the woman lunch as a thank-you. Their stop at a sub shop on the way back had given her an opportunity to get Officer Ramirez's take on the crime scene and allowed Kerrigan to pick up lunch.

With a meatball sub for him and an eggplant parm sandwich for her, she walked back into the precinct with precious little more than the day before.

They had managed to rule out the staff at Brooklyn Yacht. She'd run everyone's name and looked at them, but no one had missed work and the genuinely shell-shocked faces had suggested grief far more than nefarious dealings by Big Will's employees.

Which brought it all back to the sons.

And the increasingly sad evidence that Dyson and Decker Gentry had been running a secondary business under their father's nose.

It was the theory she'd batted around with Ramirez, and it fit.

The unregistered boat that went down in the harbor had to come from somewhere. And Big Will's sons would have access and the contacts to facilitate a purchase like that.

So why kill them now?

The boat going down in a storm was hardly their fault as the supplier. And if she circled back to her theories way back at the beginning, owning an unregistered boat would still require maintenance and the contacts to keep it running.

Why go to all the effort to find a supplier to meet your needs and then kill them?

Kerrigan hit the button for the squad room, her mind racing through the problems, when it hit. Without waiting for the elevator to arrive, she took off at a run for the stairs, racing up two stories and into the squad room.

"There's another boat!"

She hollered the realization loud enough that it had Arlo lifting his head, along with everyone else in the room.

Careful not to drop the sandwiches, she set them down on the edge of his desk, even as excitement spilled out faster than she could contain it.

He smiled at her, and she ignored the shot of pure, unadulterated lust that hit her belly at the knowing look in his eyes. She was going to have to get a handle on *that*.

But she'd deal with that later. Right now, she had a line to tug.

"I've got a theory."

"Lunch and a theory? It looks like a banner day, Officer Doyle."

"There's a second boat, Arlo. That's what went down last night at Big Will's place. That's why the cameras were off."

The smile fell, replaced by that determined cop face she had come to admire and respect and yes, *love*.

She tapped the edge of Arlo's desk, already reaching for her phone. "Let's get Wyatt. We need to get out on the water."

The police boat bobbed in the harbor near the site where the drug runners went down in the storm. Kerrigan assessed the calm waters. The harbor had a glassy look that was rare for the waters around New York, and she opted to take it as a good sign.

They'd already notified the Coast Guard and several teams were working the waters up and down the coast. But she and Arlo, along with Wyatt, Gavin, Jayden and Captain Reed, were poring over maps in the boat's wheelhouse.

None of them were convinced this spot just off Governors Island was going to be the path of another drug run, but without anything else to go on, they'd opted to start here and consider various paths from open Atlantic waters into Brooklyn.

"The working theory is they went down coming back into the harbor because they had the drugs on them in the storm. Which means they have a supplier somewhere up or down the coast and they're coming from the Atlantic." Kerrigan tapped various points on the map as she spoke. "They could be working out of Philly or Baltimore or points farther south. Providence or Boston are options, too, but the weather's going to be less favorable as it gets colder. But a boat like that could make the trip distance-wise either direction."

"But it's a haul," Wyatt added, using a ruler to point out the distance, "especially for any attempts much past DC. That's a few days' trip with a lot of cargo at risk of discovery."

Kerrigan tapped the map. "If we operate under the theory the mastermind behind this took possession of the boat last night at Brooklyn Yacht, they have to be gearing up for a run quickly."

"Did they find anything yet in the files in Gentry's offices?" Wyatt asked.

It was Arlo who took the briefing on that piece. Kerrigan had worked with Arlo before they'd headed out to the docks, that process of requesting a warrant new to her.

"The warrant came through this afternoon and the same team that was first on scene went to recover any evidence they could find, as well as take possession of the electronics."

"I've put the data team on it as top priority," Dwayne added. "But it's going to take them a while."

She was of two minds on what they were going to find but knew the digital forensics team needed the space to do their work. There was a big part of her that had to believe the Gentrys kept records of what they were handling.

And the other, bigger part of her knew there was little benefit to them to keep records.

Their cell-phone and text histories were likely going to turn up far more than computer records but they'd take what they could get. Maybe a stray email or log-ins to a personal, private email account.

Even with the potential to dig up something there, they really needed cell phones. But the last report they got from the team doing the warrants was that no cell phones had been found.

"How would you hide a boat?"

The captain's question pulled her from her thoughts. Although it was directed at all of them, Wyatt was the one to answer. "You'd need a slip for keeping it in place."

"What paperwork's needed for that?" Dwayne pressed.

"Insurance. Ownership. Registration." Wyatt ticked off each required element a purveyor of dock space would expect.

"So nowhere respectable," Dwayne added.

"The bar!" Kerrigan thought about McNulty's and Bulldog's and realized there was something there. "McNulty's has the parking lot behind it, but Bulldog's sits on the water. There's a likely chance there's a private slip back there."

"It might have even driven the decision to take the location," Arlo added. "You want to run illegals, you need a place to do it. People won't look quite as close at your boat if it's hidden on your property. No nosy paperwork, either."

Bulldog's made sense, she considered as she imagined the property and where it sat along the water. But so did McNulty's as home base. Especially if you wanted to keep attention off the boat in its hiding place.

It all fit.

It was why they kept coming back to the bar as a base of operations.

And it was also why the employees were at risk.

People might know how to keep their mouths shut for a paycheck, but it didn't mean they were blind to what went on around them.

Tia knew things. Arlo had already gotten the same

impression from the valets. And if they didn't want another one of them ending up like Tia Lutz, they needed to get this whole damn thing dismantled as fast as possible.

"We need to get to Bulldog's." Kerrigan looked at Wyatt, Gavin and Jayden. "We can dive from several yards down the dock, swim in and figure out what's going on. We'll check for serial numbers on the boat while we're at it."

"If it's stolen, we can seize the property without a warrant," Captain Reed added. "But I'm going to request one, anyway, for the dive so no one can slither out of this."

"It's stolen," Kerrigan said, convinced they were finally on the right path. "But we'll do it by the book."

She caught sight of Arlo's face as she and her fellow divers all started mapping out a plan of attack. His expression was blank, but she recognized what was there, roiling beneath the surface.

Hadn't she seen it often enough already?

He'd shut down each time she had to risk herself for this case and it was obvious he was fighting the urge to do it again.

But he'd have to deal with it.

This was something she not only had to do, but she was also the half of their partnership who had the skill to do it.

Chapter 17

Arlo considered the docks around Sunset Bay and reviewed what Kerrigan and Wyatt had worked up on the boat. He could see the dive pattern they'd mapped out. Where they'd drop into the water and where they'd come up to inspect the boat.

It was dark, murky work but they were trained for it.

And Arlo knew he had to let her go.

This was her job. Her skill set.

And it was her shot at solving this case.

She'd earned it.

Even as every fiber of his being fought the reality of what she was about to do.

He sat on stakeout down the street from the front entrance of Bulldog's with another detective he'd worked with several times in the past. Detective Tom Casey was seasoned and he knew Brooklyn like the back of his hand. He'd gotten up to speed quickly when the captain brought him in for the briefing, clear on the layout and the objectives of the dive.

He was equally clear on the protocols to move in and seize the boat once they determined it was stolen.

"Quite an operation," Casey said as he sipped from a take-out cup of coffee. "And the swath of destruction in a matter of months is incredible."

"No mercy seems to be the MO on this one."

"You're not kidding. The Papa left quite a hole." Casey let out a curse. "I'm glad you brought me in on this, but you know damn well we'll cut this node and three more will spring up in its place. It's frustrating."

It was the reality that haunted him, even as Arlo struggled with agreeing with the man.

Casey was a good cop. An honest one, too. But he'd been at it for a long time, and he'd weathered a lot.

And if he was being honest with himself, Arlo knew where the man was coming from. He'd felt that emotion and hopelessness far too keenly after the trafficking job with Vice that had gone sideways. He'd worked through it and vowed after he came out the other side that he wasn't going to give in to that way of thinking.

Not for himself. Not for the job. And not for Gabrielle.

If nothing else, he owed it to her memory to do the work and do it with the belief he was making a difference.

His comm unit crackled with an update and Arlo keyed into Wyatt's voice and off the dismal thoughts that threatened to overwhelm.

"Boat sighted in the slip," Wyatt said through their comm hookup. "Gavin and Jayden are the first team down. Kerrigan and I will go second."

Arlo knew they kept their comm limited, focused only on giving the essentials, so he avoided asking too many questions. In the meantime, he and Casey had to figure out how to get in and get out without any risk to civilians.

It was still early, which worked in their favor, but the lunch crowd would be arriving soon.

Although the plan had come together quickly, they'd all agreed as they mapped out the op that protecting civilian life was essential at all costs. Especially since they knew they were dealing with an adversary who wouldn't hesitate to kill.

"How do you like working with Harbor?" Casey asked.

"Good. Trumball and I get to pair up together often."

"And now you're mentoring Doyle? How's she working out?"

"She's doing well. She and her dive partner found the bodies on the boat mess that kicked off this investigation. She wanted more case time, so Trumball, Captain Reed and I agreed she should see it through."

"Good for her. The kid is ambitious. She's impressive to watch."

"That she is. Her instincts are rock-solid. She's coming along really well."

It felt almost clinical to speak of Kerrigan this way, yet he knew what was expected of him. Knew Detective Casey was assessing Kerrigan as a prospective partner. More, he knew his coworker was assessing Kerrigan as a talent in the department.

His feelings for her—for what they shared—had to remain separate. He owed her nothing less.

And, he realized, he owed himself nothing less.

He'd always struggled with his role in a relationship. How much he wanted to run once things got serious.

Well, what was between him and Kerrigan was serious.

And he wasn't looking to run.

So he'd pump her up and have her back and *believe* in her.

"They're a fearless bunch, that harbor crew," Casey added.

Arlo almost started laughing at Casey's assessment, Kerrigan's words at their first breakfast coming back to him.

The harbor team seems to have a special reputation. But it's like we're held separate somehow. The words are always complimentary, but we're still seen as something other from the department.

But it's also cop work in a city surrounded by water. Somebody's got to do it.

Someone did have to do it. And that special reputation was not only well-earned, but it also came with admiration when you recognized someone was the best.

Casey turned to him, about to say something, when a shot rang out, shattering the windshield and still traveling with enough force to slam into the detective's chest.

Arlo scrambled to get down, reaching over to Casey to pull him to the side and out of the line of fire.

"Tom!" he yelled. When the man didn't respond Arlo remained low, scrambling for his comm unit to call it in.

"Officer down! I repeat, officer down!" He quickly rattled off the directions along with his badge number, even as he waited for another shot to come ringing through the car.

It was only as he looked up, he saw the broad shoulders and even broader grin of the thug he'd fought at McNulty's, standing beside the car.

And a gun was pointed directly at him through the driver-side window.

Kerrigan sat beside Wyatt on the small Zodiac they'd taken to the edge of the docks. They were about three hundred yards from the boat slip at Bulldog's and they'd been monitoring Jayden and Gavin's dive. The captain had equipped them with body cameras for this dive and they'd watched on a small screen what the men saw as they moved around the boat.

"She sure is shiny and new," Wyatt muttered.

"That she is. And in every place they've checked now, unmarked."

It ate at her, the sheer magnitude of what they'd uncovered. The number of people who'd been injured along the way. And the ridiculous loss of life.

And for what?

She'd played the female angle over and over in her mind. It wasn't that she believed a woman incapable. Quite the opposite. Someone with determination and a will to succeed could be any gender. But it was the layer of dark, twisty violence that bothered her.

Because the woman behind this had decided the only way to the top was by removing every single thing that got in her way.

The Gentry brothers.

An innocent waitress.

Even the brainless thugs who should know better, but also didn't deserve to die in some ridiculous game of chicken.

A game with murderous consequences.

They'd all left their comm units open, and she could hear Gavin and Jayden's short, clipped answers to each other as they inspected the boat. Could hear the captain asking for updates where he still sat on the NYPD boat farther off the coast.

And she thought of Arlo, where he sat waiting to move in. Just waiting for the signal that the boat was dirty.

They were going to finish this.

Today.

Which made the sudden scramble on their open line a horrifying punctuation mark to the deep need she had to close this case.

To end it.

"Officer down!" Arlo's voice came through clearly in her ear, along with the resulting instructions for support.

Wyatt gave the instruction to come back to the Zodiac, affirmatives winging back from Gavin and Jayden.

But it was the words that came a short while later that stole her breath.

Arlo left the line open in the undercover vehicle and she heard a new voice. One full of menace and purpose.

"You're with me, *De-tec-tive*." There were mocking notes as the man sang out the word *detective*. "We're going to finish what you can't seem to keep your nose out of."

Although she couldn't be entirely sure, she thought she'd heard the same dark notes in the man's voice as she remembered from the alley behind McNulty's.

Which meant their thug bouncer was a bigger part of this.

"Wyatt, I need to get in there."

Wyatt had heard the same exchange on the line and shook his head at her request. "You can't approach. We'll catch them in open water."

"We can't wait for open water. You heard Jayden's description. This boat's an upgrade over the last one. Sleeker and faster, and there's no way we can let them take Arlo."

When he looked moderately swayed by her argument, she continued. "You and I both know boats. One of us can support him and the other can take out the engine."

"Kerrigan, this isn't—"

"We can't leave him!"

She was already zipping up her wet suit, prepared to ignore a direct order, when Gavin and Jayden surfaced, climbing aboard the Zodiac.

"What'd we miss?" Gavin asked.

"She's going after him," Jayden said, pride shining in his eyes. "You'd better hurry your sleek ass up. They're getting ready to move out. I heard them moving around on the deck."

Kerrigan eyed Wyatt across the Zodiac, even as she continued finalizing her equipment for a dive.

At Wyatt's muttered curse, she knew she had a partner. "I'll take the engine. You go up the side."

"There's a ladder starboard," Jayden said. "The movement all seemed to be coming from port side, where they're coming on and off against the dock entrance."

She reached over and linked hands with Jayden. His gaze was deadly serious when it landed on hers. "You watch yourself. I expect my girl back in one piece."

"That's my plan."

Before she could question the situation further, she attached her waterproof field kit, inclusive of her weapon and her badge. She checked that her bailout bottle was firmly attached and took the second Gavin handed her. "Arlo might need it."

She nodded and hoped like hell they were walking him off the boat, but it paid to be prepared.

And then she pulled down her mask and dropped backward into the water, the only sounds she could focus on coming from her comm unit and the heavy, labored breathing of Arlo's stakeout partner.

Arlo kept his gaze focused on his surroundings as he was perp-walked to the back of Bulldog's. The place looked different in the light—dingier, actually—and he counted off the steps between the front and the back entrance before catching sight of a cavernous structure that looked like a barn-door closure.

It had to be the dock, he quickly calculated, and was proven right when the doors swung open just enough for him to be pushed through from behind.

"Get in there."

Since he'd now faced the guy down twice, Arlo figured they were close enough to get on a first-name basis. "You got a name? Because you've been 'thug' in my head for a week and I figure we should know each other a bit better."

"You don't need to know my name."

"*Thug* it is," Arlo growled, not surprised when the gun at his back dug harder into a kidney.

Although he wasn't complaining, he wasn't sure why the dude hadn't shot him outright. But since he was still free of gunshot wounds, Arlo prepared himself for whatever came next.

Only to find a petite blonde in four-inch heels standing on the deck of a shiny new boat as he and Thug came up beside it.

"Mr. Prescott. Or should I call you Detective?"

A come-hither smile painted in a vibrant shade of red set off her petite features, but the look in her eyes was predatory. "Miss Parker."

"Oh, come now. You're dating my old friend from the neighborhood. You can call me Wendy."

"This is your doing?"

"I'm afraid so."

"The harbor killings and the sniper shots and the poor dead waitress?"

She made a show of glancing down at her nails in boredom before looking back up. "It's so hard to find good help. That's why I'm so lucky I have Mark."

She gestured in the direction of the man behind him and at least Arlo now had a name. It wasn't much, but they could work with it.

He *had* to work with it. There was already one man down, desperately in need of the EMTs on the other side of the building. And if things moved the way he figured they would, there was every chance he wasn't walking out of this one.

He needed to get what he could and hope he figured out a way to stay alive long enough for help to arrive.

To see Kerrigan again.

That thought struck swift and low in the gut and he forced himself to focus because he needed whatever intel he could get.

Locking away thoughts of Kerrigan, Arlo glanced

around at the firepower amassed on the boat deck. He trusted his colleagues and knew he'd had just enough time with the open comm unit in the car for them to have a sense of what happened to him and to Detective Casey, but *Mark* had ripped the one in his ear out before they were five feet away from the car.

Which meant no one knew what was happening right here.

"You've been building quite an empire for yourself." Arlo kept his attention on Wendy, well aware it was her impulsiveness that had driven every outcome so far.

Mark might have a gun pressed to his back, but Wendy held the cards and he needed to keep his full focus on her. Mark might enjoy brandishing the threat, but Arlo knew he was safe until Wendy decided he wasn't.

Which meant he had to talk fast and hope like hell the team fanning out beneath the boat could get here in time.

"This town hasn't seen anything yet," Wendy preened before him. Although he wanted to chalk up her behavior to a feral sort of madness, it was impossible to miss the clear eyes and the woman's sheer determination.

"Brooklyn's got an opening for a new crime boss, and I decided it's going to be me."

Although he hadn't climbed aboard yet, Arlo had taken note of a third person milling around the decking that led to the boat. He had a long-range sniper's rifle in his hand and a spring in his step as he headed for the entrance to the boat.

Wendy smiled at him indulgently, even as her gaze strayed to Arlo to size up his reaction. "Nice work on the cop."

Arlo fought the cold rage that burned low in his gut at the casual assessment.

"I could have taken them both," the man with the sniper's rifle bragged as he crossed to board the boat.

Wendy's smile never wavered but her tone took on a decided edge. "And carelessly leave more shell casings behind on my roof?" She shook her head before producing a gun out of her coat pocket and aiming for the man.

Without missing a beat, she fired, the shot frightfully accurate as the man fell backward.

"Get his gun," Wendy ordered Mark, all while she kept the gun in her own hand level with Arlo's chest.

Impulsive.

Brash.

Determined.

All that he and Kerrigan had puzzled through for the past week suddenly came clear in the woman that stood before him.

Wendy Parker was as lethal as she was determined.

Kerrigan kept her comm line open for everyone else to hear what was going on up on the deck. She'd waited with Wyatt while he found the engine panel, only moving on when he tapped her on the arm to proceed. She'd been careful to surface as quietly as possible, as far away from where Jayden and Gavin heard footsteps above them.

Once she was above the waterline, she moved quietly around the starboard side of the boat. The calm water had made their dive easier than usual, but it also meant there wasn't a lot of lapping water on the boat side, nor was there the cover of thick waves to keep anyone from hearing her.

She maneuvered herself toward the ladder, just where Jayden had said it would be, and heard voices above her.

A sharp spear of joy filled her when she heard Arlo's voice, bordering on insolent as he spoke with the guy that had to be their thug from the bar. The same one she'd heard in the comm unit.

She'd confirm it when she surfaced enough to see the deck, but for now, she was operating on that assumption.

But it was the woman's voice and Arlo's response that had Kerrigan stilling all movement, her fingers digging into the smooth hull.

Wendy Parker was behind this?

Rah-rah Wendy with the big smile and flirty laugh?

Even as she struggled to process that reality, she had to admit it fit. The woman's presence in McNulty's the first night she and Arlo were there.

The subtle insinuation she'd kept up with Kerrigan's life, using the old neighborhood as the excuse for the knowledge.

And the gunshots on the two boat victims, executed by someone shorter than them.

Wendy was petite, even in the heels she favored. And she had a lot of access in town, especially when her fashion business, which would undoubtedly need shipping services, was factored in.

She'd positioned herself well and Kerrigan could only imagine this was the next step for her. One that had been carefully plotted and planned.

And one she'd upended with her obvious bloodlust and uncontrolled actions.

It was a shock and yet it strangely fit.

Reining in her reaction, Kerrigan moved closer to the ladder, the conversation on board filtering over. She had to get Arlo out of there, and with any luck, Wendy and her goons would try to maneuver out of the boat slip before taking any action against him.

A trip that wouldn't be happening when she saw Wyatt surface farther up the hull, his quick thumbs-up a confirmation he'd disabled the engine.

A trip that she suddenly feared was about to turn far more deadly when Wendy's voice echoed off the water and the cavernous, covered area of the boat slip.

Followed by a gunshot.

Arlo watched the entire tableau play out, the sniper down on the deck and Mark's instructions to go after him.

He hadn't forgotten the gun pointed at his midsection—nor had he forgotten the woman who held it and her willingness to shoot fast—but he knew he wasn't getting another chance. On a deep breath, he leaped, rushing Wendy and hoping he had her just enough off guard to tackle her before the gun went off.

Her scream lit up the air and he didn't miss Mark's grunt and string of curses from the deck.

He managed to get a hold of the gun in her hand, still hot to the touch, but he ignored it as he slammed her wrist against the floor of the boat.

She continued to scream, holding tight to the gun and scratching him with her clawlike fingernails with the other hand.

And then it all stopped as one thick rubber foot came

down over Wendy's wrist, crunching hard on the delicate bones there.

"Police. You will cease and desist now."

Arlo glanced over his shoulder to see his avenging angel, water dripping heavily off her wet suit and a gun in hand as she stood over them.

Wyatt stood a few feet away, his own gun pointed at Mark on the deck.

"Wendy Parker. You're under arrest." Arlo stood to help Kerrigan cuff the woman, all while his partner read the woman her rights, followed by the list of her crimes.

Arlo was going to move off and help Wyatt once they had Wendy in cuffs, but their captain, followed by Jayden and Gavin, were already boarding and made the arrest on Mark.

He saw Gavin reach down to check the pulse of the sniper before shaking his head.

One more lost life at the hands of Wendy Parker.

Arlo turned to Kerrigan and while he wanted nothing more than to pull her into his arms, he kept his distance as the two of them dealt with the spitting cat of a criminal. Each of them took an arm and walked her off the boat.

And it was only after they had her settled in the back of a police cruiser that Arlo finally found the time to say what he wanted to say.

"You saved me."

She stared up at him, a smile twitching the corners of her lips. "I saved my partner, yes."

"That's true. You did do that today. But you saved *me*, Kerrigan. Me, Arlo. I didn't realize I needed saving until you came along, but you did."

"Well, when you put it that way, maybe we saved each other."

"You needed saving?" He pulled her close, suddenly not caring who saw them.

"I've spent my life focused on work. On what came next. On who I wanted to be. And while I don't regret a single minute of it, I didn't spend a lot of time thinking about who I wanted to spend it with."

"And now?"

"Now I still want to work hard and be the woman I know I can be. But I want to share it with you. Because I love you, Arlo Prescott."

"I love you, too."

He bent his head to kiss her, only to be interrupted by a muffled screech from the police car they'd bundled Wendy into.

"Is that her screaming?"

"I told you she's sort of a lot."

"Sort of a lot? The woman was trying to single-handedly run the drug trade in Brooklyn. She might have succeeded if she'd learned to be a little less quick with that gun."

Kerrigan nodded, her gaze solemn. "And now we have to investigate it all. How she started. Who she's involved with."

"It'll be a lot of work." He smiled as he pulled her close once more. "You up for it?"

"I think I am."

"You think?"

She wrapped her arms around his neck and pulled his head close for a kiss. "I think I need to get some pancakes first."

Arlo took her mouth in a kiss, and it was the sweetest he'd ever known.

Sweeter, even, than the syrup-laden one he laid on her a few hours later in the middle of a diner full of cops, all eating pancakes for dinner.

* * * * *

Get 3 FREE REWARDS!

We'll send you 2 FREE Books <u>plus</u> a FREE Mystery Gift.

FREE
Value Over
$20

Both the **Harlequin Intrigue®** and **Harlequin® Romantic Suspense** series feature compelling novels filled with heart-racing action-packed romance that will keep you on the edge of your seat.

YES! Please send me 2 FREE novels from the Harlequin Intrigue or Harlequin Romantic Suspense series and my FREE gift (gift is worth about $10 retail). After receiving them, if I don't wish to receive any more books, I can return the shipping statement marked "cancel." If I don't cancel, I will receive 6 brand-new Harlequin Intrigue Larger-Print books every month and be billed just $6.49 each in the U.S. or $6.99 each in Canada, a savings of at least 13% off the cover price, or 4 brand-new Harlequin Romantic Suspense books every month and be billed just $5.49 each in the U.S. or $6.24 each in Canada, a savings of at least 12% off the cover price. It's quite a bargain! Shipping and handling is just 50¢ per book in the U.S. and $1.25 per book in Canada.* I understand that accepting the 2 free books and gift places me under no obligation to buy anything. I can always return a shipment and cancel at any time by calling the number below. The free books and gift are mine to keep no matter what I decide.

Choose one:
- [ ] **Harlequin Intrigue Larger-Print** (199/399 BPA GRMX)
- [ ] **Harlequin Romantic Suspense** (240/340 BPA GRMX)
- [ ] **Or Try Both!** (199/399 & 240/340 BPA GRQD)

Name (please print)

Address _____ Apt. #

City _____ State/Province _____ Zip/Postal Code

Email: Please check this box ☐ if you would like to receive newsletters and promotional emails from Harlequin Enterprises ULC and its affiliates. You can unsubscribe anytime.

> **Mail to the Harlequin Reader Service:**
> **IN U.S.A.:** P.O. Box 1341, Buffalo, NY 14240-8531
> **IN CANADA:** P.O. Box 603, Fort Erie, Ontario L2A 5X3

Want to try 2 free books from another series? Call 1-800-873-8635 or visit www.ReaderService.com.

*Terms and prices subject to change without notice. Prices do not include sales taxes, which will be charged (if applicable) based on your state or country of residence. Canadian residents will be charged applicable taxes. Offer not valid in Quebec. This offer is limited to one order per household. Books received may not be as shown. Not valid for current subscribers to the Harlequin Intrigue or Harlequin Romantic Suspense series. All orders subject to approval. Credit or debit balances in a customer's account(s) may be offset by any other outstanding balance owed by or to the customer. Please allow 4 to 6 weeks for delivery. Offer available while quantities last.

Your Privacy—Your information is being collected by Harlequin Enterprises ULC, operating as Harlequin Reader Service. For a complete summary of the information we collect, how we use this information and to whom it is disclosed, please visit our privacy notice located at corporate.harlequin.com/privacy-notice. From time to time we may also exchange your personal information with reputable third parties. If you wish to opt out of this sharing of your personal information, please visit readerservice.com/consumerschoice or call 1-800-873-8635. **Notice to California Residents**—Under California law, you have specific rights to control and access your data. For more information on these rights and how to exercise them, visit corporate.harlequin.com/california-privacy.

HIHRS23